Write What You Know

My work was so numbing and repetitive—so dead—that my mind was forced to escape. It tended to leave me at the damnedest moments. Of course, my mind checked out when I wrote the obits, the scores and scores of obituaries. If only I could have escaped with it.

That's when it happened. That's when I came to know things about some of the dead people in the obits. I don't know how or why, and it was never something I could control. But somehow, some way, my brain went off somewhere, and when it came back, I knew things. Strange things. Secrets. The dying secrets of the dead.

Was it my drinking? At long last, was I losing my mind? Or was I merely the only one left to tell their stories?

After all, how can you explain instinct? Sometimes, you'll just get a feeling. You'll simply know certain things. All reporters do, to some degree.

That's the best I can explain it. At long, long last my reporter's instinct had returned.

I wasn't about to question it.

Fatal Dead Lines

John Luciew

POCKET BOOKS
New York London Toronto Sydney Singapore

This book is a work of fiction. Names, characters, places and incidents are products of the author's imagination or are used fictitiously. Any resemblance to actual events or locales or persons, living or dead, is entirely coincidental.

An *Original* Publication of POCKET BOOKS

POCKET BOOKS, a division of Simon & Schuster, Inc.
1230 Avenue of the Americas, New York, NY 10020

ISBN: 978-1-4516-4682-5

First Pocket Books printing November 2003

10 9 8 7 6 5 4 3 2 1

Cover design by John Vairo, Jr.
Front cover illustration by Jeff Fitz-Maurice

Manufactured in the United States of America

In memory of my mother.

Anita Louise Luciew
1940–1997

PART I

OBITUARIES

1

"How many do we got today, Lenny?" Ted Bronski, the obituary editor, asked me with a forced cheerfulness.

He was like clockwork, Bronski was, always the late afternoon, a few hours before deadline. He timed it purposely because he knew I zoned out.

My body jerked at the interruption. I mumbled "What?"

"How many?" Bronski nodded at the day's allotment of obituaries that had been faxed to me by undertakers from all over Harrisburg and beyond. The death notices were fresh additions atop my cluttered desk.

"Don't know. Got a good stack of them here, lots of death in that pile." A feeble joke, dead on arrival.

"C'mon Lenny, deadline's coming." It was a friendly warning.

"No deadlines for this lot. No more deadlines ever, the lucky bastards."

That was my life. I gave every poor sucker who passed away five column inches of news copy to prove he was somebody. I was the obit writer.

Sure, I started out a reporter, covered city hall, state politics, a couple of governors—everything that was important in this town. I was on the beat when Three Mile Island ran hot and nearly melted down, threatening to take all of Harrisburg with it. Come to think of it, that was my last big story. A few years later, a couple of hotshot managers came in from corporate and put me to pasture on the obit desk.

In the years since, I had become a sixty-one-year-old lifer at *The Harrisburg Herald.* There was little hope of retirement, thanks to my wife and her debts. A few years back, she made us buy the condo down in Orlando. She spends most of the winter and spring there. I stay up here and pay the bill.

This was the future I faced until my own obit came up, and I began losing it. I let things slip. I wasn't out on stories anymore, so I did away with my usual jacket and tie. I took to wearing sneakers to work, along with my polyester pants. I walked aimlessly around town during two-hour lunches. I had to get out of that newsroom to breathe. I had to get out from under those obits—a good twenty a day, but sometimes close to forty.

Some days—okay, most days—my afternoon wanderings led me to a bar or two. The dark rooms with a few quiet, tired-looking men huddled over their drinks were a sanctuary from the stack of death notices that I knew was piling up on my desk. The whiskey was a bracer for what was coming: those intense hours before deadline when all those death stories needed to be set into type.

Every afternoon was the same. The elevator spat me out into the newsroom, which was really starting to hum as deadline approached. Immediately, my chest tightened. I'd shuffle back to my desk, everyone pretending not to see me. I must have looked like an empty-headed zombie, the ghost of the newsroom. Sometimes, after pissing back some of the whiskey I'd drunk, I'd catch myself in the rest-room mirror. I'd not even recognize the shell staring back from the glass, his sunken cheeks, lifeless eyes, and stringy, gray hair.

Back in my swivel chair, the crush of deadline was an oppressive weight and a palpable dread. My gut rumbled. Painful gas churned through my bowels. In those hours, farting became my only pleasure. It was cleansing. I'd fart right into the cushion of my swivel chair. Sometimes, that was enough to muffle the sound. Other times, I'm sure people heard. I didn't care. They already took me for crazy. Screw-loose Lenny was what they called me, though never to my face. So what if I farted at my desk? It kept people away. It was a blessing, the only blessing.

When writing the obits, I became a complete vacuum. I looked at the words. I typed the words. But my mind was empty. I was simply a vehicle for the stories of these dead people. It was boilerplate stuff. But what if the dead person had something else to say?

Before everything happened, I never really thought about that.

I was just a ghost floating between the worlds of the living and the dead. Little did I know that my long decline as an obit writer was merely preparation for the biggest story of my life.

And, it would all start with an obit.

2

Every day people die. You never realize just how many until you are the obit writer. And then, you don't give a damn. They aren't people; they're annoyances. Pieces of paper faxed to you by an undertaker. Pieces of paper that you have to squint at to make sure you spell the names right and get the service times correct. They'll kill you if you fuck up an obit. The families read them. They want to see their loved ones' names in the paper. They want to see their own names, listed as survivors. And they want to make sure everything is just so, to get a good turnout at the funeral. After all, those goddamn things are expensive. When it's all over, they put the clipping in the family bible.

It's all very important stuff. Just not to the obit writer.

At some papers, obit duty isn't that bad. Either it's a small paper in a small town, and not that many people die in a week. Or, it's a big city, and the paper limits the full obits to a handful of notable deaths. The rest just get death notices, little more than classified ads of the obit column.

That's not the way we did it here. At the *Herald,* we wrote a full obit on everyone who died.

My work became so numbing and repetitive—so

dead—my mind was forced to escape. It tended to leave me at the damnedest moments. I could be walking around town or driving in the car, and there it would go. Of course, my mind checked out when I typed the obits, the scores and scores of obituaries. If only I could have escaped with it.

That's when it happened. That's when I came to know things about some of the dead people in the obituaries. I don't really know how, and it was never something I could control. But, somehow, some way, my brain went off somewhere, and when it came back, it knew things. Strange things. Secrets. The dying secrets of the dead people in the obits.

Believe me, I could not have told you which obit I was writing at any particular time. But my mind knew. It knew something that wasn't printed on the faxes from the undertakers. No, they'd never put this kind of stuff in an obit, but I wrote these things just the same.

Was it my drinking? At long last, was I losing my mind? Or was I merely the only one left to tell their stories?

At first, I told myself that the information was always there, somewhere in my head. Facts I had soaked up during my forty-one years in the news business. After all, Harrisburg's no metropolis. It's pretty easy to know other people's business.

Then again, maybe it was something more. After all, how can you explain instinct? Sometimes, you just get a feeling. You just know certain things. All reporters do, to some degree or another.

That's the best I can explain it. At long, long last my reporter's instinct had returned. I wasn't about to question it.

The first time I remember it happening, I didn't even know what to make of it. I was just typing along.

The keys rattled:

Russell Gardner, 72, of Middletown, died Wednesday at his home.

He was retired from Capital BlueCross and was a former employee of Bethlehem Steel Corporation. He was a member of Rotary Club and he was A DAMN DIRTY ROTTEN WIFE BEATER. HE WAS A CLOSETED HOMOSEXUAL ALL HIS MISERABLE LIFE AND HE TOOK IT OUT BY HATING EVERY WOMAN HE KNEW, MOST ESPECIALLY HIS LOVING WIFE, MARTHA. THE MESSED-UP FUCK HAD NO DESIRE FOR HIS DEVOTED WIFE, OR ANY OTHER WOMAN FOR THAT MATTER. BUT HE WAS JEALOUS OF THE ATTENTION OTHER MEN PAID THE FAIRER SEX. HE WANTED THAT ATTENTION FOR HIMSELF.

Surviving is his wife, Martha, WHO WAS HAPPY TO SEE HIM SUFFER WITH THE CANCER AND GLAD TO WATCH HIM DIE, NICE AND SLOW. The couple had no children.

Memorial services and burial will be private. MARTHA PLANS TO DUMP HIS ASHES IN THE TOILET, TAKE A NICE HEALTHY SHIT RIGHT ON TOP OF HIM, AND THEN FLUSH THE WHOLE MESS.

I didn't realize what I had written. When your mind was out to lunch, one obit blended into the other, becoming one long string of dead people's little lives. Hell, I almost sent the damn thing to the edit desk. Usually, it was automatic, but something caught my eye and broke through the dense fog shrouding my brain. I stopped my finger just before it hit the "send" button. Surely, Bronski would have taken me for a nut job had he gotten one look at that obit. Maybe, the paper would have tried to fire me. Thank God for the union.

Luckily, it never came to that. My eyes caught the word "HOMOSEXUAL," then stopped dead on the choice phrases "MESSED-UP FUCK" and "DIRTY ROTTEN WIFE BEATER." Not the kind of thing one usually writes in an obit.

I stared at the words in disbelief. What the hell was I thinking? Why did I write this? What could it possibly mean?

These questions churned inside me, but when you've been writing obituaries day after day, year after year, it takes more than a four-letter word or two in some poor schmuck's obit to get you off your ass. I was about to scold myself for what must have been some wildly excessive lunchtime drinking and then go about the task of rewriting the obit, but I stopped dead. The raw nakedness of the language struck me. I felt dirty somehow, like a Peeping Tom whacking off outside a young girl's window. Only, I was peeking into the cold, dark corner of someone's soul.

The chill that ran down the back of my neck sure got my attention. I no longer had any choice in the matter. I had to find out more. The idea came to me surprisingly clear and direct: Go see the widow.

I looked up the Gardners in the newsroom's cross directory and got the full address. In the morning, when my mind was the freshest, I'd drive out to Middletown to see the poor widow. I had no idea what I'd say or even what I was looking for. I hadn't thought that far ahead. I just had the urge to see this woman in a desperate attempt to make some sense of the odd obit I had written.

I printed out the original version; otherwise I feared I might forget the specifics. Then, I rewrote the account of Russell Gardner's life, turning it into something nice and proper, all the usual stuff people have come to expect when they read about the dead. And none of what they haven't.

The next morning, I drove to Middletown. It was a pleasant day in late June. The trees were lush green, the beneficiaries of a moist spring. The lawns were equally full, and many were meticulously manicured and accented with mulch and tanbark in all the appropriate places, around the shrubs and flower beds.

I walked up to the porch of a modest rancher, the place where Russell Gardner had died less than thirty-six hours before, the victim of a torturous case of lung cancer. The front door was open, leaving a screen as the only barrier. I could hear a woman's voice from inside. It was the one-sided conversation of someone talking on the phone. I couldn't quite make out the words, but her tone was light, her voice rising and falling in a singsong way. At regular intervals, a burst of staccato laughter punctuated the conversation. She did not sound like a woman in mourning.

I leaned my face closer to the screen, peering deeper inside. A folded-up hospital bed sat in the corner of the living room, along with other medical equipment rented to accommodate Russell's slow, agonizing demise. In the middle of the green-carpeted floor lay three black garbage bags, all stuffed to the point of bursting. Two were tied shut, but the last was open and brimming with clothes, wads and wads of men's clothes. Martha was already getting rid of dear Russell's worldly possessions. No sense letting the corpse get cold before it's out with the old, I thought.

My finger hit the bell. On cue, a woman danced around the corner from the kitchen. She glided through the living room, easily avoiding the stuffed garbage bags. She cradled a portable phone with her left shoulder and appeared to be drying her hands, as if she'd been doing a little work in the sink. Her khaki shorts rode modestly above the knee. A white cotton blouse, sleeveless and immaculately pressed, completed the outfit. The woman coming to greet me was attractive in an understated way and appeared to be a decade and a half younger than the age listed for her dead husband.

As she neared, I could hear her say, "Okay, I gotta go. Someone's at the door. Lunch sounds wonderful. It'll be great to get out. I think that's exactly what I need. You, too. Bye, Paul."

She disconnected the phone with her thumb and looked at me through the screen. A smile remained from her conversation.

"Can I help you?" she inquired politely. She did not invite me in but didn't seem apprehensive at all. I locked eyes with her and forced myself to concentrate on her features. There was something I needed to see.

"Hi, Martha." I forced a smile. "You seem to be doing well."

"Yes." A bit confused. "I'm sorry, but do I know you?"

"I was a friend of Russell's," I lied spontaneously, a talent that comes naturally to most reporters. "A rather close friend, but I guess he never told you. He liked to keep things separate, you know, the different parts of his life. He was a complicated man. I'm glad to see you're doing so well with his passing. I just stopped by to express my condolences. I read in the paper that services were private."

"Yes," she managed. The instant I mentioned her dead husband's name, the widow's mouth, which had been curled into a smile, went slack. Her eyes, once bright and welcoming, deadened. And her voice, which had been so bouncy, fell to a monotone.

"Russell didn't introduce me to many of his, uh, friends," Martha measured out her words as she folded her arms across her chest. "He kept to himself, you're quite right."

I thought I saw her tremble as she hugged herself and looked down at her shoes. Then, her hand reached for the wooden door. But before it slammed shut, Martha's eyes, now angry and teary, glanced up and found mine.

"Did he beat you, too?" She spat out the words like they tasted bad. "Or did he save it all for me?" Her tone was hot with hate, and in that second, she saw that I knew everything. "Don't come back here. Ever."

Her stern face disappeared behind the swinging door, which marked an emphatic end to our conversation.

It had all been true, everything I had written in that strange obit. Somehow, I knew I was even right about that special, shitty funeral service Russell's wife had arranged for him: she flushed the old bugger right down the commode, a few turds on top.

3

AT FIRST I DIDN'T SEE HOW I COULD USE MY NEWFOUND instincts. They were delicate and fleeting, like the vibes you sometimes picked up off a person, even someone you didn't know all that well. But so what if some closeted fag beat his wife? Who cared if a bitter Vietnam vet died painfully, tormented as much by the ulcers that ate his guts as by his conscience, which burned painful holes through his soul? I mean, these people were dead. Having suffered in life, they ought to be able to take their dying secrets to their graves in peace. The knowledge that came to me simply added to my own burden.

I admit that I often fantasized about being spoken to by some poor bastard who had a coronary while staring at a winning lotto ticket or an old, penny-pinching geezer who'd taken his last breath atop a lumpy mattress stuffed with cash. But it never happened. And I could never see what there was to do about any of it, beyond just knowing it was true.

Then there was this little girl, twelve years old and innocent. Theresa Sue Chilton. I remember typing her obit. No, I guess I don't remember the typing, actually. But I do recall what I wrote when my instinct took over and my fingers manipulated those computer keys:

Theresa Sue Chilton, 12, of Camp Hill died Friday at home of accidental asphyxiation. She is survived by her parents, Clifford and Sue Chilton. She attended the sixth grade at Hillside Elementary School.

The funeral is scheduled for 10:00 A.M. Monday at the First Episcopal Church. Visitation will be at the Glen Burns Funeral Home, but there will be no viewing. THAT'S BECAUSE THE POOR GIRL STRUNG HERSELF UP WITH HER NYLON PANTY HOSE. SHE HUNG HERSELF FROM A RAFTER IN THE BASEMENT, AND THOSE NYLONS CUT INTO THE SOFT SKIN OF HER NECK SO BAD, THE UNDERTAKER SAID HE COULDN'T MAKE IT LOOK "NATURAL." PEOPLE WOULD KNOW WHAT SHE HAD DONE. AND ONCE THEY KNEW, THEY'D ASK WHY. MAYBE THEN THEY'D SEE IT IN HER FATHER'S EYES, THE WAY HE CAN'T LOOK AT ANYONE WHEN HE TALKS ABOUT HIS SWEET LITTLE GIRL. MAYBE THEN THEY'D KNOW THAT HIS DAUGHTER WOULD RATHER DIE THAN FACE HIM AGAIN, WITH HIS BREATH STINKING OF ALCOHOL AND THAT AWFUL STIFFNESS IN HIS UNDERWEAR.

Memorial contributions may be made to a scholarship fund to be established in her name at Hillside School. Burial will be in Rolling Green Cemetery.

You don't turn away from something like that, not even if you are a burned-out obit writer. I looked into this Chilton guy. He was some big drug company executive and lived in the richest section of Camp Hill, which is saying something since Camp Hill is the most exclusive address in Harrisburg. At least poor little Theresa Sue didn't have a younger sister waiting around to become daddy's favorite little girl. Still, I wasn't letting it go.

I went to the funeral. It was a huge affair, with a long line to get in. From the look of it, the families could have been lined up to see a Disney film. Every parent in Camp Hill had brought along their kiddies for their first lesson in death.

Inside, Clifford Chilton, attired in a finely tailored suit, was trying his best to mourn and accept the outpouring of sympathy for him and his wife. Yet, there was something evasive in his manner. He didn't let anybody get too close. His wife, meanwhile, was nearly catatonic. She sat on a white folding chair next to the casket, a closed mahogany box with little lambs carved into the side, and she never moved. I'd swear she'd been drugged. Chilton wouldn't have wanted her too emotional, lest she make some wild accusation in her hour of grief. I watched, as every now and then he'd cast a cold eye on her, just to make sure she was still subdued. People bent down to hug her, but she was gone, checked out. Not once did her eyes leave that little coffin. Atop its closed lid, Theresa Sue wore a forced smile in a school photograph. Even in her sixth-grade class picture, her eyes were vacant.

But Chilton's eyes were alive, and they moved, damn it. His little girl was lying in a box less than three feet away, but he was looking at twelve-year-olds in their best dresses, nice and formal for the occasion. Chilton kept his head low and looked appropriately solemn, but I saw his eyes rolling around, lurking after all those young girls, their legs nice and smooth but their cheeks red and eyes watery from crying.

I stood in back, near where they kept the register for the mourners. I watched as little girls signed their names in the book, their signatures so big and practiced. I watched until it made me sick.

Before I left, I signed the book, too. My name appeared right under the signature of Bernice O'Toole, who wrote that she'd keep all the math homework for Theresa Sue, as if the dead girl would be out of her coffin and back at school before long.

The next day, I sent Theresa Sue's obit to her father. Her real obit. The one that could never appear in the paper. The one with things only Theresa Sue, her father, and I knew about. I sent it unsigned in a plain white envelope with no return address.

Three days later, another obit, faxed by an undertaker, came across my desk. It was for Clifford B. Chilton, age forty-three, dead of a single gunshot wound to the head.

More precisely, Chilton died after swallowing both barrels of a shotgun. A real mess, according to Whitey Weiss, the undertaker. "Couldn't do nuthin' with him," Whitey told me. "His head was just pulp."

Naturally, it was a closed-casket ceremony, held in the same funeral home from which his daughter was buried under similar circumstances just the week before.

I didn't put anything about the self-inflicted gunshot in the obit. Gotta keep it nice and proper, just five short paragraphs that the family can keep in their bible, though I doubt Chilton's obit went into any bible.

Even though I couldn't include any of what I knew, I wrote his obit with pleasure, relishing every word of the final item ever to be written about Clifford B. Chilton. As I wrote, I had the satisfaction of knowing that the last thing that went through Chilton's mind, aside from that shotgun shot, were the questions, who knew and how in the hell could they have found out?

I smiled as I typed, and my mind didn't step out on me once that entire afternoon.

4

EVEN THEN, I DIDN'T SEE THE FULL POSSIBILITIES OF MY strange instincts. Special talent or not, I was still just the obit writer, a forgotten, broken-down old hack at the newspaper.

Months passed, another spring blossomed, and then Herb Bucher died his spectacular death right in the middle of a $5,000-a-plate fund-raiser for the governor. Finally, my instincts would intersect with a story. A big story. Huge, just like Herbert Bucher.

Tremendously overweight and perpetually laboring for breath—it was a Herculean effort for his lungs to expand under all those layers of blubber—Herbie "Large Bills" Bucher dropped dead right at the head table. His fat face plopped into his plate while he was sitting next to Governor Lowell Winters. Dinner had been served not five minutes before, but Bucher had managed to swallow the better part of a slab of prime rib the size of Texas and had put a big dent in a mountain of mashed potatoes. Then, just like that, came his exit from this world and the much more tangible world of politics. Bucher would never get to see his golden boy, Winters, run for the big political prize. Under the strained assistance of no less than six EMTs, Bucher was carried feet-first from the political battlefield just as he was about to launch Winters on a race for the White House.

Bucher was Winters's chief fund-raiser, had been since the governor was a first-term state house rep from Johnstown. With the help of Bucher's considerable fund-raising skills, Winters soon found himself in Washington, where he spent ten years as a congressman. Then came the run for governor. Winters won handily his first time out, bringing with him a Republican advantage in the state house and senate. But it was his reelection in 2000 that broke all the records. Bucher raised more money than the campaign knew what to do with, especially since they were up against a lightweight. All the big-name Democrats knew there was no hope and had stayed away.

The historic landslide ignited the presidential talk, and Bucher kept right on raising the money, the sums ever increasing. By the time that February rolled around—a full year before the crucial New Hampshire primary—the political buzz around Winters had reached a fever pitch. He'd raised more money than any other Republican in the country, but he still hadn't announced for president. Speculation had it that he was aiming for a late-spring kickoff for the campaign. The mere formality of an announcement did not slow down the fund-raising, however. The late-April soiree in Hershey, the one where "Large Bills" finally cashed out, was the biggest yet.

I wasn't there, of course. What would an old obituary writer be doing at a ritzy political affair featuring the hottest governor in the country? But I heard all about it. The juicy gossip circulated all around town and even managed to filter down to the dive bars I frequented. From the sound of it, the bigwig donors got every bit of their money's worth that Thursday night, a story to tell for years. Of course, none of the juiciest details were ever reported by the *Herald*'s very own political ace, A. Abraham Braxton. But I relate them here, nonetheless.

By all accounts, the governor was quite startled when Bucher dove headfirst into his plate. Someone said it looked as if Winters tried to duck under the table. Perhaps, he thought someone was shooting at him and had hit poor Herb instead. After all, Winters was a precious political commodity, just one press conference away from being the Republican front-runner for president.

Once Winters regained his composure, he tried to help, figuring he'd best look decisive and cool in front of all of those important supporters. A state trooper dressed in a suit, part of Winters's security detail, was at Bucher's right, trying to lift the fat man out of his plate. Winters aided from the left. Neither man could get his arms even halfway around Herb Bucher's prodigious girth. Instead, the two men counted down to synchronize their exertion and finally managed to move Herb's torso back. But the dead man's considerable weight shifted to the left, leaving the governor—a slight man with a shock of perfectly styled gray hair—with more of a load than he could handle. Winters tried his best to brace the leaning weight, but it was like trying to stop a falling maple. People said it was as if Bucher's limp body went into a slow tilt. Just like that, both Herb and Winters disappeared under the table.

There was a mad scramble to free the governor. One reliable witness, an undertaker friend of mine who happened to be a top donor, told me he could hear Winters's muffled but panicked screams. "I can't breathe," the governor was heard to have said. "Get this fat fuck off me."

In the end, it took six men, some knocking over chairs and one splitting his tuxedo pants, to roll Bucher, finally freeing the governor. Two troopers on security detail grabbed Winters under either arm and raised him to his feet. They motioned for one of the rushing EMTs to take a look at the governor, but to his credit, Winters wouldn't hear of it. He gestured instead to Bucher's sprawled and bloated body.

None of the governor's bumbling made it into the breathlessly dramatic yet sympathy-laced story by A. Abraham Braxton. Winters came off as a fast-acting hero trying to help a beloved friend. But there was no mistaking the panic etched on Winters's face in the picture snapped in the unguarded seconds before he could collect himself. It told the real story.

For six years, Pennsylvanians had become accustomed to seeing their governor wearing his best smile or a decidedly determined furrowed brow. He had been produced, packaged, and delivered to the public by his handlers, as if they were selling toothpaste or underarm deodorant. But there he was on the front page looking rattled, disheveled, and unprepared. The governor's hair was matted; his eyes were confused; and his tux shirt was slathered with mashed potatoes and gravy from where Bucher's messy face had sunk into his chest. Quite simply, Winters looked terrified, like any fifty-eight-year-old man who had just watched his fat friend die. A man who just seconds before had nearly been buried alive under an avalanche of blubber.

He did not look presidential.

That's what I remember thinking when I saw the newspaper. Looking back on it now, knowing everything that would happen, that's when fortunes started to turn for Lowell Winters. And it's when my fortunes turned, as well.

Of course, I didn't know of the changing tides of fate on that Friday morning when I first saw the photo of our disheveled governor in the *Herald.* But I would soon enough. Herb Bucher would come to see me. I received his obit later that day.

5

As much as it pains me to admit it, I can't tell my story without telling the story of Arthur Abraham Braxton. I can't call him my nemesis, for he never really acknowledged my existence. But I sensed that he hated me, or at least my kind, the moment he swept into the newsroom three years before, propelled by the urgent force of his self-promoted talent.

Those who know said Braxton had the editors, especially city editor Bill Sharps, eating out of his hand in the job interview. In fact, it wasn't so much that Braxton, a cub reporter with exactly one year's experience, was being interviewed for a job. He was interviewing the editors, seeing if he deigned to work here. Braxton fully believed that he was better, smarter, and quicker than anyone else at the paper the moment he stepped into the newsroom for that first interview. His effusive self-confidence wowed the editors in no time. It was no coincidence that he had just spent a year at a small but respected paper in New Hampshire, the major proving ground in presidential politics. And it was soon agreed that Braxton would have the best beat at the paper: covering the governor's reelection bid. Even back then, talk was building that

Winters would be a front-runner for president in the next national election cycle. Braxton knew it, too. He wanted a front-row seat in Harrisburg, a chance to follow Winters all the way to the White House. It was too perfect. He was too perfect.

The assignment represented an unbelievable opportunity for someone a year removed from journalism school, even if it was a master's program, completed after Braxton had taken off a few years following his undergrad courses to travel the world. It was the kind of opportunity that could make a career. Who knew, there might have been a book deal in it: the inside story of a Pennsylvania president. It's why Braxton had chosen us.

He was a prodigy, no doubt about that. African American, but only by genetics. Everything else about him was New England blue blood. He had a pedigree, for Christ's sake. His family was old-time Boston, with one of his ancestors a major force in the freedom movement before the Civil War. His father was a renowned heart surgeon and his mother a Harvard professor. He smelled of money and privilege, an odor detected instinctively in any newsroom. It's no secret that newspapering is not a profession in which you get rich, or even all that comfortable. And I have always resented the people from money who came to journalism as some sort of public service, as if their work was a noble hobby, some sort of charity. For the rest of us, who really did have to subsist on the meager money we earned, these crusaders made us feel like suckers. Braxton made me feel this way, and worse.

When my mind permitted me to focus, I watched him. For three years, I watched him, and I read all his stories. There was something about Braxton that just demanded attention. He was good-looking as all hell. Six feet, three inches and lean muscled, with soft, pleasant and, yes, trusting features. He was country club, through and through, and the best dresser I ever saw. Clothes just loved him. It helped that his entire wardrobe was expertly tailored, but the effect was glorious. When he'd doff his jacket in the newsroom, his shirts were the whitest white, with never so much as a stain under the arms. The only marks I ever saw on his clothes were the monograms on his cuffs. No buttons, he wore cufflinks.

But the most distinctive and beguiling thing about Braxton was his skin. It had the sumptuous, inviting color of a cup of coffee with plenty of cream. I never saw a single blemish on his countenance and never detected so much as razor stubble on his chin. His shaved head was perfectly shaped, completing his look.

Braxton's acceptance in the halls of the state capitol was immediate. Officials actually *liked* talking to him. He could hold a compelling conversation on any subject and was more than happy to spend hours chatting about things that would never show up in print. He did not have to hound, harass, or pump people for his stories. He had the quiet, dignified confidence of a reporter who knew all his bases were covered.

It helped that he was unfailingly accurate in his writing, with a great eye for detail yet an ability to communicate plainly, with a keen discernment of what was important and what wasn't. Still, his most controversial stories contained a certain edge, a definite agenda, if you will. Nothing as obvious as a slant, but subtle shadings that put certain facts in one light, while glossing over others. Such was the case with his story about Herb Bucher's noteworthy death. Braxton played up the governor's efforts to save the fat fund-raiser without getting into the nettlesome details of Winters nearly getting squashed to death. Since whatever edge unfailingly favored the governor, Braxton's steady flow of tips and exclusives continued uninterrupted.

I was never sure myself how extensive Braxton's sources were, but there was no doubting that he had a direct pipeline into Winters's office. It was often discussed among jealous reporters that Winters had been as taken with Abe Braxton as anyone. The governor clearly enjoyed his company, not to mention the favorable play his administration received in his stories.

No, I didn't like him. Perhaps it was because he made me feel worse about myself than I usually did. Then again, all the new ones made me feel that way, as they blew into the newsroom so brash, young, and confident. I'd seen plenty of young reporters come up in my time. Like the spring ducklings hatching down by the Susquehanna, every year there'd be another hot-shit reporter. They'd put in twelve-hour days mining the little stories for that one big one. They'd tell themselves they were here for a cup of coffee on their way up to the Philly *Inquirer, The Boston Globe,* or the goddamn *New York Times.* If that didn't quite work out, it would be off to law school or back to some university for a master's or a Ph.D. Perhaps, they'd land in some cushy public relations job, or become a press secretary for the state. The future was bright.

The only time these hotshot rookies got a little nervous that their plans might not succeed was when they looked at me. They'd see me scratching my head over yet another obit, and they'd be shaken for just a second that it could happen to them. Then, just as suddenly, they'd laugh it off. No, they'd never end up like me, walking around the newsroom like a zombie.

What they never realized was, somebody has to

type the obits. And what these young kids never understood was, a newsroom is really a place filled with misfits, people who could never hope to make it in the real world. In that respect, I fit in just fine. I was part of the mix of intellect, ego, and garbage collector that defines any newsroom. I've often thought that, deep down, there was a part inside each one of them that knew we were the same. They just needed a few decades in this business to find out how similar.

What really got them, these young ones, was sticking them with a day of writing obits. Oh my, you'd hear them holler and complain, trying anything to get out of it. But most reporters had to do their share on the way up, all part of paying dues. They got a taste, just a taste. And they hated it.

One young reporter who never got his taste was Abe Braxton. When he'd hear one of his young colleagues complaining about weekend obit duty, Braxton would proudly announce that he'd never written a single obituary—and never would. He wore the fact like a badge of honor, as if he were better than the rest of us for having never dirtied his hands with the stories of the dead.

I didn't like him from the very first. Maybe it was my own jealousy. I admit I envied him. Maybe, it was something more. My instinct, perhaps, trying to tell me something.

In any case, I'm sure he didn't think much of me. In fact, I know it. Who would have guessed that we'd end up working together on the biggest story of our lives?

6

The fax came in at ten in the morning that Friday. From the start, I knew this would not be a by-the-numbers obit. But I had no idea how far from the ordinary the death of Herb Bucher would take me.

Not all obituaries are created equal. Some lives are just more important than others. A local butcher is more interesting than a housewife. A long-time restaurant owner or a well-known bartender will get special treatment, usually a few quotes from old customers waxing sentimental. Priests and bishops are always a big deal. We newspaper people like to make a fuss when one of our own cashes out. It's one of the few perks of this business. But by far, the most lengthy and lavish obits are reserved for public figures. When a well-known actor dies, it's national news, even if he or she hasn't appeared in a film in decades. Same with a head of state. In Harrisburg, where state government is the number-one industry, about the biggest thing you can be is a political player.

Herb Bucher may have never held public office, but everyone who was anyone in state politics knew him. Plus, Bucher was hard to miss, weighing as he did about four hundred pounds. And he was a constant fixture in the trendiest downtown bars, where he picked up the check without fail. Many would mourn him for this reason alone. It didn't take much more than that to score a person one hell of a big obituary in the *Herald.* And unlike typical obits, these stories carried the byline of the writer. In some small way, my name would be forever linked to that of Herb Bucher.

I knew I'd have to write a tribute to Bucher. I'd give him his life's due in death. I didn't know it then, but in turn, Bucher would give me my own life back, my life as a reporter.

I had plenty for this obit. In addition to the usual material from the undertaker, every politician in town had faxed over statements on Bucher's passing. You could always tell when it was a political person who died by all the written statements from colleagues and friends. It was so the politicians weren't misquoted. Plus, by releasing their comments in writing, they could avoid wasting time on the phone with an obit writer like me. My job was to make it all sound good, to give it a writer's touch. I knew the editors were expecting something special. City Editor Bill Sharps even forced himself to speak to me. He tried way too hard to adopt a casual manner, as if we chatted all the time.

"Hi, Lenny." Sharps oozed discomfort.

I grunted acknowledgment but didn't face him.

"I have you on the story budget for the Bucher obit. That'll run as part of the package with Braxton's follow-up, so it's going to go news side, not with the other obits, okay?"

I nodded and grunted again.

"If you have any problems let me know." Sharps was already retreating from my cubicle. "You can let it run for twenty inches. Make it a good read, plenty of quotes."

Twenty inches, I thought, as Bill Sharps returned to the warm glow of his computer screen, where he was most secure and comfortable. Twenty inches was four times the size of an ordinary obit. It had been a long time since I had written twenty inches. Sure I had typed thousands and thousands of inches, but it was something altogether different to write at length about any one thing.

I was rusty, but I began as I always did—with the name, age, and the date of death. As I wrote, the boilerplate became inspired. And the tribute I offered was rewarded with a mysterious tip, which flowed through my typing fingers and onto my computer screen, along with the rest of Herbert Bucher's obituary.

GOVERNOR'S FUND-RAISER DIES; LEAVES POLITICAL LEGACY, BIG VOID IN WINTERS ADMINISTRATION

By Lenny Holcomb

Herbert V. Bucher, chief fund-raiser for Gov. Lowell Winters, died Thursday night after suffering a heart attack at a black-tie Republican dinner in Hershey. He was 44.

Known to most business and political leaders simply as "Herbie," Bucher revolutionized political fund-raising in Pennsylvania, raising millions for Governor Winters, who won two terms in office largely on the backing of Bucher's efforts.

His official title was political director of the Winters Leadership Fund, the governor's political action committee, and therefore was not a state-paid employee. His main function was raising money. Politicians and businessmen remembered him fondly for his favorite line, "How much shall I put you down for?"

During fund-raising pushes, he often made up to 200 phone calls a day. Co-workers said his right index finder was permanently callused from all of the dialing.

In recent months, political speculation mounted that Bucher was helping prime the donation pump for Winters's biggest campaign yet. The governor is reportedly weighing a run for the Republican nomination for president. Ironically, Bucher's death occurred at a $5,000-a-plate fund-raiser that was the unofficial campaign's biggest moneymaker yet.

Bucher's loss to Winters, the candidate, is incalculable, analysts said. But the governor refused to talk politics in speaking of Bucher's death. His prepared statement read simply that a dear friend was gone.

"A kind spirit and a bright light has been extinguished in my life and in the lives of so many in Harrisburg," Winters said. "Herbie's appetite for life was legendary and his loyalty as a friend was unwavering. His hearty laugh, his warm smile and his unmistakably optimistic voice will long be remembered. I will miss him always."

Winters is slated to deliver the eulogy at Bucher's funeral service, which is set for Monday at St. Patrick's Cathedral in Harrisburg. The event is expected to attract the political A-list from Harrisburg and around the state.

Bucher's ultimate legacy will depend largely on the outcome of Winters's expected presidential bid. But many of the changes Bucher wrought on the fund-raising scene were controversial, as money became the wheel grease of Pennsylvania politics.

In his own defense, Bucher often said money was a political reality, like poll taking and kissing babies. "You need money to get your message out," he had said. "That's the bottom line for everybody in this business, and I mean the donors and the candidates."

Social to a fault, Bucher often held court at his favorite restaurants and watering holes around town.

"I must say that I was never permitted to buy a single drink when I was in his presence," said state Majority Leader Sen. Pete O'Leary. "To this old Irishman, that's as fine an epitaph as a man can have. Herbie wasn't Irish, but he had smiling eyes. And he kept so many others smiling with him. The pubs won't be the same without him."

BUT BUCHER'S PERSONAL LARGESSE BEGS THE QUESTION AS TO THE SOURCE OF HIS GENEROSITY. HIS SALARY WAS A MODEST $79,000, BUT BUCHER RAN UP BAR AND RESTAURANT TABS TOTALING $12,000 A MONTH OR MORE. THAT'S ACCORDING TO SOURCES KNOWN ONLY TO THIS REPORTER.

ACCEPTANCE TO BUCHER'S INNER CIRCLE WAS FREE ADMITTANCE TO AN ENDLESS BUFFET OF BOOZE AND SCHMOOZE—ALL DELIVERED ILLEGALLY AT THE EXPENSE OF WINTERS'S CAMPAIGN FUNDS.

IT WAS NO SECRET THAT BUCHER LOVED MONEY. IT WAS THE MAIN REASON HE WAS SO GOOD AT RAISING SUCH VAST SUMS. BUT HE ALSO LIKED TO SPEND IT, LOTS OF IT. IT WAS A NATURAL STEP THAT HE SHOULD TAKE FROM THE CAMPAIGN. AFTER ALL, IT SEEMED LIKE HIS MONEY. HIS EFFORTS HAD PRODUCED IT.

SO HE SPENT MIGHTILY AND RECKLESSLY. BUT BUCHER WAS SO VITAL TO THE GOVER-

NOR AND SO OBVIOUSLY BELOVED, NO ONE ELSE IN THE CAMPAIGN OR THE ADMINISTRATION DARED QUESTION HIM.

WITH HIS CHIEF FUND-RAISER NOW DEAD, WINTERS MUST KNOW HIS CAMPAIGN IS SUDDENLY VULNERABLE, GIVEN THE UNGODLY AMOUNTS THAT IT WILL TAKE TO COMPETE IN A PRESIDENTIAL RACE. BUT THAT WOULD BE THE LEAST OF THE GOVERNOR'S WORRIES IF IT EVER GOT OUT THAT BUCHER STAYED FAT AND HAPPY BY EMBEZZLING FROM THE CAMPAIGN.

WINTERS WOULD BECOME THE UNWILLING POSTER BOY FOR CAMPAIGN FINANCE REFORM. NOT ONLY THAT, ONCE-LOYAL DONORS COULD GROW HESITANT, KNOWING THAT THEIR MONEY WAS MISSPENT BEFORE.

IN THIS ONE VERY IMPORTANT WAY, BUCHER'S EPITAPH HAS YET TO BE WRITTEN.

Once again, I didn't realize what I had written. The writing had been an unconscious act. My fingers simply moved over the keyboard and words populated my screen.

As I read over it, I was struck first by the quality. This wasn't a by-the-numbers obit. It flowed, had style, a good pace. There was a nice sprinkling of quotes and some insight into the man. I had nailed it.

Then, I read down to the parts that talked about my special source and the things about Bucher's spending and where he got his money. What to make of this?

I paged through my notes and faxes. None of the documents listed Bucher's salary, yet I had a figure in the story. I punched Bucher's name into the paper's database. Up popped the annual story in which we published the salaries of certain public officials. People loved that stuff, especially in Harrisburg, where so many people on state and political payrolls wanted to know what the big shots made. Sure enough, according to the most recent listing, Bucher was pulling in $79,000 from the governor's political action committee. Exactly what I had in the story. I could have remembered it, I told myself.

But what about Bucher's drawing money from the campaign accounts and how, if it ever got out, it could sink the governor's campaign? Could this be right, too?

If it was, I'd have myself a real story, front page for sure.

In journalism, however, instinct will take you only so far. A hunch is but the first step. All those things about Bucher wouldn't mean spit unless I could nail them down. If I ever hoped to see a word of it in print, I needed facts, documents, and evidence. I'd have to prove everything to Bill Sharps and the other editors before the paper would run a word.

I dared not say anything to anyone. They'd just think I was crazy. I'd have to work this one alone, keeping it nice and quiet. In that adrenaline-fueled moment, I really believed I could do it, too. And why wouldn't I? Things were coming to me, now, and my mind was getting sharper and sharper, like the old days. For the first time in a long time, I felt like a reporter.

But I was still the obit writer. First, I had to file Herb Bucher's obit, minus all those things about embezzlement and the sinking of Winters's political fortunes. I quickly reworked the story and sent it off to the city desk. Then I started making my calls.

7

I HADN'T MADE A CALL AS A REPORTER IN OVER FIFTEEN years. Sure, I phoned undertakers nearly every day to double-check the spelling of a name or a service time. But I hadn't worked on a story, a real story, since I was put on obits. I didn't even have a phone book at my desk. But I did know who I would call.

Edmund Moore had worked at the paper for eighteen years when he got out. He was a good reporter, covering state government mostly. We worked the Three Mile Island disaster together back in 79. I was out at the scene, near as I could get to the shadow of those four cooling towers that soon would personify the threat posed by every nuke plant in the country. Moore stayed back at the paper, working his state sources, running out to press conferences, and lead-writing most of the coverage.

When I wasn't worrying about radiating my balls off, I'd shoot the shit with the other reporters or a few of the plant security guards. And every day like clockwork, I'd call Eddie with the latest line being dished out by power company officials.

That was going on twenty-five years ago, now. Eddie

went to work for the state soon afterward, parlaying his name recognition on TMI into a spot as press secretary for the state environmental protection department. From there, he went on to Capital City Bank, ending up as their communications officer, a post whose demands consisted mainly of attending business lunches and city groundbreakings outfitted in $1,500 business suits. I'd see him from time to time, mostly over the lunch hour when I'd be wandering around downtown, and he would be striding purposefully to some important meeting. We never really talked, but he always extended a cordial hello as we passed, even if I was too dazed to respond.

He had done well for himself, Eddie had. He had gotten out of the paper at the right time, that was for sure. Somehow, I knew he'd do me a good turn. Even in our quick passings on the street, I got the feeling that Eddie realized he could have very easily ended up just like me, had things been different and he stayed. I saw it in his eyes, which had the hollow look of a man staring at his own ghost.

Basically, he pitied me, but I didn't care. I'd use whatever juice I had.

I flipped through a phone book I purloined from a nearby desk and found the bank headquarters' number. I dialed, and a sweet-voiced secretary purred into my ear.

"Good afternoon, Capital Bank. Mr. Moore's office, this is Sylvia speaking. May I help you?"

"Uh, hello," I managed. "Uh, can I talk to Mr. Moore?"

I spoke tentatively, lacking the tone of privilege, urgency, and entitlement that most reporters managed to strike when they just *had* to talk to someone. I had it once, but I'd been talking to undertakers too long.

"Whom shall I say is calling?"

"Uh, Lenny, Lenny Holcomb from the *Herald.* He knows me. We go back a ways."

"Thank you, Mr. Holbrook. Please hold."

"Holcomb," I said desperately as the earpiece swelled with classical music.

I don't know how long I was on hold. My mind started taking a walk on me, but a distantly familiar voice spoke through the phone, bringing me back just in time.

"Lenny?" Edmund Moore asked.

"Eddie," I said, relieved. "Good to hear your voice."

"You, too." Eddie always had a welcoming nature that put people at ease. It had helped him get a ton of good stories over the years. "Been a long time. You doin' all right?"

"Yeah." It was all I could muster.

"Hearing from you brings me back. Those were some times back in the day." Eddie chuckled with the fondness of someone long enough removed to remember only the good times. "What are you up to these days?"

"I'm still at the paper, Eddie." My tone was flat, dead.

"How long's it been now?"

"Forty-one years, but don't remind me." I couldn't mask my self-loathing.

"What do they have you doin' these days? Last I remember of us working together, all of Harrisburg thought they'd be glowing in the dark."

"Not too much excitement like that these days. They have me on obits."

"Oh," Eddie managed as the air went out of him. "What can I do you for, buddy?"

"I got something here, Eddie." My hushed tones indicated importance. "Are you in a position to talk a bit of business, something a little sensitive."

"Sounds serious." He was interested, or at least intrigued.

"I got a story, Eddie. A real story. You remember what that feels like?"

"I do, but it's been a while. I've been out of the game."

"So have I." I couldn't help but sound desperate, because I was. "The hell kind of life you think it's been for me, typin' obits all day long? I been doing that shit for twenty years."

The other end of the phone was deadly silent as Eddie Moore listened to my pleadings.

"You were smart to get out when you did, and I don't begrudge you one bit of your success. You deserve it. But I didn't get out. Now, I got a chance to show those bastards that I can do more than type obits. But I need you to do me a favor, Eddie, a big one."

"Tell me, Lenny. If I can, I will."

"I knew it," I said, relaxing. "Somehow, I knew you would."

"So, what's this about?"

"You know the guy who just died? The governor's fund-raiser?"

"Herbie Bucher? Shit, yeah. I ran into him quite a bit. I'm a donor myself. Herbie hit me up pretty regular. He sure had a way of separating people from their money."

"That ain't the half of it," I muttered into the phone, careful that my voice would not carry beyond the fabric walls of my cubicle. "Some of that money of yours probably ended up in his personal account. He's been pocketing the spoils for years. I have some good sources on this. I just need his bank records showing the deposits. That's where you come in."

"Jesus Christ, Lenny," he gulped. "I don't know. There's going to be some heavy fallout on this, and I don't want to involve the bank. I mean, we can't be caught handing out our customers' account records to the goddamn newspaper."

"Don't worry, Eddie," I assured, gaining confidence now. "I'll protect you and the bank. We'll just print that the records were obtained by the paper, and leave it at that. The documents will never leave my hands. And with the lawyers already involved in Bucher's estate, the paper trail could have come from anywhere. The newspaper could have gotten hold of the records from any number of sources. You and the bank will have plenty of cover, believe me. As soon as someone with a political ax to grind sees those records, copies will be all over town, anyway. But then, I miss my shot. I got the tip, but I need those documents to run with it."

There was a long silence. I could barely breathe.

"I like you, Lenny," Eddie said, finally. "I'll see what I can do."

"Wait a minute," I interjected in a sudden, sickening realization of my mistake. "What about your secretary? I mean, she got my name wrong, but I told her I was with the paper. She might put two and two together. I knew I'd screw things up. Fuck."

"Don't sweat it," Eddie said, sure of himself. "I'll make like you called about some other story. I'll even have her fax you the latest press release on our economic development project with the city. She won't think a thing, believe me. Reporters call me all the time. After all, I am the spokesman for the largest bank in town." Eddie let loose a sly chuckle, and the pleasing sound of it quelled my own doubts.

"Right," I said, allowing myself to laugh with him.

"It's probably not a bad idea to avoid my office, though," Eddie continued, back to business now. "Meet me tonight, around eight, at The Passway. We'll have a couple of drinks for old times' sake, and maybe I'll have something for you. Something that'll get you off that obit desk."

"Sure," I said, surprised at the excitement in my own voice. "The Passway. The old haunt. That'd be great. And thanks, Eddie. I owe you big."

"See you on Page One." It was something we used to say to each other when one of us was working on a big story. I was surprised Eddie remembered. He really did miss it. So did I.

I hung up the phone, and my heart raced. I felt like a cub reporter on his first story. I wanted to jump out of my chair and race over to the city desk to start selling my story onto the front page. I wanted to pant about it breathlessly for Bill Sharps, hoping he'd pat me on the head like a good dog who'd just brought his master a bone.

I stopped myself, of course. I'd have my moment, but not yet. The political fallout surrounding Bucher's death would remain Braxton's story for a while longer. I couldn't make my move until I had the proof. I was still just the crazy obit writer talkin' shit until I got those records. But I'd forgotten the adrenaline rush of a good story. It was one of the best things about this job. It made you feel young. Young and alive, the exact opposite of writing obituaries.

8

I HADN'T BEEN TO THE PASSWAY CAFE IN DECADES. EVEN MY afternoon wanderings to escape the obits, which led me to many a downtown tavern, had not taken me there. The location was a bit away from downtown, on Herr Street, near Cameron. But that wasn't it. I had purposely avoided the place because it had been the scene of too many good times in the old days. I just couldn't stomach the place in the state I was in.

In the old days, the tavern and restaurant named for a nearby underpass was the newspaper bar, every reporter's after-work destination. Many a story had been told, rehashed, exaggerated, and told again in that small, smoke-filled bar. Back then, a fastidious Italian couple ran the place. Food was decent. Great, in fact, if it was after deadline and after hours. The lady sat in back, counting the money near closing time, while the old man worked the bar. The boys and I would be laughing and drinking, clanking glasses and washing away the day. Nothing, I mean nothing, went better after racing a deadline than some whiskey shots and beer chasers. It was a signal to your brain that it could finally slow down and relax. There was no guilt in the many hours my colleagues and I spent in that little bar. Even our wives, who we knew didn't like it much, wouldn't say a thing. We were newspapermen.

I still respected that old place. That's why I took the trouble of sprucing up a bit before heading over, donning a fresh shirt, knotting a tie that was new in the 1980s and slipping on a jacket that smelled strongly of mothballs. Walking into the bar, I wondered if it had been worth the effort. Nothing much at all had changed—the same tables, chairs, and barstools—but everything was badly worn. Plastic flowers were buried under layers of dust. The walls were sticky with grease and nicotine. There was a detectable haze of cigarette smoke, stale beer, and must. Even the old Italian couple, now dead but immortalized in a black-and-white portrait hung lovingly above the bar, looked weary. It had been too long for us all.

At least the bar was clean under the quick rag of a young keeper sporting a prominent beer belly. He was short and looked Italian, perhaps a relative of the former owners. I didn't ask. I couldn't afford to think about such things. I needed all my concentration for Eddie Moore and what I hoped he would bring.

"What can I get you?" the barkeep asked, his rag hand taking another swipe across his very clean bar.

Down the bar, a couple of guys were huddled over their drinks and staring into the glow of a muted television tuned to some second-rate sporting event featuring grotesquely huge men pulling tractor-trailers. No one was in any of the booths, and the place felt ghostly. I could almost hear the echoes of my own laughter from years long gone.

"Whatta ya got on tap?" I asked as I mounted a stool. I made the same query wherever I went, even where I was a regular. How was I to remember what beer various taverns kept on tap?

"Just Yuengling," he said, as if this were common knowledge. The regional brew, originally known as a coal miner's beer, was now the trendy beer in town.

"All right, a Yuengling. That'll do her."

I retrieved my wallet from my back pocket and slapped a twenty on the bar. In exchange, the bartender presented me a glass of the amber lager, which I gripped with both hands, carefully raising it to my mouth. I wasn't as steady as I used to be, especially when I went the whole day without a drink, as I had today. I took a long, continuous draw, slurping down half a glass before I rested.

Just then, still exhaling from the pleasure of the day's first taste, I felt a hand on my shoulder and heard a familiar voice. For a moment, it seemed like twenty years ago.

"Hey, Lenny," Eddie Moore said.

I turned to see a man I barely recognized. He looked taller, him standing and me on the stool. He was handsome and seemed youthful, though he was a year or two older than me. His gray hair was perfectly barbered and his nails shone from a recent manicure. His suit fit just right.

"Jesus, Eddie," I gasped, shocked by my first close-up look at how different we'd become. Back when we frequented this bar, we both bought our suits at Sears and were partial to drab, narrow ties. "You look like a million bucks."

He smiled uneasily, but I continued on, knowing I made him uncomfortable by pointing out his success. "I got you out slumming tonight. Bet you haven't been in this old place since you quit the paper, eh?"

Eddie adopted a look of reflection and nodded as

he settled on the stool next to mine. "About that, about that. I miss it, though. I miss the times here, and believe it or not, I miss the paper."

"Staying would have cured you of that. No, Eddie, you did the right thing. You rode Three Mile Island for all it was worth and you got the hell out. You miss what it was and what we were once. That was a long time ago. It ain't that now, and believe me, neither are we. Hell, you're a big-shot banker, and I'm an obit writer."

"You're wrong, Lenny. You're a reporter." Eddie Moore held up a thick manila envelope.

"You were right," he went on. "Your source was right on. Bucher has been cashing checks written from campaign accounts for the last four years. That's going back to before the second governor's race, when Bucher raised all that cash. Looks like he was depositing an average of about $15,000 a month. From the looks of it, he pretty much controlled at least one of the campaign accounts, so he could write himself checks and deposit them, just like that."

Eddie spoke with the unmasked enthusiasm of an old municipal reporter who once got hard-ons chasing down stories about city councilmen getting kickbacks from contractors and school board members packing the payroll with relatives in do-nothing jobs. It wasn't Watergate, but so what? For a reporter, there was nothing better than nailing a dirty public official. It was how you earned notches in your typewriter. And damn if it wasn't fun.

"If it was that simple, how come he never got caught?" I asked, trying to focus my mind, which was already swimming with the possibility of a front-page banner headline.

"Well, he was smart enough to keep his personal account at a different bank," Eddie said. "So, it would've taken some legwork to follow the money across the different institutions. And he wrote notations on the checks, as if they were going to cover cash expenses. But I doubt there were ever any legitimate vouchers to back them up. Reimbursements wouldn't be handled that way, anyhow, with a guy cutting himself checks from accounts he controlled. Truth is, the campaign probably didn't want to know what was going on. The money that Bucher was putting in his pocket was a pittance compared to the millions he was bringing in. It was better for Winters that Herb stay fat and happy."

"And that he did," I said.

"Big-time," Eddie laughed. "No wonder that bastard was such a big spender all over town. He was always closing the bars, buying round after round of fancy martinis all night long. I always thought he had some kind of liberal expense account with the campaign. Turns out he did—one he opened for himself."

"What are you giving me?" I gestured to the envelope.

"You've got four years' worth of activity records for both the campaign accounts, which were kept at my bank, and Bucher's personal account, which was held at City Savings. There are also copies of canceled checks from the campaign account that were endorsed and deposited by Bucher into his own account. The checks have the memo notations I told you about, Bucher's half-assed attempts to mask the payments as reimbursements. But the amounts are just too large and too regular. Greed makes people stupid, I guess."

My eyes focused on the envelope. I had my story.

"You don't know what this means, Eddie." I actually felt myself tearing up.

"At least offer to buy me a beer?" Eddie cracked, forcing a laugh to lift the awkwardness of my unexpected sentimentality.

"Sure," I coughed, choking it back. "My privilege."

"Antonio," I commanded, pretending to know the barkeep's name. "I'd like to buy my friend a beer, if you please."

Eddie slid the envelope across the bar. I picked it up, felt its weight, and marveled at the mere envelope, not even opening it. I tucked it into the back of my pants so there would be no danger of me drinking too much and forgetting it at the bar.

The beer arrived and Eddie leaned over to me with his full glass.

"To old times and old newspapermen," he said, smiling.

9

THE FOLLOWING MONDAY, I ARRIVED AT WORK EARLY, WELL before eight. It was a sharp break in my usual pattern, one of the many that day. I'd spent the entire weekend preparing for my moment. If I had gone over the contents of Eddie's envelope once, I'd done it a dozen times. Then on Sunday night, I laid out my best pair of slacks, dug through my closet for a clean, unwrinkled shirt, and spent an hour holding up hopelessly out-of-fashion ties, to see which of them matched best. And knowing my sneakers weren't going to cut it in my play for the front page, I rubbed a shine into my wingtips.

Still, as I walked into the newspaper lobby that morning, doubt choked me. I felt like a forgery, some counterfeit reporter in a period costume. Then, our kindly black security guard at the front desk, a man who noticed everything but whose face rarely registered a thing, did a double take when he saw me. He glanced subtly at his wristwatch, noting the early hour, and then looked at me with a surprised, satisfied smile. Without saying a word, he reached a hand to his forehead, tipped his blue cap, and nodded approvingly as his eyes scanned all the way down to my spit-shined shoes.

As I smiled back, I discovered the spring in my step. I was ready, I decided then. Awake, alert, and as ready as I'd ever be. I punched the button for the elevator.

The newsroom was nearly empty at that hour, and I traversed the floor unnoticed. I placed the all-important envelope on my cluttered desk, only to find the nearby fax machine spitting out an obit. A couple of the local undertakers were early risers, preferring to do their embalming first thing. Maybe, such early glimpses of the dead reminded them that they'd been granted another day and had best enjoy it, just as soon as they finished with the corpse. I paid the incoming fax no mind, though, technically, I was still the obit writer. Perhaps not much longer, not once the contents of that plain-looking envelope had its say.

I looked over those records one more time, just to keep my confidence up. The pages were filled with figures, and I could see where Eddie had used a black marker to ink out certain codes, so the documents were not immediately recognizable as printouts from his bank. What was recognizable on each page was Herb Bucher's name and account number and his lengthy history of deposits and withdrawals. The man was burning through incredible sums of money. But despite all those extra, illegal deposits, Bucher's balance was only about $10,000. He was spending nearly everything he was taking in, and having the time of his life doing it. I did not begrudge him this. Bucher knew when to get out. He coded into a pile of mashed potatoes, and now all of this was someone else's problem. More precisely, it was Governor Winters's problem.

Like I said, it wasn't Watergate. But I knew the paper would jump at the story—and so would every other newspaper in the state and, probably, the country. After all, what was Watergate anyway, but a bungled office break-in? It was an old maxim in journalism that the biggest stories often started small, just tiny pieces of a much larger puzzle. It was the reporter's job to gather up all those tiny facts and build.

That's what I was determined to do. But not in my wildest dreams or my darkest nightmares did I have any idea of the colossal events I was about to set into motion—all the pain, death, and danger I would cause. Back on that Monday morning, I was just itching to be a reporter again. Knowing everything that would happen, I sometimes think that it would have been better if I'd just thrown those damn documents right into the trash and got going on the morning's death notices. Then again, no reporter would have done that. Not even me.

I was still fingering those records and working up my nerve when Abe Braxton breezed into the newsroom. As usual, he made a beeline for Bill Sharps to begin promoting whatever story he was offering up next.

The untimely death of Herb Bucher had proven to be quite the media sensation. More interesting than the death itself were the implications for Governor Winters's expected presidential run. Politicos all over town were debating the scenarios, but Winters seemed content to ride the public's sympathy for now. Bereavement translated just fine in the polls. And Braxton was right on board. The governor's favorite reporter had them weeping in their breakfast cereal. His sorrow-soaked reaction stories ran Page One.

"A shocked Governor Lowell Winters could not even think about politics or campaigns," read one of the articles. "This was my friend," the governor was quoted as saying. "This is the time to remember a friend, not to think of politics."

Naturally, the governor would get around to talking politics soon enough, pointing out "Herbie's" crucial role in past campaigns. "He leaves a big void in our operation," Winters said later in the story. "I know a lot of people are talking about us making a run for the presidency, but this is a blow. Herbie has been behind me since I was a state rep. He saw me through many, many elections. If we do decide to run, the hardest part will be running without him. It's a big loss, what can I say?"

That morning, I overheard Braxton pitching more such coverage. I lingered about the fax machine, pretending to collect the early obits, while my ears were tuned to the conversation at the city desk. Neither Braxton nor Sharps noticed me, despite my newly polished appearance. Nor would they have given it a second thought if they had.

"Five days ago, I would have bet anything that Winters would announce this week, but with all this going on, no way," Braxton said, disappointed. "Of course, the governor will deliver the eulogy at the funeral today. I've got an advance copy, quite eloquent. I think we ought to run the entire speech as a sidebar. People are going to want to read it, and just pulling out quotes isn't going to capture it."

"Good idea," Sharps admired, "but what about the political fallout?" Sharps prodded carefully here, lest Braxton think he was trying to trip him.

"Well, they're going to have to get someone to fill Herb's shoes—and quick," Braxton acknowledged. "But the way he brought in the money, he won't be easily replaced. There are some names floating around, but nothing's confirmed."

Both men nodded thoughtfully.

" 'Course, there are some people who think this

whole thing could be a boost to Winters in the long run," Braxton added. "That it could become the emotional center of his campaign, if you will. My sources think that when Winters finally does announce, he'll dedicate the race to Bucher. It'd go over big with the staff. They all loved the guy. Could be worth a story on how the emotion of this tragic event may translate to the race. It could add a human element to the usual campaign stuff."

Sharps's eyes brightened. Boy, could this kid shovel it. He just about had me buying it. Sharps was already sold.

"That's the kind of story we can do that the competition can't," Sharps enthused. "We're gonna have media swarming all over this place when the official announcement finally comes. But this is still our backyard. We gotta show people that we own this town. Your story will be a good example. Nice work, Abe."

I couldn't take any more. At long last, I spoke. It was the first time either of them had heard me utter a full sentence in months, years perhaps. Up until that moment, I'd been a ghost, neither seen nor heard at *The Harrisburg Herald.*

"I guess we're just going to keep soft-pedaling this story with all this sentimental shit."

Both men's heads swiveled to face me. That same instant and to my great dismay, the fax machine started spitting out yet another death notice, as if to curse me. But I pressed on. There was no going back now.

"Yeah, it looks like we'll just do the weepy, sappy shit, but we won't cover the real story, the real news. Seems like we're more interested in giving Winters good PR than we are at getting at the truth about this cocksucker Bucher."

If they missed it the first time, I could see that they

took my meaning now. Braxton's full lips tightened, baring teeth. His forehead wrinkled in anger, and I could see veins bulging in his neck. Sharps, the little guy, was slack jawed.

"What in the hell are you talking about?" Braxton's words were long, slow, and indignant.

Sure, I'd poured it on a little thick, felt I had to, just to get their attention. Besides, that's the way we reporters talked around the newsroom back in the day, before we gave up the First Amendment in the name of political correctness and sexual harassment. I saw a sensitive spot, and I scratched it.

"You know what I mean, Braxton." I nodded knowingly, then paused. "Or maybe you don't. Maybe you're too busy suckin' the governor's dick that you don't see the story right in front of you."

I shook my head in bewilderment as Braxton went off.

"I don't have to take this," he huffed, folding his arms in a cue for Sharps to leap to his defense.

"Wait a minute, Lenny," Sharps managed. "You can't talk like that. It's totally uncalled for. It's not constructive criticism."

Sharps sounded like a kindergarten teacher on a school yard. No, even a kindergarten teacher would've had more balls. Before that moment, I never realized what lightweights I was dealing with. In my day, every other word out of an editor's mouth was fuck this or fuck that. Those ink-stained dinosaurs wouldn't blink at calling any politician a cocksucker right to his face. Now, we were whoring for the governor and we couldn't be honest enough with ourselves to call it what it was.

"You're right," I said, soft and defeated. "Guess we don't care that this motherfucker Bucher, who everyone's been crying over, has had his hand in the till for years."

For a long moment, there was silence. I had stunned them again. Finally, Braxton spoke.

"I suppose a little birdie told you that," he scoffed. "Be nice if you could prove it. You're out of your league, obit man. Why don't you go back to your dead people? I'm sure you have a fresh corpse or two to write about, don't you?"

"Matter of fact, I do. I got Bucher to write about. And it's a hell of a story, too. The prick's been milking the governor's campaign for years, to the tune of $650,000. That's if my math is right. I'm a reporter after all, not an accountant."

"Lenny, where'd you get this?" Sharps choked on his words, every bit as much as he was choking on my story. One thing about Sharps, he got a hard-on for a good story, he didn't care where it came from.

"I got it confirmed."

Sharps's obvious excitement over my story didn't play well with Braxton. "Who the fuck's your source?" he shouted at me.

"Who the fuck are you to ask me that?" I matched him.

We stared coldly at each other, and I realized then that I had him. Deep down, this cocky bastard was unsure of himself, afraid I'd scooped him, beat him at his own game.

"I have sources, too, you know. Forty-one years on this newspaper, and you think I don't have sources? Maybe you should talk to people outside the governor's staff. You've let them piss in your ear so long, you don't hear nuthin else. My guy would never come to you with something like this. He reads the paper. He knows you've been givin' Winters one big blow job."

"We're going to need more than a source on this, Lenny." Sharps broke in before it became a real dick-measuring contest.

"I know. That's why I got these." I held up the envelope, which I'd been hiding under a few of those early-morning obit faxes.

"What's that?" Sharps salivated.

"Bank records. Deposits for Bucher's personal account. Shows he's been depositing checks drawn on the campaign account. Rings up to more than $650,000 over the last four years. I wonder if the governor will be weeping over his good buddy now?"

Braxton coughed. "Let me see those."

"I don't think so. I can go over the stuff with Bill later. I think I should be at the funeral today. That way, I can ask the governor about these accounts in person. Can't wait to see his face when I give him a peek at these records. 'Course, we'll let him deliver his eulogy, first. Wouldn't want to spoil all that good grieving, would we? Heard it's a hell of a eulogy. I'll catch Winters on his way out of church. Sound okay, Bill?"

I couldn't suppress a grin. I had gone from hardly speaking to Sharps to casually calling him by his first name.

"Uh, yeah," Sharps said. "By the way, Lenny, you did a good job on the Bucher obit. Looks like you're back in the game."

"Whenever you have some time, we can go over the records," I replied, ignoring Braxton as if he'd disappeared. "You'll see, it's all there, just like I said."

"I want in on this," Braxton snapped. "I want to see the records so I can start checking with *my* sources."

"I think we ought to wait on that," I said. "Your sources will just tip off the governor, then I won't have the pleasure of the look on his face. By the time this day's through, he'll want to piss on Bucher's grave, 'stead of cry over it. 'Sides, you're covering the funeral, and I know you'll want to get right to work on that story about how the tragedy will be the emotional springboard for the campaign."

Braxton turned to Sharps for the call. "Bill, I think this is a mistake. This guy's an obit writer, for Christ's sake."

"No," I corrected. "I'm a reporter. I'm a reporter who just ate your lunch on this story. And I'm a reporter who won't be writing obits today. Will I, Bill?"

"No," Sharps said, stunned both at me and at himself for agreeing. "Bronski can get someone to cover. You go to the funeral, talk to the governor. You have Page One tomorrow, Lenny. And Abe," Sharps shot Braxton a look. "Don't talk to anyone about this until after the funeral. Lenny sees the governor first. He gets first crack, okay?"

Braxton didn't acknowledge him, but I did.

"Sounds like a plan."

I handed the obit faxes to Sharps, cracked a sneer at Braxton, and turned on a heel toward my cubicle. I was a reporter with a front-page story.

10

HERBERT BUCHER'S FUNERAL WAS A GRAND AFFAIR AT St. Patrick's Cathedral on State Street, in the shadow of the capitol dome. It was a fine spring day, with trees and flowers in bloom all around. The funeral had presented the state's elite with the chance to see and be seen, and few had resisted. Politicians of every political stripe came to pay homage to the most prodigious fund-raiser Pennsylvania politics had ever seen.

TV vans were parked across the street, their towering satellite dishes raised to the sky for live broadcast. About twenty reporters and photographers had been admitted inside the church to cover the service, but all were relegated to the balcony. I did not have the proper credentials to gain entry. My faded press pass barely got me past the sidewalk barricades, which kept the public at bay as the limos rolled up to deposit one guest after another. Dressed in black and properly somber, they filed into church in reverse order of importance.

The governor was last, of course. He couldn't help but make a few gestures to the gathered crowd. I must admit, he looked presidential in a finely tailored suit. His gray-white hair was perfectly coifed, and just the right amount of wisdom wrinkles bloomed around his eyes each time he smiled at admirers. I knew he'd serve up one hell of a eulogy in memory of Herb Bucher. It would be soggy with emotion yet laced with the unfinished political aspirations that he just knew Bucher would want him to carry out.

Later, the send-off would be completed with a grand wake at the Zembo Temple. It would be all the food and booze one could eat and drink, and I wondered if the bill would be paid out of the campaign money. It'd be fitting, I thought, knowing how much of that money Bucher had already spent indulging his considerable appetites.

Finally, the guest of honor himself was wheeled into the church in a piano case of a coffin. Encased in mahogany, Bucher's body became the center of attention in front of the cavernous cathedral.

I waited outside, sitting on one of the church's concrete steps, enjoying the cool spring air. I didn't even fret over the questions I would ask the governor when the time came. I was gaining confidence now, and I counted on the words and the questions being there when I needed them.

Later, the bells tolled for Herb Bucher. Those somber, relentless bells were my signal. To a very real extent, they were tolling for Gov. Lowell Winters, as well. I stood, brushed off my pants, and took my notebook and pen in hand.

Winters was among the first to emerge from the church. He exited with no warning or advance staff, and I had to hustle to intercept him. "Excuse me, Governor, may I ask a couple of questions?" I blurted out as he strode toward a waiting limo.

He was flanked by two dark-suited state troopers,

part of the governor's security detail. Two more waited near the converted black Lincoln Town Car. Looking somber but striding purposefully, Winters seemed in a rush to leave before the rest of the crowd and, more importantly, the media disgorged from the church. He didn't even have an aide with him, which I thought unusual.

"Governor, Lenny Holcomb from the *Herald*. I have something important. Just a few questions, please."

Finally, Winters slowed and trained his focus on me. He seemed perplexed, wondering who I was. The capitol press corps was an insular bunch, and I was an unfamiliar face. I grabbed my press ID from my pocket. Obit writer or not, I carried my press pass as a measure of self-respect.

"Lenny Holcomb, Governor," I repeated, holding up the ID. I extended my hand for a shake.

"Hi there," he said tentatively. "I must apologize, it's kind of a tough day, and I don't really have the time."

"Governor, I just need a comment." I was walking with him now. "We have a story running tomorrow, and I think you'll want to respond."

The governor furrowed his brow. I could tell he was both intrigued and wary.

"Where's Braxton? He's the one I usually deal with at your paper." Winters stopped again, this time near his elongated and customized Town Car. He could relax a bit, knowing escape was at hand.

"Probably still inside covering the funeral," I answered.

"Yes, that's just it. I really don't want to comment on anything else. My eulogy speaks for itself. This is Herb's day. I don't want to step on his news cycle. You can understand."

"Sure Governor, but—" Before I could continue, he

made a move toward the opened rear door of the limo.

"But Governor," I shouted. "My story is *about* Herb Bucher. An issue concerning him and your campaign operations."

His eyes sharpened on me, revealing the stern side of this man. A governor, for all the politicking and baby kissing, is still a CEO, and bosses have a ruthless side. "Today is for mourning, not for politics."

"All due respect, sir, it's not a political story. It's a crime story."

That stopped him cold. His curiosity took control, anchoring him to that spot on the sidewalk.

"Excuse me? What do you mean, a crime story?"

"Turns out that records and documents obtained by the *Herald* show Bucher was embezzling money from your campaign. The documents we have go back about four years and the total amount is upward of $650,000. Governor, I'm told that Bucher maintained quite an excessive lifestyle, spending well more than he was making. Did you have any idea this was going on?"

I never once took my eyes off him, even as his face burned with increasing anger.

"What is this?" His words were halting and indignant. "Is this some kind of ambush here? Have you no decency? We're at the man's funeral."

"All due respect, Governor, we have the documents and we're ready to go with a story, bad timing or not. I thought you'd want to comment. Otherwise, we can let your gushing eulogy stand as your statement. So, how does it feel, Governor, having just eulogized an embezzler? The man was robbing you blind, and you just kissed his cold, dead ass."

"You think you can talk to me like that?" Winters was clearly used to the kid-glove treatment from the likes of Braxton. "I'm done with you, and I'm done with your paper. You tell Braxton he tricked me. Ambush me with this dirt, will you? Your paper's cut off. You'll get nothing from me or my administration. You tell Braxton he's on the outs. You don't ambush me at a goddamn funeral."

His face glowed, and I finally had to glance away, as if protecting myself from the intense heat of his rage. Just then, I glimpsed a blond woman in a black dress that revealed quite a bit of leg for a funeral. She seemed to have noticed the animated nature of our exchange and rushed toward us.

A press aide, I thought. Politicians liked pretty blond mouthpieces, but she had not been there when it counted. She had not been there when the governor needed her to charm me or shoo me away. Now, she was racing to assess the damage and salvage what she could.

"Christy Denza, aide to the governor. Can I help you?" She was still catching her breath, but she fake smiled and extended me her hand. Then, she did a double take of the governor's perturbed countenance.

"Lenny Holcomb, with the *Herald.* I was just asking the governor, here, if he was aware that Herb Bucher was embezzling money from his campaign. Looks like $650,000 over four years. We've got the documents."

Christy swung her head to steal another glance at Winters, who seemed to have gone from anger to numb acceptance.

"Braxton tricked us," Winters mumbled, as if in disbelief. Christy immediately reached for his arm and squeezed it—hard. "Ah, I see," she broke in loudly, cutting off the governor's rambling accusations.

That was the second time with the Braxton stuff, I thought. Why was Winters so pissed? After all, Braxton may have been known for his favorable press coverage, but no reporter worth his salt could be expected to tip off a public official about a major story before it broke. There was a line. We, the press—and I guess I'd have to include Braxton in that—were on one side, and the politicians were on the other. That was the way it had to be.

"We'll have to take this under advisement," Christy continued, her arm now protectively around the governor, directing him toward the backseat of the limo. "If you want to fax us your documents, we'll issue a response later today. It'll be in time for your deadline, I promise."

She extended me her business card. I took it.

"I don't know if I'm comfortable with that." It was a mild protest. Christy was beautiful and it was hard to talk to her forcefully. "I mean, this is an exclusive. I really don't want the data out of my hands. It was supplied by a confidential source, and by distributing the documents, I risk breaching that confidentiality."

"I understand. Let me give you a call when I get back to the office. We'll work something out. There'll be a statement by the end of the day. Do you have a card?"

"Uh, sorry, no." I felt inadequate.

"What's your direct line, then?" she asked hurriedly. I gave it to her.

"You'll be my first call when we have something."

She climbed into the recesses of the limo, disappearing as the door closed.

Just before the long, black car motored off, I caught sight of the governor's silhouette through a tinted window. He was rubbing his forehead worriedly as he slumped in his seat.

He did not look presidential.

11

THE NEXT MORNING WHEN I WALKED INTO THE NEWSROOM, the world had changed.

I had left the paper quietly the evening before, having written and filed my story on Herb Bucher's embezzlement. Parts of the article read much like the mysterious passages in Bucher's obituary. But in writing this story, I did not need my instinct. I had facts.

A mere twelve hours later, I felt different and I must have looked different, because people noticed me. And it wasn't just my sharper wardrobe, which I continued to select more carefully now. After twenty years of doing obits, I'd been reborn. I wasn't Lenny the crazy obit guy. I was Lenny on Page One with the biggest exclusive of the year. With that single story, my image had been recast.

Co-workers who had not so much as glanced at me in the past said, "Hi, Lenny." Others smiled and gushed, "Great story today, Len."

I accepted the hellos and kudos as I walked to my desk. Waiting atop a pile of early obit faxes was a fresh copy of the morning paper, delivered to each desk by a clerk. The banner headline was in bold, block type that ran across the top of the front page: "GOV. EULO-

GIZES TOP STAFFER AS ACCUSATIONS ARISE." Underneath the banner were two subheads, one to introduce Abe Braxton's funeral story and one over my piece on Bucher's embezzlement. The head over Braxton's story read: "WINTERS GIVES TOUCHING TRIBUTE BUT LATER BACKPEDALS." It detailed the funeral and Winters's sugarcoated ramblings of a eulogy. The story was serviceable but had none of Braxton's usual style. Absent were those telling details that always cast Winters in the best possible light.

Not only was his writing flat, but Braxton himself had been painfully subdued all day yesterday. After our morning argument in the newsroom, he dutifully went off to cover the Bucher funeral, while I lay in wait outside. When we returned to the paper, it was I who drew Bill Sharps's attention. He came to *my* desk to hear about *my* story. Braxton remained quietly ensconced in his cubicle. Most of the time, he was on the phone, talking in hushed tones. Later, he left the office for long stretches, sort of like me on a typical day of typing death notices. Then, very near deadline—too close for comfort, really—he dropped off a copy of the governor's statement responding to the Bucher charges. Braxton didn't even look at me, much less speak. He just flung it on my desk as casually as if it were an obit.

It didn't matter, anyway. Christy Denza had faxed me a copy an hour before. She also called to give me plenty of off-the-record background, which I guessed was what they called spin control. Back in the day, we just called it bullshit. Nonetheless, I found myself liking her.

We chatted a bit, and Christy seemed somewhat perplexed that I also served as the paper's obituary writer. She couldn't understand why I was suddenly covering a major political scandal. Christy played off her interest in my obit duties by noting that she was a local girl, from Mechanicsburg, and had the small-town habit of checking the obituary page before anything else in the paper. Of all the things she tried to sell me on, that was the one thing I believed. She was humble and without question a hard, diligent worker who had no use for the easy way when it came to anything. I got the impression, just in our brief conversation, that she had scratched and clawed her way up and was trying desperately to hold on. My ambush outside the funeral had made it that much tougher on her. There was a hint of desperation in her voice as she asked again and again if I needed anything else for the story. Desperation because she would get the blame for the bad publicity the administration was about to receive.

She did her best to make Winters look good, a tough task after he had so publicly tied his fortunes to the cold carcass of Herb Bucher. Christy explained how emotionally upset the governor had been over the death. The allegations of Bucher's embezzlement were doubly devastating, making the day one of "conflicted emotions" for the governor.

Winters's written statement called for a "full, open and independent" investigation, while adding that the governor was "saddened and disappointed" to hear of the allegations against a trusted friend and longtime aide.

Since the governor's office was responding directly to questions raised by the *Herald,* his staff agreed to issue the statement to us alone for the first twelve hours, preserving our exclusive. The rest of the news outlets in town and around the state would get a press release first thing the next day. But by then, we would already be on the street, on people's lawns and unfolded over their breakfast tables. It was our story. It was my story.

Mostly out of sympathy for Christy Denza, I made sure to use much of what the governor had to say. It even gave me a punchier lead, with the governor calling for an investigation. Of course, I pointed out that official records obtained by the *Herald* were what prompted the governor's actions. And I included that Winters appeared confused and reacted with hostility when first confronted with the information.

"FUND-RAISER EMBEZZLED FROM CAMPAIGN, RECORDS SHOW; STATE TO INVESTIGATE," read the subhead over my story. And just below that, were the words *By Lenny Holcomb, Herald Staff Writer.*

As I sat at my desk the next morning, I took a long, slow drink of that front page, not even reading it. Just looking, admiring.

Just then, I felt a presence behind me. I sat frozen and prayed they'd go away.

"Excuse me, Mr. Holcomb," said a feminine voice. "I'm Jacquelyn Towers. I don't think we've met."

I had not counted on this. Who knew my story would prompt staffers to actually visit me at my desk? Reluctantly, I turned to see an athletic-looking woman of twenty-six or -seven, very attractive with a girlish smile that immediately disarmed me. I had noticed her byline before, but I would have never placed it with this cute face. She didn't look like a reporter, whatever one was supposed to look like. Believe me, this was a compliment.

She smiled and I could see how her girlish looks could work for her. That shy smile could disarm an army of state politicians. They'd forget themselves, talk off the cuff, and veer from the talking points. In no time, they've said too much, and Jacquelyn Towers had herself another Page One story. Yes, I could see how she could easily be underestimated and use it to her considerable advantage.

"Hello," I ventured. "What can I do for you?"

"Just want to say, that was a great story today. Musta had one hell of a source. The timing was perfect, too, right at the funeral. I can't even imagine the look on Winters's face. He always comes off so polished and controlled when he sticks to the script, but it's a short trip to get him flustered. That's my take on him, at least, the few times I've interviewed him."

She extended a hand over my cubicle wall. I gripped it lightly, then let go just as quickly.

" 'Course, Braxton gets most of the face time these days," she added sourly. Towers had been toiling in the capitol bureau a full year before Braxton came aboard. Conventional wisdom had her next in line to cover the governor. Conventional wisdom was wrong.

"I'm still not convinced Winters is a national contender," she went on. "I can see him blowing it if something extemporaneous comes up, and your story is about as extemporaneous as it gets. I like how you wrote it, too, that he was flustered when you confronted him. I'm surprised we ran it that way, given the paper's reputation of favorable coverage, 'specially since Braxton took over the beat."

I nodded. We had something in common. We both hated Braxton.

"What I really want," she began, then paused. "I'd like to work with you, Mr. Holcomb."

My eyes widened. I was about to speak, but she cut me off.

"I promise you, I am not trying to horn in on your story." She held out her hands, a gesture of innocent intentions. "You have the sources on this. You broke it. It's yours, no question. But I think you're a hell of a reporter. You've been around town forever and you obviously know a lot of people. I just want a piece. I'll help you with anything you want. I could learn a lot from you. Whadda ya think?"

She flashed another smile, but I must have looked stunned. I mean, what was she talking about? I wrote one story, but I was done. There were no more sources. My main source was a dead guy.

"I don't think so," I stammered. "I really don't know what else there is for me to do. Probably, Braxton's gonna take it from here. I mean, he still covers the governor. It's his beat."

I pointed out a painful fact and believed I had successfully quashed her idea.

Me? I was content to accept a few congratulations and quietly go back to typing obits. Looking back, it would have been so much easier that way.

"I can understand if you don't want to work with me," she frowned. "But it's your story. You're on the budget to cover the governor's press conference this afternoon. Sides, Braxton called in sick today."

"Press conference?"

"Yeah, probably just a rehash of what we've had. The governor's office has to update the rest of the media on the story. Still, they might release some records, and they could have something new on the investigation. You should definitely be there."

I was already feeling in over my head. At least I had the sense to realize it. I knew I needed help, and Jacquelyn Towers looked to be about the best help around. To top it all, she'd think I was doing her a favor.

"I guess if we're going to work together, you better call me Lenny."

"Jack," she said. "Call me Jack."

"So Braxton's out today?"

"Yeah, poor bastard's probably in a good sulk, too embarrassed to show his face after getting shown up by the obit writer. Sorry, no offense." She added the apology with the embarrassed surprise of someone who sometimes speaks before she thinks. I didn't mind. I found Jack Towers completely refreshing.

"None taken."

It was something else Jack said that concerned me. I was thinking about Braxton. I didn't believe he was home sulking. He was too good for that. No, he was thinking of a way to get back on top. I was sure of it.

But even those thoughts receded as I looked up at Jack. Worries were for another day, I decided, and so were the obits. I snatched the fresh faxes from my desk.

"Looks like I'll have to find another home for these," I said, holding up the death notices. "Bronski will just have to assign someone else. I'm covering the governor today."

"Damn right, Lenny," Jack cheered. "You tell those dead fuckers to go screw themselves."

12

I FELT THE EYES OF THE CAPITOL PRESS CORPS UPON ME. Working as they did for newspapers around the state out of a cramped newsroom located inside the capitol building, most of these reporters did not know me. They had never heard the vicious rumors that have circulated about me at my own newspaper. Still, I wasn't any more comfortable. These reporters may not have known about me, but they did know my name. It was printed on the press pass strung around my neck, and it had appeared atop this morning's story. I was very sure these reporters disliked me as someone who had trespassed on their turf and made them look foolish by scooping them. But they were also curious. They must have wondered about me. *Who was this old guy? How did he get that damn story?*

I was equally intrigued. The capitol press corps was comprised of about twenty reporters, including three-person contingents from the Pittsburgh and Philadelphia papers. The others hailed from much smaller outfits, some working for collections of six or seven papers in the tiny towns scattered across the state. The majority were newspaper reporters, although a few full-time radio reporters toiled there as well. Television reporters swooped down only when events warranted. They were all here for this one. The focal point of Pennsylvania's press was a vacant podium emblazoned with the state seal.

It was a motley group, a mix of old and young, metropolitan types and small-timers. Some of the older guys had grown fat and lazy over decades of slopping up the political stories that ran like tap beer around the capitol. A few sported guts that rivaled beach balls, and they looked interminably tired and uncomfortable. They had fed at the trough of meals and drinks on the tabs of lobbyists and lawmakers. It was a grand tradition here, and it amused me to think that some of them had grown fat and happy on the illicit generosity of Herb Bucher, the very impropriety that we had all gathered to pick over, bemoan, and exploit.

The younger journalists still had the look of hunger in their eyes. They had come in quest of that one elusive story that could make a career. This was the archetype for which Braxton could be the poster boy, that was, if he were there. But there were plenty more just like him, salivating over what was about to be served up and all the career advancement possibilities it entailed.

I found it strange that I didn't recognize anyone, not even the older guys. After all, we were all reporters in the same small city. But the capitol was a different world, an island in the middle of Harrisburg. The reporters there rarely ventured off that island, and when they did it was only to visit the exclusive set of trendy bars and restaurants favored by the capitol crowd. Now, at long last, I'd been granted admittance.

Above all, I watched Jacquelyn Towers as she worked the room that day, chatting with various reporters, some of whom she probably hadn't seen since

Braxton took over covering the governor. I overheard reporters ask her about my story. Perhaps by her presence there, they assumed she had some part in it. If they did think this, Jack was not about to correct them. She basked in the attention.

When people asked about Braxton's very notable absence, Jack offered only a blank shrug. She could have dismissed the intrigue by simply noting that he was out sick. Instead, she left them to think the worst: Braxton had gotten beat on the story and had been reassigned.

Finally, a wooden door behind the blue podium opened and Christy Denza, burdened by a pile of documents, walked awkwardly into the room. She paused briefly at the microphone. "I apologize. The governor is running a bit late. We expect him in about five minutes. Meanwhile, I have copies of the press release and records of campaign accounts showing the abnormalities. I'll pass them out to get you started."

Christy's young face looked drawn, as if she hadn't slept much the night before. Her eyes had the wear of more than a few hours spent crying, and strands of her blond hair had pulled free from the perfect arrangement I had noticed yesterday. Even her suit, obviously a designer label, looked a bit wrinkled.

And it was odd, at least to me, to see a press secretary passing out papers to reporters. Didn't she have an assistant or some deputy for that? The reporters hardly looked at her as they grabbed greedily for the documents, crowding around the young girl like wolves. A fat man, not content to wait his turn, tried to pull a copy of the stapled packets from the bottom, causing Christy to lose control of the pile. Papers covered the floor.

"I'm sorry," she said, stooping to retrieve them.

The gathered reporters didn't make a move to help, choosing instead to watch with pathetic expressions.

I didn't know it then, but the scene was a perfect symbol of how far Christy had fallen. The revelations of Herb Bucher's improper borrowing and spending were now chained to her like a weight.

Jack Towers returned with two of the packets, handing me one, then taking the seat next to me.

She thumbed through the report. "Doesn't look like there's anything here that you didn't have, Lenny."

I peered seriously at the documents but could not focus. "Uhm-hm."

"So what's your play?" she asked. "Those sources of yours have anything else?"

"No, they're hanging back, waiting to see Winters's move. By the looks of it, he's in full disclosure mode. Doubt we'll get the chance to spring any more surprises."

"Crisis mode, is what he's in," Jack purred so that only I could hear. "Looks like the scandal you unleashed has already claimed its first victim. Word around here has it that Christy's out as press secretary."

My eyes widened, beckoning more.

"Yeah," Jack whispered, holding the thick packet of documents to her mouth. "With the shit storm raging, word is Winters is thinking about bringing in someone new, someone from the outside, to turn things around. You know, an image maker, a fixer. He sacrifices Miss Miniskirt to the scandal, brings in somebody with a name, and soon enough, Bucher's old news and the press is writing about how the campaign is staging a comeback. It's all about appearances and momentum and conventional wisdom. You have to counter every story. That's why he'll make the move."

I nodded with admiration. It was too damn easy to

forget that Jack had a hell of a brain working behind that cute smile of hers.

"I assume you'll want to handle the questions." Jack nodded at the podium, where the governor would be standing in a couple of minutes.

"No, you take it. Maybe you have something fresh. I've been working the story too long. I'm too close." It sounded like a reasonable excuse, and I knew Jack would jump at the chance.

"All right, Lenny, I will. Thanks." Jack considered me and smiled. "You're okay, not at all egotistical and territorial like most of the assholes in this room."

"Being an obit writer kind of cures you of your ego," I confided. "And it sure as hell makes you realize that life's too short for such shit."

Jack's smile widened. She liked me, I thought, and I sure as hell liked her.

Jack was predictably brilliant at the news conference. As representative of the newspaper that broke the story, she received the much-sought-after press conference honor of asking the first question. She wasted no time putting Winters on the spot.

"How could you, personally, Governor, not have known?" she pressed in firm, even tones.

Jack refused to wilt under the heat of all those television lights, not to mention Winters's own intimidating glare. She followed up with one of those patented three-part zingers that managed to touch on disillusioned donors, campaign finance reform, and Winters's suddenly precarious status in a Republican presidential field that many had expected him to dominate.

"How 'bout it, Governor, what can you say to all those loyal supporters who gave to your cause, only to see their money go toward your top aide's bar bill?"

I watched Jack belting out her questions and, afterward, scrambling to interview a couple of key lawmakers. And I realized I was witnessing someone doing the exact job she was born to do. She reveled in the moment, thriving on the thrill of news gathering.

But, give him his due, Winters was pretty good, too. He would not allow himself to be buttonholed nor become flustered, even mildly annoyed. He must have been impeccably coached. Perhaps that outside fixer who Jack had speculated about was already working behind the scenes.

Winters even managed to deflect a couple of the tougher questions with well-timed jokes. He labeled the $650,000 that his fat fund-raiser had siphoned from the accounts "the bar tab of the century," earning an outburst of authentic laughter from the jaded press corps. The governor's lighthearted characterization would make the lead paragraphs, if not the headlines, of most news stories on the event. It was a shrewd, coded signal to the masses that this wasn't such a big deal.

But Winters's best defense was his candid full disclosure. It's always the best strategy in such situations. Journalists quickly lose interest in stories when they can no longer play the gotcha game. It's much more fun when politicians try to duck and weave, and deny and hide. Despite this exercise in openness, there wasn't a lot of new information. Aided by the combination of my instincts and Eddie Moore's records, I had gotten most of it. Still, this didn't diminish Jack's journalism-fueled adrenaline rush. It was the grand, tingling feeling of being high on a story. As I recall the sensation, it's an urge to sing, dance, jump and fuck—all at the same time.

Perhaps controlled by such urges, Jack just happened to brush into a young fellow on our walk back to the paper. He was a tall, handsome young man dressed in a suit that managed to compliment his fit, well-muscled body. The two chatted, while I waited at a discreet distance on the capitol mall. They made moon eyes at each other and couldn't seem to talk without touching one another. There was no particularly intimate contact. But it all was happening out in the open near the capitol fountain, which on this fine day had attracted a throng of state workers on their lunch breaks. My old-fashioned mind feared that such a cozy display could ruin Jack's reputation as a reporter, especially if the guy was a political player. I was embarrassed for her. Or perhaps, I was feeling something else. Jealousy?

After more touching and a parting hug, Jack trotted back to me. I tried to pretend the whole thing hadn't happened, but before I could think of something to change the subject, she offered a voluntary explanation.

"We dated. Big ego and major shortcomings elsewhere, if you know what I mean." She laughed, then continued. "Still, I'd do him again. Got great abs. I like feeling the ripples. Sorry I took so long, Lenny. Horny, I guess."

I could hardly breathe at the thought of her having sex. Sure, I could imagine it, but I had a hard time digesting her openness about it. Of course, I had encountered plenty of broads in my day, especially in this business. But I had always shied away from them, ending up with repressed virginal types, instead. But after forty years of living inside the cold front that descended over my marriage, Jack's sexual frankness excited me. My pulse raced, but it seemed best to get back to the business at hand.

"Why don't you go ahead and write the story, Jack,"

I announced, knowing she'd want to. "I'll check with my sources again," I lied. "They might have something more, but I doubt it. Sorry to disappoint."

"Don't sweat it. This is all happening because of you. Enjoy it. Besides, there's no Braxton to deal with. I owe you big just for that."

Perhaps in repayment, Jack gave my byline a free ride on her story. To make matters worse, she put my name before hers, an honor usually reserved for the lead writer. I felt guilty, like a freeloader. I promised myself I'd get something new. I didn't want Jacquelyn Towers to think I was a washed-up obit writer with only one good story in him. But my fears whispered that I was exactly that.

13

The next day, I arrived at the office well before 8:00 a.m. My undeserved byline over Jack's story mocked me. I had to find something new. I was a reporter, I told myself. I could still do this job. I'd make a few calls, starting with Eddie Moore. Maybe he'd have something more. At the very least, I'd thank him again for the records.

But my heart sank as I neared my cubicle. Abe Braxton was back, neatly dressed and already on the phone, no doubt working to reclaim his beat. My confidence flagged. I was a fluke. He was the reporter; I was the obit writer.

Braxton was hunched over his desk and talking quietly. I couldn't hear the conversation because the police scanner was spitting static nearby. I walked closer, ostensibly to glance at the fax machine. Three obits already. I was about to turn down the volume of the scanner when an emergency dispatch came over the air.

"County Control to Harrisburg River Rescue. Cell phone caller traveling on I-83 bridge advises seeing a body in the Susquehanna River, near Dock Street Dam."

I felt the momentary rush of breaking news: a possible floater in the river. Just as quickly, the wave of excitement passed and the knowledge gained through years of working in Harrisburg sobered me. It was probably just a log, I told myself. The river was up due to the spring rains and the snowmelt from up north. I had seen that current carry many strange things through Harrisburg. Often, the debris ended up getting caught in the churning, powerful current created by the falls of the Dock Street dam, a low-head dam that deepened the river for boating.

Rush-hour motorists who glimpsed large, bobbing objects in the throes of that current often mistook them for bodies. False alarms came in all the time. Still, River Rescue had to send out a crew and a rescue boat, just in case. A morning of playing cards at the station would be shot all to hell.

I was about to dismiss the report when a state cop radioed in.

"Unit two-zero-niner reporting an abandoned vehicle on I-81, northbound lane, a quarter-mile before the Front Street exit to Harrisburg. The bridge is narrow there and the vehicle is obstructing traffic. There's a mile backlog on the Harrisburg approach, and it's just going to get worse. Request towing service to my location. Subject vehicle is a black Volkswagen Beetle, PA plates CLD GOP. Over."

"Roger that," the county dispatcher replied. "Towing service en route. Keep traffic moving as best you can."

I found myself staring at the scanner, which was nestled under a snowdrift of faxed police reports on the cop reporter's messy desk. It was as if my looking at that black box would somehow increase my understanding of the sometimes garbled voices that spoke from it and reveal the significance of these calls. I did not immediately notice that Abe Braxton had emerged from his cubicle and trained his attention there, as well.

When the voices fell silent and the scratchy, irritating crackle returned, I finally glanced up. Braxton looked as if he were being held in suspense. He appeared to know something, yet was anticipating more.

"My, my Braxton," I said with as much sarcasm as I could muster, "you constantly surprise me with the breadth and depth of your interest in news. Now you're covering traffic reports? It's just an abandoned car that's fucking up rush hour."

He broke his stare as annoyance swept his face. He clicked his tongue and said, "You don't know anything."

"But you know something, Braxton, don't you? What is it?"

"I know that car," he said in a soft voice. It wasn't so much that he was answering me, he was merely saying the words out loud, so he could believe them himself. His eyes returned to the scanner, still waiting.

"So what?" I said. "It's an abandoned car, probably ran out of gas. Cops only called it in because of the rush-hour traffic on the ramp."

He didn't answer.

Just then, the scanner crackled, cutting me silent and commanding our attention.

"River Rescue to dispatch. Confirm report of human victim at Dock Street. Repeat, visual sighting confirmed. We'll need a second boat to effect rescue. Body is in the thick of the current. We'll need an anchor boat to tether the rescue craft. Please advise."

"Copy. Dispatching second craft now. Any chance of a rescue? Over."

"Negative. No signs of life. This is a body recovery at this point. Rescue Unit One will stand down and wait for second craft. Over."

I looked at Braxton, his jaw hanging open. My brain was rapidly connecting pieces of information. He knows the car, I thought. But what does he care about the floater? It's probably a homeless person, some desperate drunk, an unlucky fisherman, or a pathetically depressed lost soul.

Braxton's eyes didn't budge from the scanner, which came to life yet again.

"State unit two-zero-niner to dispatch. Advise you to cancel tow to 81 bridge. Abandoned vehicle is unlocked, keys in ignition, and plenty of fuel. I can drive it off the bridge myself. I have the vehicle started and idling, so it's not mechanical. Found a pair of high-heel shoes on the curb, though. We may be looking at a jumper. Please advise."

"Two-zero-niner, copy. Move car as indicated but wear gloves. Car is a possible suicide scene. River Rescue has identified a body at Dock Street. Could be your motorist. Employ crime scene techniques. Over."

"Copy," the officer said before the scanner belched static.

I faced Braxton. "Whose car?" I demanded.

He looked at me, his eyes wide with fear and understanding.

"The vanity plate. CLD GOP. Christy L. Denza. GOP, as in the Republicans," he said dryly, with no attitude at all.

His eyes dropped to the still-crackling scanner. "She must have jumped," he continued in not much more than a whisper. "I heard she got fired yesterday. I'm sure she was upset, but I can't believe this. This is crazy."

Now, it was my mouth hanging open. That girl, that's all she really was, a beautiful girl with a big job and an important title in a political town. A town where when you are up, you are everything, but when you slip, there's no one to catch your fall. Damn, I hated politics.

Braxton retreated to his cubicle. In an instant, he was back on the phone, whispering to someone. As he talked, he grabbed for a fresh notepad and a pen, and he slipped a slim, silver microcassette recorder into his pants pocket.

I, too, gathered myself. I would go to the recovery scene. I wasn't the cop reporter, but death was my business. It was close enough, and no one else was around, anyway.

Braxton hung up and bolted from his chair. He pulled on an overcoat as he strode across the newsroom, toward the elevator.

"Where are you going?" I asked, following with my windbreaker in hand.

"Down there."

"So am I."

"Since when are you a cop reporter?" he asked.

"Since when are you?"

We exchanged looks but kept walking toward the elevator. We shared the ride but didn't speak another word. I could hear each of us breathing, though, as the elevator settled on the ground floor. When the bell rang and the door opened, Braxton headed for his black BMW in the parking lot. I walked the eight blocks to the river.

14

By the time I arrived at Dock Street, situated along the raging Susquehanna, rescue crews had two boats in the water. TV trucks had rolled up, and photographers trained cameras on the unfolding action.

The dam's strong current had captured the body of Christy Denza in its ever-churning rotation and would not let it go. Her body bobbed up and down, almost comically. It'd float away from the dam a couple of feet only to have the undertow pull it back. This endless cycle continued for the better part of twenty minutes, until the two recovery boats, working together, could get into position. I couldn't help but watch that lifeless body, which just the day before had been such a beautiful, vital girl working in the shadow of the governor.

The recovery played out like a silent movie, all sounds masked by the deafening roar of the water rushing over the dam, not to mention the constant flow of traffic over the interstate bridge above.

I looked up at the bridge. That's where the motorist had spotted her, I thought. Then, I looked north, up the wide mouth of the river to the second interstate bridge, about seven miles in the distance. That's where the cop found Christy Denza's abandoned Volkswagen Beetle. It's where she jumped, I guessed. Those rushing waters had carried her all the way down here, the debris in the river clawing at her, stripping her clothes and tearing her flesh the entire time.

The massive reverse current created by the dam was the only thing that kept her body from floating farther. I've heard that the only way to escape the dam's grip is to dive down to the very bottom and swim out underneath those turbulent waters, though I don't know anyone who's tried it and lived.

That current sure was trouble for the men trying to retrieve Christy's body. I've seen uninitiated boaters attempt to approach the dam from downstream, only to get sucked in. Before the boaters could react, the current had pulled them into the water rushing over the dam, swamping their boats and tipping them right over. That's why the recovery boat was tethered to the second craft, aimed in the opposite direction, motor running. When the time came, that second boat would pull the recovery vessel from the current's grip.

By the time the team's long hooks extended for Christy's bobbing body, a good crowd had gathered on the paved platform under the bridge. More watched from atop the riverbank, where Harrisburg's exclusive Shipoke neighborhood overlooked the water. Our cop reporter, Robert Macy, had arrived and begun talking to the idle police, who were themselves nothing more than spectators. Television reporters interviewed a few of the gawkers, gathering useless comments on such obvious things as the danger of the river during the swollen months of spring. I didn't bother talking to anyone. And neither did Abe Braxton, who stood alone on the concrete, near the rushing waters of the dam. He still wore that expectant look. He wanted to see for himself what had happened to Christy.

Finally, the men pulled Christy's half-naked body from the water and placed it in the boat. It disappeared from view as the men laid it on the floor of the craft. Then, they unfolded a black plastic body bag. They always bagged the body before bringing it to shore.

I knew then why I was there. I was the obit writer. I would tell Christy's final story. The all-too-early last chapter of a life that had been full of potential. Hopes raised by all her ambition were now dashed. She had lost her job and mistaken it for a failure so great that she couldn't bear to live. Foolish.

Standing there, seemingly paralyzed by it all, I felt a strange kinship with her. We were both outcasts at the very places to which we had devoted our lives. Then and there, I promised myself—and I made a silent promise to Christy, as well—that I would tell her story, and tell it right.

Usually, the newspaper doesn't make a big deal over suicides. If you do it in the privacy of your own home, the unpleasant circumstances never need be mentioned. When I write these obits, I simply state that so-and-so died at home. In rare cases, mostly deaths of those under the age of thirty, we may list the cause of death—a gunshot, for instance—but never the manner of death. No one has to know. But when someone decides to jump from the interstate bridge at rush hour and her body floats down to the dam for every motorist on I-83 to see, we have to say something. We have to explain that. The fact that up until yesterday Christy Denza was the governor's press secretary would make it front-page news. She was Winters's second top aide to die in as many weeks. Not a good track record for anyone, let alone someone who sees himself a top contender for the White House. He was sure to look like a villain for having just fired the poor girl.

Maybe that's why Braxton was there. He knew there would be political fallout. Perhaps he'd try to pitch another story on how this tragedy will add emotional heft to Winters's campaign. I'd like to see him try. It was all crumbling for him now. Braxton had been so determined to cover a presidential campaign that he handpicked Harrisburg, believing Winters to be the favorite. Now the campaign was imploding before it even began. Maybe Braxton was contemplating his ruined plans as he stared out at the river. He seemed hypnotized, like I so often had been when writing my obits.

The rescue team delivered the lumpy black body bag to the waiting ambulance gurney. Blue-uniformed attendants wheeled it to the wagon, which had backed down the boat launch to make the loading easier. The ambulance pulled away in no great hurry, lights but no siren. I knew where it was headed. I'd pay a visit there soon.

But first, I had a job to do. I had an obit to write. It was a pressing matter, but not so that I couldn't stop off at the Pepper Grill on my way back. A few whiskeys would help me face the task. I knew I'd hate my job that day. But I hated Governor Winters even more. I hated him for firing Christy Denza.

When I got back to the paper, I found Bill Sharps perversely excited by the whole thing. What luck for him and the newspaper that Christy Denza would hurl herself into the swirling Susquehanna the day after being fired by the governor.

"I can't believe this," he enthused in an impish way that made me feel all the more slimy and sick about my job.

He seemed to have all the confidence in me, however. If he smelled the whiskey on my breath, it didn't diminish his faith.

"We'll want a front-page obit, of course." His words came in a torrent. "She was a local girl, grew up in Mechanicsburg. We'll need to talk to parents and friends. I want a full sketch of her education and career. This was a hometown girl who made good. Press secretary at twenty-four, and now this. It's a tragedy that everyone's going to be talking about."

I eyed him, hoping he'd display at least a molecule of embarrassment over his enthusiasm. He didn't, merely continued with his grand journalistic plans for covering the suicide of Christy Denza.

"Braxton will do the reaction story with the governor. Where is Abe, anyway?"

"Last I saw, he was at the scene," I said.

"I think he was pretty close to Christy," Sharps added thoughtfully, only now realizing a flesh-and-blood person was gone. It wasn't just some abstract story to drool over. "Probably a tough one for him."

"Tough, all right." It was my turn to be crass. "Braxton's watching his man Winters's political career go up in smoke, or should I say, down the river. I think that's what he's really depressed over."

Sharps wore a confused smile. He didn't get it.

"Anyway, Jacqueline volunteered to help with this, so why don't you two team up," he instructed. "You two seem to be working well together."

"Yes, I could use the help. A lot of interviews for the obit."

"Make it sing," Sharps cheered as he scurried back to his place at the city desk. "This is emotional stuff. Really hit the human element, Lenny."

What would you know about being human? I asked silently, flashing Sharps a shit-eating grin.

• • •

Later, I don't know how much later because my mind checked out a while, Jacquelyn Towers startled me out of a stupor. She had that way of walking up from behind and jolting the shit out of me. She never seemed to announce herself, just started right up with conversation.

"So, did you see her?" she buzzed from behind my head. My mind raced back to respond.

"What?" I muttered, twisting in my swivel chair to see her leaning over my cubicle wall. With her arms folded over the divider and her eager face leaning in to hear the dish, she reminded me of a teenager begging for gossip about a boy.

"Christy! Did you see them pull her body out? I can't believe this! Everyone's talking about it. She did look kind of flustered at yesterday's press conference, didn't she? Like she knew she was getting the ax."

Jack's mouth moved so fast, it was making me dizzy. Or maybe it was the whiskey. Either way, her youth and enthusiasm were tiring.

"I saw enough. It wasn't quite the excitement that you and Sharps seem to think. Or maybe my years of writing obits have numbed me to the point where I can't get excited over a good suicide."

It was true. As somberly and seriously as most people treated death, at newspapers it was good copy, nothing more. Human decay and moral mayhem were somehow transformed into excitement and adrenaline. The more bizarre or spectacular the death and the bigger the death toll—whether an accident, murder spree, or natural disaster—the better the story. My years on the obit desk had cured me of this outlook. In this small way, it had made me more human.

"You're in a mood," Jack scolded, as if I were one

of her girlfriends. "By the way, was it Jack or Jim?"

"What?"

"The whiskey on your breath." She acted as if I were trying to bluff and she had called me on it. "Jack Daniel's or Jim Beam?"

"Neither," I said, correcting her for the cardinal sin of mixing up her whiskey. "Johnnie Walker this morning. I like scotch when I have to write a tough obit. Puts me in mind of good, hard-drinking wakes."

"Whatever," she said. "Here, take a Tic Tac. You'll knock people out with that breath."

"Thanks." I dutifully deposited the mint.

"Well, what do you want me to do?" She was still deferring to me, whiskey breakfast or not.

"Why don't you go out and start the interviews, since your breath is better?"

She smiled smartly back.

"You feed me the quotes," I added. "I'll start writing the obit."

PART II

INVESTIGATION

15

CHRISTY DENZA WOULD NOT BE REWARDED WITH THE FINAL dignity of a pretty obit. I knew that well before I started writing, the scotch whiskey still a faint haze at the corners of my brain. This would be more of a news story than an obit. It would include all the ugly details of her suicide, make that her apparent suicide. In the news business, one must always qualify such things until the county coroner makes his official ruling. And knowing old Buzz Swanson, a former undertaker who graduated to a fresher grade of corpse, he'd take his own dawdling time.

Not that the public or even the press need wait for such formalities. They wouldn't require much proof beyond Christy's Beetle parked on the bridge, keys in the ignition, and her high heels on the curb—not to mention the small detail of her body turning up at the dam for all of Harrisburg to see. It would all be there, in her obit, and Christy's entire life, packed full of accomplishments though it was, would be forever overshadowed by the manner of her death.

Not for me, though. In researching her life that afternoon, her death became secondary.

Christy was an honors graduate from Penn who

worked on two successful state house campaigns before landing a spot on the governor's staff. She'd even interned one summer at the *Herald*, though I didn't remember her. She'd been at the top of her class since the second grade. At least that's what it said in an old story on the area's top high school graduates, called the "Best and Brightest." It was just one of the dozens of articles that popped up when I typed Christy's name into the newspaper's electronic database. I read them all, every word.

Somewhere in college, the political bug bit. As a freshman, she ran for secretary of the student government. She lost to some sorority girl, but never lost another election. Before graduation, she worked an internship in D.C., but after school, she promptly returned to Harrisburg to make her mark at the state level. She volunteered on the campaign staff of some newcomer running for state house. Out of nowhere, the guy won, and Christy made a name for herself. A few years later, she landed a job on Winters's staff and rose from there.

There was no boyfriend that we could find. Seemed odd at first, then I concluded she probably didn't have the time. These days, many women focused on careers first, seeming not to want or need relationships. If they wanted sex, they could get it and not feel a bit ashamed, as Jack Towers had so capably demonstrated.

What remained unclear in the information Jack and I gathered that day was what drove Christy. She had none of the earmarks of someone destined for such lofty heights. She wasn't a blue blood, like Abe Braxton. Far from it. Her old man worked construction, and her mother did time in a sewing factory. As blue collar as her family was, she would have known about hard work and must have realized it was her only advantage.

Oddly, those blue-collar roots didn't foreshadow her Republican affiliation, but it was the right side to be on if you wanted a top political job in Harrisburg. Christy had certainly wanted that.

Her drive to succeed hadn't rubbed off on her older brother and only sibling, Danny, however. He worked construction, like his old man, and still lived at home at age thirty-one. His one area of expertise was explosives. When I typed Danny's name into the newspaper's database, a single article came back. It was dated a few years ago when they imploded the state transportation building, a twenty-story, state-issue structure that had been badly damaged in a fire the year before. The building was such an architectural albatross that everyone was glad to see it blow. In the articles we wrote about the building's demise, Danny Denza's name came up in a story about the crew rigging the building with explosives. It was quite a science, apparently, to dissect a building's strengths and weaknesses in order to place the charges just so. I'll say this, Danny's crew knew what it was doing because that ugly eyesore of a building came down without a hitch. I woke early that Saturday, along with a crowd of about ten thousand others, to watch her go.

As good as he may have been with his dynamite, Danny Denza was nothing like his sister. He was about removing landmarks. She was all about making her mark. She had been doing just that until it all started to unravel the night fat Herb Bucher went facedown into his mashed potatoes. How could that have led to this?

It's the kind of question that could turn Christy Denza and all her accomplishments into one big, pathetic melodrama. She wouldn't get respect, or even sympathy. Christy could expect only pity now. The fact that she was so young, pretty, and accomplished would only increase her portion.

What was worse, she had become someone the governor could now easily explain away: a person obviously too emotional for the rigors of her job. When asked why he thought she did it, the governor could just stare blankly and say, "I don't know." The implication would be clear: To do what she'd done, Christy *had* to be a little unbalanced.

Winters's threat to no longer talk to the paper sure didn't last long. Braxton was back squarely in the governor's good graces and gathering Winters's self-serving quotes. And why not? Politicians must get their message out. And Braxton had always handled Winters's message oh so carefully. He would this time, as well.

Me? I'd tell Christy's story. But I wondered, who would care? Her family was devastated beyond mere grief. This girl, who had been such a source of pride for them, had now opened a great well of embarrassment. Surely, someone who committed suicide must have been disturbed. Perhaps, she wasn't raised properly. That's what people would think. There'd be anger, too. For now, the family would direct its rage at Christy, for doing what she'd done. Surely, there'd be resentment left over for the governor, too, the man who had fired her. But how does one get back at a governor? Winters would peer into those television cameras, shake his head in bewilderment and mutter, "I don't know. I just don't know." Everyone would know just what he meant.

I knew all of these things as I started Christy's obit that day. I knew what people would think. I knew what her friends and acquaintances would say in the quotes Jack Towers would gather. I knew what I'd have to write, and I knew it would be ugly. But there was nothing I could do about any of it.

FIRED WINTERS AIDE FOUND DEAD IN RIVER IN APPARENT SUICIDE

By Lenny Holcomb and Jacquelyn Towers

Christy L. Denza, a native of Mechanicsburg who held the state's top public relations spot as press secretary for Gov. Lowell P. Winters, died yesterday, an apparent suicide from the Interstate 81 bridge over the Susquehanna River. She was 26.

She is the second Winters aide to die in as many weeks. Fund-raiser Herbert Bucher collapsed of a heart attack last Thursday, just days before this newspaper would reveal his alleged role in embezzling Winters campaign funds.

Denza, a striking blonde whose rise to power in the Winters administration was meteoric, was head of communications as the Bucher controversy broke. She was abruptly fired late Tuesday, following a press conference at which Winters was grilled about the extent of his knowledge of Bucher's embezzlement.

Early Wednesday, her car and belongings were found abandoned on the I-81 bridge, the point from which authorities believe she jumped into the river. Later that same morning, rescuers recovered her body from the river about seven miles south, near the Dock Street Dam.

Denza's dismissal was seen as a calculated move by the administration. Winters, a top contender for the GOP nomination for president next year, is ex-

pected to bring on a new communications director to rejuvenate his flickering election hopes. However, that move may have to wait, given the sensitivity surrounding Denza's death, sources said.

For his part, Winters said he was "shocked and saddened" by Denza's apparent suicide, but he refused to speculate on whether her firing was her motive.

NO! NO! NO! MEXICO, GOTTA GO TO MEXICO. JUST LIKE IN THAT JAMES TAYLOR SONG. I LOVED THAT SONG.

"In the game of politics, and many times it is just that—a game—sometimes you have to change players," Winters explained. "Unfortunately, we felt we had to make a change when it came to Christy. My administration and the possibility of a presidential campaign needed a new direction and a new voice. It was my decision, and one I believe Christy fully understood. She was a professional. I am totally devastated by this turn of events."

HE LIKED THE BIKINI, REALLY LIKED IT. THEY BOTH DID.

It has not been determined exactly when Denza allegedly jumped and no witnesses have come forward, police said. She was last seen leaving the capitol at about 10:00 P.M. Tuesday. Police are checking the phone records to her midtown apartment, as well as to her cellular phone. An autopsy by County Coroner Harold "Buzz" Swanson was set for Thursday.

YOU'LL NEVER UNDERSTAND WITHOUT MEXICO. IT ALL STARTS IN MEXICO.

Friends of Denza said her job as the governor's press secretary had been "her life" and expressed shock over her firing.

"I can't believe it," said Julie Martin, a longtime

friend. "She put in so many hours at the capitol. She was always working, even on the weekends. She loved her job. It meant the world to her. I can't believe she was fired, just like that. It had to break her heart."

Police have not found a suicide note, and investigators cautioned that it would be premature to ascribe a motive.

IT'S ALL THERE. SWEET BABY JAMES KNEW WHAT HE WAS SINGING ABOUT. ALL THE REASONS ARE THERE.

Her family spent yesterday in their Mechanicsburg home. Parents Jeb and Mary Denza refused all requests for interviews. But her older brother and lone sibling, Daniel Denza, emerged and angrily ordered the media from the property. Asked about his sister's death, Daniel Denza called the preliminary ruling of suicide "a lie."

"I know she didn't do it," he said. "My sister was a worker and a fighter. Losing her job would just be something for her to bounce back from. There was no quit in that girl."

Asked about evidence pointing to suicide, Denza shot back: "Did they find a note? No. Christy wrote notes and memos about everything. No way she's going to kill herself and not write a note to her family. None of it makes sense."

Christy Denza's death cuts short a fast-rising career in the capital city. She joined Winters's staff nearly three years ago as a policy aide and in a year was named press secretary. Even those who knew her best were left to wonder what went wrong.

"Everyone asks the same question—why," said Joe DiSilva, her high school principal at Mechanicsburg, where she was class valedictorian. "It's some-

thing we'll never know and never understand. That's what makes it so difficult to deal with. That, and it's such a waste."

NOOOOOO! MEXICO. GO DOWN.

I finished in a flurry of keystrokes, just as Jack signaled me from across the chaotic newsroom. A phone glued to her ear and furiously scribbling notes, she gestured that she had more information on the way. She must have reached Christy's college roommate, someone she'd been trying to get all afternoon. Now, Jack wanted to add a few more quotes to our story. Personally, I thought we had enough. Jack had done well to get one friend, the principal and her brother, who was so adamant that it wasn't a suicide. But the story was as much Jack's as it was mine, and if she wanted to add something, she could go right ahead.

I felt proud as I sent the story off to her. As distasteful as it was, I knew it was good. My efforts were payback for the time Jack had carried my byline on the press conference story. This time, I had done the heavy lifting and was glad I could.

But stupidly, in those chaotic, confusing minutes before deadline, I had sent the story to Jack unread. Not five minutes later, I spotted her striding across the newsroom in my direction. I assumed she was coming to congratulate me. She waltzed up and leaned over the wall of my cubicle, her elbows sticking out over the top and her chin resting on her crossed arms.

"Okay, Mr. Lenny, what gives?"

"What?" I stared blankly. I never knew when she was kidding, or really serious. Perhaps, she was perturbed that I'd neglected to use one of the quotes that she'd spent all afternoon gathering.

"You're a little bit of a perv, aren't ya, Lenny," she goaded me. "C'mon, you can tell ol' Jack."

I felt a queasiness creep through my bowels as I realized what must have happened. There was something in Christy's obit *besides* her obit, something I hadn't realized I'd written, but something that could prove very important, just like those times before. It was my instinct, making itself known again.

All I could think was, I had to read that obit. I prayed Jack hadn't changed anything. At the same time, I knew I had to play dumb. She would never understand how my instincts sometimes came to me. I gave her my best blank stare.

"Guess that stuff was for me, Lenny," she continued as if I knew exactly what she meant, as if it was our little secret. "I gotta say, I'm a little flattered and surprised. Must be one of those old guy things, that it?"

She laughed. "You want to blow your retirement savings on the cute, young girl. Take her down to Mexico in one last, desperate bid to recapture your youth before it's too late. It's a nice thought. Maybe even a little tempting. I said a *little* tempting. But don'tcha think we have enough on our plates? I mean, we're kind of in the middle of a political crisis. Not the time to be thinking about vacations to Mexico."

Jack smiled devilishly at me.

"I'm sorry, Jack," I stammered. "I don't know what you're talking about."

And I really didn't. All the stuff about Mexico was lost on me. But it had to mean something.

"Lenny," she scolded. "Mexico! James Taylor! You practically quoted the song in Christy's obit. Not the best venue to make a pass at a girl, I might add. But you've been out of practice, I understand."

I furrowed my brow. "Mexico? James Taylor?"

"Yeah," she said, growing more annoyed. "You know," she began singing the song, then looked somewhat offended that I hadn't appreciated her voice a bit more. "You know. You must. It's all over the obit. That and some rather clumsy hints that you'd prefer me in a bikini and you like going down. I mean, come on."

I didn't know what to say.

"Lenny, you were hinting that you and I should jet off to *Meh-he-co* for a little sex vacation. You're all embarrassed now. It's okay. I give you points for the effort, but I say we get back to work."

"Yeah," I muttered. "Good idea."

"Do you want to clean up the obit, or shall I?" she said, losing a battle to contain an ever-widening smile. Jack enjoyed knowing her attractiveness held power over men. I was merely her latest form of amusement.

"No," I snapped, sounding way too overanxious. "I'll do it. My mess, I'll clean it up."

I shot her a forced grin.

As much as it may have crossed my mind, the mysterious passages in Christy's obit certainly weren't my attempt at making a pass at Jack Towers. That was truly a suicide mission.

"I don't know what the hell I was thinking, Jack." I tried to chuckle it away. "Sorry if I offended you. My wife has been wintering in Orlando. Guess it's left me harder up than I'd realized." I smiled a guilty smile.

"Just don't get weird on me, okay?" Jack said, not buying my explanation.

"Send the story back. I'll clean it up, then send it along to Sharps."

"Okay, Len." She studied me hard for a long second, before walking away. Was she actually weighing my nonoffer to go to Mexico? I couldn't think about that now.

The story popped back into my computer file, and I rushed to open it. Maybe something in the context would reveal the meaning.

I must have read the story ten times, but I couldn't make sense of any of it.

In the past, when I got a feeling about a story, it materialized all spelled out. This time, it was just James Taylor, Mexico, and bikinis—a hodgepodge if I ever heard one. But there never was any rhyme or reason when it came to my instincts. I knew it had to mean something, but what?

I had heard the James Taylor song before. Jack's rendition did a little to jog my memory. As I recalled, it's basically an ode to escaping south of the border for a little fun in the sun. Did that mean that I should go to Mexico? That a piece of Christy Denza's story was to be found there? It was out of the question, really. The newspaper would never go for it, not on the vague hunch of an obit writer. And I sure as hell couldn't pay for such a trip myself, not with my dear wife Maddie's debts dragging me down.

Then, there was the mention of the bikini. *HE LIKED THE BIKINI, REALLY LIKED IT.*

Whose bikini? I assumed Christy's. But who was the *he?* Having seen Christy's curves up close, I had trouble imagining a man who wouldn't like her in a bikini. On the other hand, bikinis and Mexico go together. Perhaps, it had something to do with a bikini she had worn in Mexico.

THEY BOTH DID.

Again, they who?

First things first, I'd have to find out if Christy had, in fact, been to Mexico, and if so, when and with whom. I furiously jotted notes on the back of an old obit fax.

All of my questions seemed to be leading me to one place: her apartment. If there were secrets, they'd be there. But getting in would not be easy.

For now, though, deadline was fast approaching. I had no choice but to clean up the story and pass it along to the city desk. Before doing so, I printed out the original version so I could puzzle on it some more.

A nagging uneasiness swept over me right then, a feeling that there was more to Christy's death. Something I was missing. But at that moment, I had no choice but to file Christy Denza's obit, pathetic as it would make her appear to all the world.

16

By the time I departed the paper that Wednesday, it was well past six. For the most part, they rolled up the sidewalks in Harrisburg at 5:00 p.m., a half hour after a flood of state workers poured out of town and headed for the burbs. There wasn't much left for me to do that day, anyway. Even if there was, I didn't have the energy.

Tomorrow would be worse still. I'd visit Buzz Swanson tomorrow. I'd go to his offices in the basement of the county nursing home, a strange but somehow appropriate place for the county morgue. That's where Buzz did his postmortems. He liked to start around noon on autopsy days. Buzz could abide a drink before the noon hour, but he could never seem to stomach all that cutting and sawing much before lunchtime.

Good thing, because neither could I. I was used to dealing with the dead on paper. Seeing them pull Christy Denza's ghost-pale body from the cold, swirling river had thrown me. I was not looking forward to seeing her sprawled out on that steel table with half her guts hanging out. But something told me I had to go. There was something to be discovered, and somehow I knew Buzz Swanson would find it. It was a good thing he and I went way back to the days when he just prettied up the stiffs, instead of cutting their lungs out. I looked forward to seeing him, just not the other things I would see.

Walking toward home with the sun setting beyond the capitol dome and my wingtips striking the sidewalk, I realized there was really nothing for me to go home to. Just a dusty, empty row house piled high with old newspapers and musty books. If Maddie saw the place in its present condition, she'd hang me for sure. But who was I kidding? She wasn't returning from Orlando anytime soon. Maybe never. Just as well, I didn't miss her. But I did miss company, the physical presence of another human being, even one I didn't like talking to very much. Feeling this need, I decided I'd stop by The Passway Café, just like the old days. After all, I was a reporter again. I deserved a drink in the old reporters' haunt.

I carried the printout of Christy Denza's obit in my pants pocket. Maybe puzzling over it with a cold lager in hand would help. As I rounded Herr Street, The Passway's large neon sign with most of the letters burned out came into view. I warned myself that it would have to be an early night, one beer and then go. Okay, maybe two. I opened the door and dropped inside. The fat Italian bartender was cleaning his bar. I smiled at him.

Late the next morning, with the sun high above the river splashing golden light, I headed off to see Buzz Swanson, as planned. I ended up drinking much more than I should have last night, and the beer left a faint pain behind my eyes. Predictably, the alcohol hadn't done a damn thing to help solve the puzzle of Christy Denza's obit, but I was optimistic that I'd find something today.

I walked around back of the gothic-looking building

that served as the county nursing home. The structure loomed above me, looking as drab, old, and tired as many of its inhabitants, who were uniformly those people who could not afford any other facility. There in back, a garage door stood open. I knew Buzz Swanson kept it that way when he was cutting. It helped ventilate the place, especially when he had a decomp case. The coroner's offices were pitifully outdated.

As I neared the place, I wondered what the nursing home residents thought of these grim facilities in the basement, knowing it would be their final destination in this building. Not everyone would be autopsied, of course. But they would all need death certificates, and Buzz would be down there waiting to stamp their tickets. The old folks's only way out of this place would be an elevator ride down to these dark corridors. Later, an undertaker would wheel them out through the garage. It was a model of efficient planning, really. Of course, there was another reason the county put the morgue here. It was cheap, and none of the customers would ever complain.

I walked through the garage, passing old, mildewed hospital beds and rusted wheelchairs. I came to a long, hot corridor. At the far end of the hallway, the boiler room produced the smothering heat. The nearest door led into the operating room.

Well, that's what they called it, anyway. It was really a glorified broom closet. As opposed to the state-of-the-art medical examiner facilities you might find in some cities, there were no amenities here. No tile walls that could be easily washed clean, just painted cinderblocks that soaked up the germs and smells from each case like a sponge. And where in most modern morgues you'd find purified, negative-flow ventilation systems to snuff out airborne threats such as tuberculosis that sometimes spewed from the bodies and blood of the deceased, a lone window-mounted air conditioner served as the only ventilation in Buzz's operating room.

As I peered through the smudged glass, Buzz didn't appear to mind his surroundings all that much. His broad, fleshy face was filled with anticipation. He was engrossed in Christy Denza's gross anatomy.

She still wore the few scraps of clothing that managed to cling to her during her seven-mile journey in the swollen river. Her pale body was facedown on the steel table. Buzz once told me that he liked to get a dorsal view and a couple of pictures before flipping the body and beginning the cutting, which always started with the Y incision that laid bare the entire torso.

It appeared Christy had a small tree growing out of her back. The thick branch poked through right where her left kidney would be. She'd been impaled by debris, which had been transformed into a lethal weapon by the violently turbulent waters. Buzz snapped a couple of pictures, while the young resident brought in to do the actual cutting snapped on a pair of gloves. See, Buzz wasn't an M.D. and had never even worked in a pathologist's office. His prime qualification for the elected post of county coroner was his status as a former undertaker. In Pennsylvania, it didn't matter. No actual qualifications were stipulated in order to run for coroner. Buzz's main function was to certify all the deaths in the county, a matter of paperwork, not blood and guts. Still, Buzz was sure to be there for every autopsy. He loved his work and actually helped out quite a bit. He knew what he was doing.

In the operating room, Buzz never bothered with a surgical mask or hair cap. There was no need to be sterile there. Still, the resident chose to shroud his face for his own protection and the psychological separation that most of us need from the dead. Buzz didn't need any such separation. He had been around dead bodies since he was knee-high, I'd guess. His father was an undertaker and so was his father's father.

As he studied the remains of Christy Denza, he wore a bemused look. His salt-and-pepper hair was thin on top but a bushy tangle on the sides and in back. His eyebrows were equally unruly, a pair of thick caterpillars wiggling up and down above his inquisitive eyes, registering each of his discoveries. Always trying to understand the ways of death, he poked a finger at the branch jutting out of Christy's back. More often than not, Buzz could tell what had gotten them.

Buzz's intense blue eyes were running up the length of that tree branch when they caught sight of me staring through the glass. At first, he looked perplexed, as if he were trying to place me. Buzz had told me before that he'd had problems with distraught family members showing up at the morgue and walking right in. As soon as they caught sight of their loved ones on the table with everything hanging out for God and the world to see, they'd pass out right on that dirty floor, stained as it was with the blood of countless cases. Sometimes, with gang killings, rival factions had been known to arrive to finish the battle right outside the morgue door. Not that Buzz necessarily minded another fresh one for the table.

Buzz's eyes softened with recognition as he waved me in. "I'll be damned," he exclaimed, as I entered the room. "If it ain't Lenny Holcomb. I've seen your name all over the paper. What'd you do, get a promotion?"

"Got lucky, is all." I downplayed it. "Had a tip and it led to a couple of stories, but you're only as good as your last story. I'm here to get something new."

In his position as coroner, Buzz often dealt with the younger reporters who covered the real news. Probably, none of them had ever thought to drop by when Buzz was in the middle of a job.

"Well, you didn't miss nuthin'," he said, looking down at Christy. "I like to take my time with things. It'd be rude, I think, to start cutting without getting to know the person."

This old undertaker was talking as if he and Christy were having a conversation. Given the strange obits I'd been writing, I guessed anything was possible.

"We've just been snappin' a few pictures of the young lady, seein' what her skin can tell us," he went on, eyes trained on the body. "Most of these young cutters," Buzz waved a gloved hand at the anxious pathologist on the other side of the table, "they can't wait to get inside. They're like a teenager with a hard-on. They think that's where all the answers are. But skin can tell you a lot. How 'bout that branch, Lenny? Damnedest things can happen to the human body, eh?"

I nodded but didn't really want to look anymore.

"You really want to see something, you got to see a decomp case," Buzz added enthusiastically. "The human body is one hundred percent recyclable. Amazing. I can tell how long they've been out and in what weather just by the smell. Most people don't want to smell it, but it's evidence. Gotta consider all evidence in this business. It's them trying to talk to you. The dead can't talk the regular way, so they find other ways. They say things with their bodies, the way their bodies look, what color they've turned, the pattern of bleeding and lividity, the marks and wounds left behind, and of course, the smell. They talk with the smell, too. Do you hear it, Lenny? Do you hear her talkin'?"

I stared blankly at Buzz Swanson. Shit, I thought,

this bastard's crazier than I am. He gets a whiff of putrid air, and he thinks it's a dead body saying "hello."

Buzz slid along the length of the table, maneuvering in the confined room, to examine the back of Christy's head. He ran his fingers through her matted hair almost lovingly. Christy's locks had none of the blond shine that I remembered, and it struck me how we are diminished in death. We actually look smaller, less real. So much like a discarded shell. I felt my stomach coming up, though I knew there was nothing down there. I never had much of an appetite any time of day, but especially in the morning. I suppressed the urge to heave and looked up at the ceiling, which beat down on me with intense operating room lights.

"Look at this," Buzz said, his voice lost in his intense focus. "It's a pretty significant hematoma. Her scalp is bruised from the bleeding underneath. Looks like this young lady was struck on the head."

Buzz's discovery brought the young cutter out of his impatient funk. He joined Buzz over the back of Christy's head.

"You're right," the young one said. "I didn't see the contusion, but we would have found it when we opened the skull. We'll be able to judge the amount of bleeding and place a time on the injury once we get inside."

I didn't understand why the two of them were making such a fuss over a bump on the head. Christy got tossed around that river for miles. She had a tree branch sticking through her, for Christ sake. What was a bump on the head?

"My guess is the bleeding will show that the blow was less than an hour previous, give or take," said Buzz, still running his gloved hands over Christy's scalp, ever so gently.

"Maybe," the young pathologist allowed. "But, how 'bout we flip her so we can get in there and find out for sure. This could necessitate a change in the manner of death ruling."

"What's going on, Buzz?" I asked, bewildered.

"Looks like you got your story, Lenny." He looked up at me with steel blue eyes and spoke with authority and seriousness. He was talking for the dead now. "That wound to her head, which appears to be from some kind of blunt object, would've knocked her unconscious. Happened less than an hour before her death."

"I don't get it," I muttered, frustrated. "She didn't die in the river?"

"Oh, she drowned, all right."

"Then she coulda bumped her head getting washed over all those rocks in the Susquehanna," I protested. "It's a miracle you've got a whole body to work on. That current ain't too kind to things."

"She got bounced around but good," Buzz agreed. "Busted ribs, a broken arm, and a cracked leg—compound fracture, no less. Maybe more, once we get all the X rays back. But the blow to the head happened before she ever went into the water."

"With all those injuries, how can you tell?"

"The bleeding, Lenny," he said. "There's too much blood. She'd been bleeding under her skin for a good while. Woulda had a huge bump on her head and probably a concussion. It almost certainly would have knocked her unconscious. Now, take a look at the skin where that branch is poking through. No bruises, no bleeding. She was already dead when that tore through her. Her heart wasn't pumping, so there's hardly any blood."

"You're saying she didn't jump?" I asked in disbelief.

"I don't see how she could've." Buzz looked down at

Christy affectionately. "We'll know for sure once we do the procedure. We're going to have to get to work here, Lenny." It was a warning. "You're welcome to watch."

I felt my stomach lurching again. "No thanks. I'll wait outside. Then you'll give me the official ruling?"

"Anything for the *Herald*'s ace reporter." Buzz smiled.

I backed away from the steel table, taking one last look at Christy's gray body. As I exited the small, dirty operating room, I heard Buzz's soft, sympathetic voice.

"Okay, let's turn the young lady. We'll take care of her now."

It struck me then how Buzz and I were the same. We both spoke for the dead. I did it with my obits, and he with his careful examinations. We were both good at it, in our ways. Maybe, that's why so many gave up their secrets to Buzz Swanson. And perhaps it was why some trusted me with their special secrets. But while what I did put a fitting cap to a life, pointing out all the best of a life lived, Buzz's procedure, as crucial as it was, diminished the dead. It reduced them to a mere assemblage of pieces and parts.

That wasn't Christy in there anymore. The person I wrote about in her obit was long gone.

About an hour later, Buzz Swanson emerged from the small operating room, dark blood covering his once white plastic smock.

"Here's the way I can put this." Buzz spoke slowly and clearly, a cue for me to pull out my notebook, which was sticking out of my back pocket.

"Christy Denza received a blow to her head about thirty minutes prior to her death. It was delivered by a blunt object, and it almost certainly rendered her unconscious. She entered the river, probably at the point her car was found on I-81. The condition of the body is consistent with having traveled five to seven miles in the current. The cause of death was drowning. The head wound was not lethal."

Buzz paused for effect.

"But the forensic evidence shows this wasn't any suicide," he said.

I finished scribbling and raised my eyes to his. He nodded his head, a display of confidence in me.

"Someone knocked her out and dumped her," he said. "I'm ruling it a homicide. I'll be sending my report to the D.A.'s office late this afternoon. That should give you a big head start, maybe even a scoop."

Then, Buzz's eyes bored into mine. "You do what you have to do, Lenny, wherever it leads."

What was he saying? Did Christy tell him something more? Or was Buzz reading my mind? Was he telling me, as my own suspicions were, that Christy Denza's death would somehow lead to Gov. Lowell Winters?

17

AS I WALKED BACK TO THE PAPER, I COULD FEEL THE BLOOD pumping in my head as the questions and self-recriminations circled my mind. My heart was pounding, and my face was hot and sweaty in the afternoon sun. It wasn't a reporter's high brought on by a good story, though I did have a hell of a story. This time, it was rage. I was mad at myself for writing that ugly obit immortalizing Christy Denza as a pathetic, lost, and wounded creature who couldn't handle getting fired. It was so damn condescending. Winters had all but called her a little girl who couldn't hack playing with the big boys. Such bullshit. Worst of all, I was the one who dished it out to three hundred thousand readers.

More than anything, I was angry with the governor, who I now believed had something to do with Christy's death. That involvement was no longer something as diffuse and indirect as firing her the day before she died. I was sure the undiscovered secrets of her obit held the key.

For now, though, the cranial bleeding Buzz found was damning enough. Evidence of murder, because unconscious women can't jump off bridges. But they can be driven there and dumped off, late at night when the highway traffic is one or two tractor-trailers screaming through the darkness. The location of Christy's abandoned car was a mere two-mile walk to the governor's mansion. So it was possible. Winters could be involved, somehow. I didn't have the proof to give voice to my accusations. But I did have the coroner's ruling. It was a homicide now. That alone was sure to rock Harrisburg.

"Bill, I got something," I said to Sharps the very moment I reached his desk. I was out of breath from running the three flights to the newsroom. Christy's story couldn't wait for the elevator.

Bill Sharps looked at me with grave concern. "Lenny, are you okay?" He shot to his feet and guided me to a swivel chair. "You're red in the face, and the sweat's just pouring off you. You look like you're having a heart attack."

"I probably should be," I spat out between breaths. I must not have realized how fast I'd been going. The final ascent up those stairs had done me in.

"I'm not ready for my obit just yet," I protested. "Got too much work to do. You'll want to hear this. I just got back from the morgue."

Sharps's attention shifted from the question of my health to the information I was about to reveal. "Go on."

"It's Christy Denza," I said, shaking my head. "We were wrong, Bill. She didn't commit suicide." I talked as if the very thought was absurd.

"It was murder." I felt myself tearing up and didn't know why. "They killed her. They hit her on the head, and they dumped her. Made it look like a suicide, but Buzz found the bleeding. She was hit less than a half hour before she ever went into that river. She was alive but unconscious, and they threw her in. Dead people don't bleed, that's how Buzz knew."

I swung my head, glancing around the newsroom, looking for Jack but not seeing her. My eyes caught Abe Braxton, instead. His bald, perfectly shaped head peered over the wall of his cubicle. He was watching me.

"Is this official, Lenny?" Sharps asked, vying for my attention. "Swanson's ruling it a homicide?"

I nodded tiredly. "It's our story, too. D.A.'s getting the report late. Doubt it will get out for the six o'clock news. Knowing what a camera hog Nash is, he'll call a big press conference tomorrow."

"What made you think to go down there?" Sharps asked. "The cops had called it a suicide. No one had reason to think any different. Yet, you went to that autopsy suspecting something."

"That I did. Don't know why. Something didn't feel right. Just a hunch, I guess. My reporter's instinct."

"Well, your instincts have been pretty damn good lately." Sharps smiled. "Got any more?"

"Not that I can say right now."

Sharps looked at me quizzically, and I answered him with a flat stare.

"You've got enough for today, anyway," Sharps allowed. "Need any help?"

"I'll work with Towers. She around?" I scanned the newsroom again. "And I guess Braxton will get another useless response from the governor," I added sourly. "Only this time, Winters'll have to answer why he thinks someone on his staff was murdered."

"I want you at the next press conference Winters holds, Lenny," Sharps said, looking at me very seriously.

"Braxton won't like it," I pointed out. "He thinks I've been making his life hell, ruining his relationship with Winters."

"I'll handle Braxton. You work your hunches, and you go and ask a few questions of your own. Braxton's our line into Winters's office, but press conferences are an open field. That's when you fire away."

I felt emboldened. It was as if Sharps had just given me license to ask the governor of Pennsylvania if he had anything to do with Christy Denza's murder. Surely he had read the code in my eyes and realized my suspicions.

"I'm there," I said.

"Good," Sharps concluded. "Winters has one about every other week, so you won't have to wait long. Meanwhile, get to work on the Denza story. Grab Towers, she's around here, somewhere."

I returned to my cubicle to find Jack Towers leaning on the corner of my desk, sifting through an old pile of obits. She looked up at me with emerald eyes.

"Jesus, Lenny, you look like you've seen a ghost."

"Maybe I did. Christy Denza was murdered."

"Get out," she gushed. "You went to the autopsy? Why the hell didn't you tell me? I would have gone, too."

"You didn't miss anything worth seeing, believe me," I said. "I like to see your eyes nice and bright and full of hope. After eyes look at something like an autopsy, they just don't shine as bright. The fewer ugly things you see in life, the better."

"What do you mean?"

"Look at me, look at my eyes."

She stared into my droopy, lifeless eyes until I felt uncomfortable. "See that? That's what happens from looking at too much death and typing too many obits. You start to go dead, yourself."

"I don't care," she said with the foolishness of the young. "I want to see. It's my job."

I shook my head but couldn't help but smile at her. She was something.

"Right now, let's just see to Christy Denza," I said. "We called her a suicide and she wasn't. We owe her the truth."

"Wasn't our fault. It's what the cops said."

"It doesn't matter. We didn't get her story right, and she sure as hell can't tell it for herself."

"What should I do?" she asked.

"The usual interviews. But hold your calls till later. We don't want to tip off anyone. If we keep this off TV, we can break it tomorrow morning. D.A.'s getting the coroner's report late."

"Got it."

"Inform Braxton," I added with distaste. "We'll need something from the governor, but make sure Braxton knows to handle it as an exclusive. We don't want the capitol press getting wind. The later we approach people, the better."

"Right," Jack said.

"I'm going to see the brother myself," I added. "He suspected something all along. I want to see what he knows."

Already focused on the mission I had laid out, Jack was about to head for her desk.

"One more thing," I said, my voice low and confidential. "I may have something else for us to work on. There could be more to this story, a lot more than anyone imagines. We should talk. Privately. See me after deadline."

Jack's eyes widened with the impatience of a little girl. I should have known it would kill her to whet her appetite and then hold out. She was about to protest my cruelty in this regard, but I cut her off.

"Nuh-uh. No. I don't even want to hear it. Christy's story first," I said. "Page One tomorrow, and we tell the truth this time. We make it right."

18

THE CURTAINS REMAINED DRAWN ON THE DENZAS' VERY modest home just outside Mechanicsburg, a suburb on Harrisburg's west shore. It was much too far for me to walk, forcing me into my old Fiesta. I avoided driving as often as I could. Behind the wheel wasn't the place for someone whose mind had a tendency to wander. But being off the obit grind and with my rebirth as a reporter, my concentration had noticeably improved. If my mind was turning now, it was thinking about Christy Denza and Governor Winters, not meandering to some far-off, foggy place. I had a newfound presence of mind.

As I sat in my car in front of the Denza house, I wasn't sure how I'd approach Danny. He'd done a pretty good job of running off the last bunch of reporters who visited. And I couldn't very well just blurt out that his sister had been murdered. I felt he should hear most of the details from the cops or the D.A. But I needed him to trust me, or at least agree to talk.

Clouds blocked the sun as I walked up to ring the buzzer. I didn't carry a notebook, and I felt that for once, my appearance might work for me. I didn't look like some slick media hound. And I certainly wasn't a threat.

The door opened suddenly and Danny Denza filled the frame. He wore a T-shirt and jeans and carried a Budweiser bottle in his left hand.

"Who're you?"

"Name's Holcomb, Lenny Holcomb." I offered no more information than he'd demanded.

"I know that name." He shook the half-empty beer bottle accusingly. Then, as if just noticing the bottle, Danny swung back his head, drained the remaining beer, then wiped the back of his hand across his face. His movements were unsteady and overly exaggerated. He had been drinking for some time, though the afternoon was only a couple of hours old.

"You're that bastard that lied about my sister in the paper today." It wasn't a question; it was an accusation. His eyes narrowed. With his long nose, small, thin mouth and close-cropped brown hair, he had the look of a hawk, an angry bird. Danny Denza seemed prone to losing his temper. The beer just made it a shorter trip for him.

"Got a lot of nerve showing up here, mister," he continued, waving the empty bottle close to my face. "You're one slimy son of a bitch. You and the other one who's been calling."

"I'm here to say you're right."

He didn't know what to make of my agreeing with him.

"We were wrong. We realize that now, and we're working on another story to set the record straight."

"What do you mean, you was wrong?" he asked, skeptically. "How do I know to believe you? Maybe you're two-faced. I talk to you, then you turn around and print how I'm *agitated,* make me sound like I'm crazy 'n' shit."

"Enough people have accused me of that very

thing," I said. "Being crazy, I mean, not two-faced. I wouldn't do that to you."

He folded his arms. He was listening.

"There's going to be a major change in this case," I explained. "The story we published today—as accurate as it was at the time and based on police statements—was, as I've said, incorrect. I'm sure your family will be hearing from the police or the D.A. very soon. A story running tomorrow will detail the new findings."

Danny seemed relieved, relieved and vindicated. He took it as license to lecture me.

"You guys made her into some weak little girl who couldn't handle herself," he said, emotion cracking his voice. "Christy wasn't that at all. Killing yourself, that's givin' up. She'd never give up. That's me, not her. She was murdered. I tried to tell 'em, but no one would listen."

"I'm listening, Danny. What can you tell me about your sister?"

"If we're gonna talk, why don't you come in." He held the door for me, and I entered the Denzas' small house. "My parents are down at the funeral home, picking out the casket. 'Course, Christy's still over at the morgue. We got to wait till they're done with her."

He talked as if an autopsy was a distasteful procedure, and I guess it was to many people.

"I know Buzz Swanson," I said, as I followed him. "He takes good care of things. She'll be along soon, I'm sure. If it wasn't for Buzz, this might have gone into the books a suicide."

"Never woulda believed it," Danny said as he led me to the kitchen. "It's murder. Everyone will know that now. You'll write it in the paper. And it'll be solved, if I have any say. I'll get the bastard that did it. Swear I will."

Danny's voice rose with his vow to get Christy's killer, and I felt real anger in him then—anger mixed with a frustrated impotence that nagged at him. It could be summed up in one troubling question: *Why couldn't I protect my little sister?* He must have been asking himself that over and over.

Danny headed right for the magnet-covered fridge and retrieved two more bottles of beer. As he did, I noticed an erasable marker board on the refrigerator door. At the top were the words "Funeral Home" and a number. Just below that, there was a familiar name. It read "Braxton—Herald, 555-3241." Why the hell would Danny Denza have Abe Braxton's phone number? Then I remembered, Danny had said another reporter had been calling. I assumed it was Jack Towers, who'd already spoken to him once. What the hell could Braxton want?

Before I could ponder the scenarios, Danny interrupted me.

"Don't suppose you're the type who'd mind a little drink in the middle of the afternoon?" He smiled as I surveyed the collection of bottles on the Formica table. If Christy's brother wanted me to drink with him, he would not have to twist my arm. I sat down across the table as he slid me one of the bottles. Danny cracked the lid on his and guzzled half of it before I had the top off mine.

"Guess we're not waiting for a toast," I chuckled.

"Ain't nothing in this family to toast anymore. Mom's half outta her mind with all this. It killed her that Christy's gone, but she practically went catatonic when the police started talkin' 'bout suicide. Dad's just angry and mean. Christy was the one good thing ever come out of this house."

He tipped his bottle, drank hard, then slammed the empty vessel on the table.

"Life's a bitch," Danny said. He leaned back on his chair, tilting it on two legs, and reached into the refrigerator for another beer. It was a practiced move, one I was sure he performed quite a bit.

"C'mon man, you're just mouthing that bottle," he protested.

As I watched him, I thought of the many ways death hangs over us. In this house, Christy Denza's death seemed to have wiped away all the hope these people ever had. Just anger remained. And as I watched Danny drain another beer, I thought alcohol was as good a way as any to numb it.

"It's the goddamn governor, isn't it?" Danny's question caught me off guard. "He had something to do with it, didn't he?"

The hair on the back of my neck prickled with anticipation as I hoped for real evidence. "What makes you say that?"

"He's a phony fucking prick, that's what. He used my sister, and he'd do anything to get elected. I wish't Christy never met him."

"Do you think they were having a relationship?"

At first, I didn't know where the question came from. Then, I realized it was all there in the references in Christy's obit. Mexican vacations and bikinis—they all pointed to sex in their own way. Maybe that's what it meant, Christy and Winters were having an affair, an affair that went bad just as he was about to seek the highest office in the land. No stronger motive to kill somebody than that, I thought.

"No," Danny answered, deflating my hopes. "If anything, she was havin' the relationship; he was just screwin' her. That what you think, they were screwin'?"

"Don't know. Do you know if she'd been to Mexico recently?"

"No . . . I don't know," Danny said, shaking his head and tiring of the questions. "Christy traveled all the time, all over the place. She loved it. She was gettin' to see the world."

I was about to fire another question, but Danny interrupted.

"Mexico did you say?"

"Uh-huh. Did she visit there recently?"

Forehead ruffled, Danny forced his mind to make connections through the haze of alcohol. "Mexico, Mexico?" he pondered. "Hmmm. I think she was there. Yeah, I remember getting a postcard, pretty sure it was Mexico. Musta been back in January, right around the time we got that big snow. I remember her writin' that the trip was something for work. I thought to myself, yeah sure, work. It was just a politician's excuse to get a little sun in the middle of winter—all at taxpayers' expense."

"Mexico?" I pressed, "You're sure?" My own mind was searching for something.

"Yeah, I guess. Why?"

Yes, I did recall something about Mexico. It *was* this past January. The governor attended some trade conference there. I must admit, it sounded like a political junket to me, too. Now, it was a crucial connection. Winters and Christy were there together. But that wasn't enough. She was his press secretary, of course she'd go. I fired another question.

"Did you and Christy talk much? Were you close?"

"Not really." He shook his head and frowned. "Winters took her away from us, and she changed. Christy was swimmin' with the big fish now, hangin' at all the 'in' bars, goin' to the right parties and all the happenin' places. Do I look like I hang at the downtown martini bars?"

I shook my head and smiled.

"This was her big chance," he continued. "She was taking her shot. Everybody's gotta try. But she wasn't a phony, not like the others. She had all the clothes, the downtown apartment, all the right friends, but this is where she comes from." He waved a hand, gesturing at the modest house. "Figured she'd get sick of it sooner or later, that it'd wear off. Either she'd end up seein' through those people, or they'd get done usin' her."

"The fact that she was distant with the family, did that hurt any feelings around here?" I had to consider that if Christy's relationship with her own family was strained, maybe a motive for her killing existed there.

"Not really." Danny wasn't the least defensive. Perhaps it was the lubrication of alcohol, but he was completely open. "Fact, I think it made it easier on everyone. My parents aren't the type to approve of everything she was doin' over there in Harrisburg. My mom gives me hell for my beer, so I don't think they really wanted to know that their only daughter was sittin' around trendy bars sippin' martinis in skirts cut up to her ass, while she entertained passes from old men."

Danny took a long swallow, washing away the distaste of the image he had just conjured.

"No, it was much easier if she was the good little daughter with this big job across the river," he continued. "She and her job stayed over there, and my parents stayed here. She'd call once in a while, talk about her latest accomplishments, and my parents were free to brag about her to all their friends. They'd never have to know the dirty little details."

"If your sister and the governor were—" I searched for the right word, "having some type of sexual relationship, would there be any friends who'd know the details, be aware of her private life?"

"First, I don't call any of the people she hung out with over there 'friends,' " he answered sharply. "They'd have no loyalty to her, anyway. In this town, all loyalty goes to Winters. 'Sides, if they were havin' an affair, or fuckin' each other, or whatever you want to call it, Christy wouldn'ta told anyone. That girl knew how to keep a secret. She was best at separatin' her life into little compartments that never had to meet. Sort of like what she did with us. The governor woulda known he could trust her."

Danny reached for the fridge again and my eyes found the marker board once more. Abe Braxton's name and number reminded me that he was hard at work on something. Something big, to get back in the game. I needed more.

"What's Christy's apartment like?"

"Don't really know," Danny said after his first draw on a fresh bottle. "None of us been over there since we moved her in. That was years ago now. It's a building on Second Street. She had the second floor. That's about all I remember."

"You mean neither you nor your parents have been over there since she died?"

"Nope. Cops went through the place lookin' for a suicide note, just like they searched her car. Said they didn't find anything. Haven't really thought about it since."

"I think we should go over there," I pressed anxiously. The way the day's events had unfolded, I'd managed to bond with Danny Denza, the one person who could take me into Christy's world.

Danny didn't answer. He appeared content to keep drinking his beer all afternoon. There was a time not too long ago when I would have been just as content. But not now, with Christy's story there for me to uncover.

"Think about it," I prodded. "We know Christy didn't commit suicide, so naturally there was no note. But this case is about to get bumped up to a homicide, and when it does her apartment and everything in it gets sealed. Now's our only chance."

If I sounded urgent, it's because I was.

"Find what?" Danny snapped. I must have come off too much like a reporter salivating over a story.

"Don't know." My voice was softer now, reasonable. "But there's something, I just know it. And I have a feeling that Winters or one of his guys has already had a look. We should look, too."

"I don't even have a key." He was thinking of excuses now. "She kept her Harrisburg life separate, I told you."

"Do you know the landlord?"

"Yeah, maybe," he said, annoyed. "Some old lady with about fifty cats. She lives on the first floor. I met her when we moved Christy in. The woman is a couple bricks shy, know what I mean?" Danny rotated his index finger around his right ear, the universal sign for crazy. "Hell, the lady stinks of cat piss. My mom damn near passed out right then and there when she saw what Christy was gettin' into over in the city."

It never ceased to amaze me how West Shore folks thought of little old Harrisburg as this wild urban jungle. That was part of the reason so many in the western suburbs, like the Denzas, stayed away. It was also how Christy could have her separate life in the city.

"The landlady'll let you in," I said, more excitedly than was professional. "She has to, you're next of kin. Let's go, I'll drive."

"Hold on," Danny protested. "I ain't finished my beer. Don't you know it's a sin to leave a beer to waste?"

I looked at him, still slouched in that kitchen chair and cradling the dark bottle in his left hand.

"Of course." I smiled. "First things first."

19

Driving over to his dead sister's apartment, I felt Danny Denza grow increasingly tense the closer we got to the city. As we made the approach to the Harvey Taylor Bridge, which carries thousands of cars each day over the Susquehanna and into the heart of the city, his breathing became labored. Perhaps it was all that beer finally catching up with him. Or maybe it was the fact that we were riding over the very river from which his sister's body had been pulled less than forty-eight hours before.

The capitol dome dominated the city skyline as we left the bridge and entered Harrisburg. The preeminence of the green dome with the golden lady of Pennsylvania perched high atop it was, of course, a symbol of how state politics ruled all of Harrisburg, from the tops of state office buildings by day to the trendy bars the lobbyists and lawmakers infested each night. Governor Winters was atop this political food chain. All power in Harrisburg flowed from and through him. Christy Denza had been close enough to that power to feel it.

I made the left onto Second Street and drove into the city's Midtown neighborhood, where Christy had lived on the 1400 block on the second floor of a spacious, old row home. This area had become a haven for single professionals and yuppie couples with no kids. It was a good bet that all of them had ties to state government. Either they worked for the government directly—for Winters himself or in one of the state departments—or their company did business with the state. Either way, their income and their livelihoods were owed to the capital city's political machinery.

At night, these streets would be parked thick with Volkswagens, Hondas, and Acuras. Now, those cars were safely lodged in downtown parking garages while their owners toiled. I pulled easily into a parking space along the street. I slid the key from the ignition and glanced over at Danny. He hadn't spoken since we left his parents' house and seemed to have fallen into a deep stupor.

"We're here," I said, startling Danny from his alcoholic trance. "I think you should talk to the landlady," I advised. "Might want to say you've come to pick out a dress for the funeral. Something like that."

"Yeah, whatever," he said, absently reaching for the door handle.

The now bright sun overwhelmed Danny as he rose from the low-riding compact. He raised a hand to shield his eyes and walked unsteadily to the sidewalk.

"Damn," he said, looking wobbly. "I don't know if this was such a good idea. Don't feel so good."

"Lean on me a little," I offered. "It'll be okay."

We stepped inside the vestibule of the apartment building, and I immediately smelled the cat urine. Danny looked as if he was about to hurl his Budweiser any second. If leaving an unfinished beer was a sin, I wondered what kind of transgression puking it up was.

"Fuckin' cats," he said. "Don't for the life of me know why Christy stayed here."

"Probably doesn't bother you on the second floor," I offered.

I rang the bell marked One. The nameplate said M. Blimpton.

We stood at the door for quite a while, listening to all manner of noises behind it. Finally, locks unlatched and the door swept open. An intense smell of cat urine struck us as a large woman dressed in a mumu appeared. About five cats swirled around her bare feet, brushing their heads and bodies up against her meaty calves, which were prickly with stubble. Strands of cat hair clung to the jagged bristles of her unshaven legs. I peeked beyond her and saw still more cats marauding or lounging. The throw rugs and most of the furniture appeared covered in cat hair, tumbleweeds of which blew across the wood floor like it was a desert.

"You boys lookin' for a place?" said the woman, who wasn't wearing a bra, allowing her breasts to droop to somewhere very near her belly button. "Just happen to have one comin' available. Let's just say the tenant had a falling out."

Her smile was evil and absent teeth.

"You boys queer?" she asked, darting her head back and forth between us. "I ain't got no prejudice. I like renting to queers. They're nice and neat. Just no blacks. They don't pay. Stiff you on the rent, they will."

I glanced at Danny, who appeared even sicker from the sights and smells. I knew the success of our visit rested with me now.

"Hello, ma'am," I ventured, a fake smile plastered on my face. "This here's Daniel Denza." I directed a hand Danny's way. "He's the grieving brother of Christy Denza. I believe she was your tenant, ma'am."

"Oh my." She raised a fat fist to her face.

I nodded my head solemnly and locked eyes with her.

"That was a terrible tragedy," she said. "That young woman shoulda been married, had a man to take care of her. She'd come home at all hours. I wasn't spying, mind you, but my cats would hear her. Worked and played herself to the bone, that one did, till it all got to be too much."

"Guess we'll never know." I glanced at the floor and shook my head for effect.

"The only blessing is that she didn't do it here," the fat woman offered, then clicked her tongue. "I'd never be able to rent that apartment. Oh Lord, no."

Danny's eyes widened in anger. Discreetly, I grabbed his forearm to steady him.

"She's gone beyond now," I said. "Ain't polite to talk about the dead. The family's got to get their girl ready for her grave now. That's what brings us here today, ma'am. Her brother come to pick something out, so she can be laid to rest nice and proper."

" 'Course," the woman said, looking as if she might cry. "Family's gots to take care of their dead. It's only proper."

"I knew you'd be the kind, respectful woman you are," I said. "Now if you'll just give us the key so we can pick out that dress. In all the tragedy and upheaval, the family can't find a spare key, and of course, the police are notoriously slow in releasing personal effects."

"Why, yes." She turned to fetch a spare set, but then stopped. "Say," she said, accusingly, "how do I know who you are?"

"Dan, show the lady your ID."

Danny reached into the back pocket of his jeans, pulled out his wallet, but made no move to open it. I took it from him and plucked out his driver's license.

"See, ma'am," I said. "Daniel Denza, says right there."

"Oh, fiddlesticks," she scoffed, not even trying to read it. "I can't see straight, anyway. Just thought I should ask before I gave you the key. They always ask for ID on them TV cop shows."

"Sure enough, they do," I agreed. "Now the key, please, ma'am."

She brought back a single key attached to a ring fashioned into the shape of a sleeping kitty.

"Bring it back, now," she said. "I'll be here."

Danny and I climbed the steps, then he waited while I worked the lock on the big wooden door. It was old and tricky, but the door finally opened to reveal Christy Denza's private world. Suddenly, as if awakened from the half-trance he'd been in since we left Mechanicsburg, Danny brushed by me into the apartment. I followed and closed the door. It was a spacious one-bedroom with a decent kitchen, but it wasn't fancy by any means, especially the sparse furnishings. Christy had grown up without frills, and she had continued to live without them, even though I was sure she could have afforded better.

A wooden futon, the kind that converts into an uncomfortable bed, outfitted the living room. Probably a holdover from her college years, I thought. A couple of folding metal chairs, the kind often found in church basements, were stacked against the wall, and a particle-board bookshelf held an impressive collection of literature, along with plenty of self-help books and feminist manifestos.

My eyes scanned the room as I heard sounds of Danny in the kitchen. There was the familiar rattle of bottles and the hissing exhale of a beer as its top was popped. Danny was back at it.

Other than a plethora of candles scattered about the place, the decor was spare. The television was small and old and wasn't hooked up to cable. Then, I noticed the stack of policy papers and photocopied press clippings, and realized why Christy had no need for entertainment. She brought work home, lots of it. The mass of papers on the floor near the futon wasn't so much a neat stack as it was a messy pile, with stray papers scattered here and there, even under the futon. Perhaps the mess was created when the governor sent one of his own to look around the place, checking for anything incriminating, as I was sure he had.

I picked up a thick handful, sat on the futon, and began thumbing through the documents. Many of the papers were stapled packets of proposed legislation, drafts of speeches, or the administration's latest policy pronouncements, all bearing the state seal. Christy had used a highlighter to mark some of the passages. The documents were thick with words, the stilted language of law and the bloated rhetoric of politics—polar opposites, yet both part of the same elitist system. They bored me, and I rifled through them quickly.

But mixed in with the boring policy papers, I found printouts of E-mails. At the very top was Christy's own E-mail address, cdenza@pagov.state.us. Her work address, of course.

But even as I leafed through these dispatches, nothing commanded my attention as particularly important. Much of the correspondence concerned meetings and press events, draft versions of press releases, or changes to the governor's event schedule. I noted the addresses of the people Christy corresponded with in her work life, but none of the names meant anything. There were no messages from Winters. Oddly, quite a few of the notes were from Christy—to herself.

These amounted to little more than personal reminders: *"Don't forget to schedule the interview with the Pittsburgh edit board,"* said one. *"The VFW speech is too damn long, and the governor says it doesn't sound like him. Rework it! Brainstorm for ideas and the proper tone,"* read the next one. Another was simply a reminder to pick up the dry cleaning: *"You need your black suit for the funeral."* It was dated the Friday before Bucher's funeral, before everything started going bad for Christy.

I read over page after page, but it seemed pointless. It was just minutiae about proper punctuation in press releases and other seemingly trivial concerns of someone who speaks for a governor. Certainly, nothing that related to her murder, not even a reference to Mexico.

I was about to move on when something caught my eye. Not all of the E-mails were addressed to Christy's work account, I noticed. Some had been sent to her personal address. I recognized it as one of those on-line E-mail services that can be accessed from anywhere over the Web. I was far from an Internet surfer myself, but I knew about E-mail in all its various forms. Had to. More and more local undertakers were e-mailing their obits. With this type of Web account, all one needed was an address and password to send and receive mail. Christy's personal address was denza2010@mailnow.com.

Yet, even these dispatches lacked intrigue. One was a girlfriend asking Christy to meet her for a drink at Scottie's, one of the fancy downtown bars where the beers are expensive and the shots are short. And there were more messages from Christy to herself. It was a neat little system she had, much easier and far better than writing herself notes. After all, you can't lose an E-mail in the shuffle of paper on a desk. An electronic memo would be there waiting anytime she checked her mail.

Christy had sent these messages using her private account. I could see why. They struck me as much more personal, Christy's system of dealing with on-the-job stress, perhaps. One of the passages embedded itself in my brain:

> *Why did you want this fucking job in the first place? Do you even remember? And you say you want to run for office one day? Become the head asshole? Better think again. But if you go ahead and do it, and you win, you better not be just another gutless politician who can't make a move without taking a poll or reading tea leaves or checking his goddamn horoscope. Do yourself a big favor, keep this message so you can remember what it feels like be a young, frustrated idealist working for someone like that. Someone who could never possibly live up to the hopes you had for him. Don't you become like that. Ever!*

I couldn't help but smile. In those few times I encountered her, Christy had been professional and polished. There didn't seem to be a trace of doubt behind her penetrating eyes. Deep down, though, she was just a dreamer, someone who wanted to reach for something bigger and do some good. Then, I understood. Denza2010—it was her own personal target date, the appointed time when she'd emerge from the shadows of other politicians and run for something herself. Now all of that, everything she'd hoped to become, had been taken away.

I kept that printout, folded it and slipped it into the front pocket of my doubleknits. I hadn't learned any more about Christy's murder, but I'd discovered something about her as a person. To me, this was just as valuable.

At the opposite end of the futon, a yellow legal pad rested on the floor and a fancy pen lay at a slant on top. She'd been writing, but had put it aside. I picked up the tablet and read Christy's notes. I was holding a very rough draft of Winters's official announcement for president, a speech he hadn't yet delivered and now may never get the chance, given all the scandals. I shook my head. Christy's own death may see to it that her last speech never sees the light of day. The irony kicked me hard.

I put aside the tablet and pushed myself up from the futon. I decided to skip the kitchen for now, figuring I'd leave Danny alone with his beer a while longer. I headed through the long rectangular apartment, which was connected by an extended hallway.

First stop was the bathroom. It was clean, with a big claw-foot tub. I stepped on the fuzzy pink bathroom rug and opened the medicine cabinet. Aspirin, Midol, and a circular container of birth control pills. Did this mean she had a boyfriend, or at least a regular sex partner? I was surer than ever that it was Winters, but couldn't prove a damn thing. I returned the pills and moved on to the bedroom.

A crucifix hung nailed above the light switch near the door, and a puffy comforter and plenty of pillows outfitted the bed. A couple of novels rested on the nightstand and a rather large closet brimmed with top-label suits and dresses. The floor of the closet was piled high with shoe boxes. Christy dressed well, but the bright on-sale tags still clinging to some of Christy's newest acquisitions testified that she didn't pay full price. Christy had been raised working-class, and she shopped for the bargains.

My eyes settled on a framed picture that rested prominently on Christy's nightstand. I sat on the edge of her bed and picked up the frame. A smiling little girl of about twelve, freckles on her cheeks, was happily kissing her older brother. She was loving it, but the boy looked more than a little embarrassed standing next to a guy dressed as a Reese's Peanut Butter Cup at Hersheypark. Christy and Danny as kids. It was the image that Christy had chosen to look at every single night. She may have lived a separate life from her family, but she still loved her big brother.

Looking at that picture was like staring at a couple of ghosts. Christy was dead, and Danny was all but dead inside. It was one happy moment frozen in time. I ran a finger across the dusty glass, and brought the frame closer to my face. The image was slightly out of focus, and the picture itself looked worn, even bent, as if it had been handled many times by a little girl, before being preserved under glass. Then, I noticed the square outline of something pressed against the old photo from underneath.

I turned the frame over. In the practiced hand of a little girl, Christy had written, "Danny and Me at Hersheypark—1989" on the cardboard backing. I flipped open the little latches holding the backing in place and lifted it off. There was more cardboard and some white matting behind the picture. I lifted that, too. That's when I saw it, the back of another picture, one placed directly behind the old photo from Hersheypark.

Except this second picture wasn't old. It was the instant kind, with shiny black backing. A Polaroid that developed right in your hand as you watched.

I reached for it, waited a beat, then turned it over. All at once, those mysterious clues from Christy Denza's obit fell into place.

20

I WAS LOOKING DOWN AT A VERY DIFFERENT IMAGE OF CHRISTY Denza. She was blond and beautiful, with a sly look on her tanned face. A confident, sexual woman now, she was clad in a blue bikini. The setting was a beach. She had her arms wrapped around a man, an older man. Her head was turned in profile to give him a kiss, the kind with tongues involved. The man's head was turned as well, but his identity was clear. Governor Lowell Winters was French-kissing his press secretary on a beach.

But not just any beach. There was a guy wearing a sombrero in the deep background.

Mexico.

The two had traveled there for the winter trade conference, but more went on than state business.

Probably a beach hustler trying to make a fast five bucks selling Polaroids had snapped the image. And Christy bought it, bought it and kept it. Then, she filed it away, hid it.

But why? Did she know she was in danger? Was she trying to protect the proof of their relationship?

In the white space underneath the photo, there was a single word written in black marker: *Freezer.* The kitchen would be my very next stop. But first, I slipped the Polaroid into my pocket, then repaired the frame, and replaced it on the nightstand. It would be very useful when the time came. Then, I resumed my search.

From her bed, I pulled open the drawers of her nightstand. A couple of sticks of incense and a strip of condoms. Rubbers and pills? Christy was either very careful, or perhaps the rubbers were for random encounters—onetime lovers she wasn't that sure about and, therefore, had to be more cautious to guard against disease. I didn't know. I knew nothing about these young women of today.

I got up, the soft bed creaking in relief, and moved to Christy's dresser, sliding open the wooden drawers carefully so as not to make a sound. The top drawer contained underwear, panties mostly. The next one was bras, all those C cups pointing north. That's when I saw it: The brilliant blue material from the Polaroid. Her bikini. Its bright color shone from the bottom of the drawer. I reached for it, but retrieved only a scrap of material. It had been cut into pieces. Christy had sliced and diced the very garment that had ignited Winters's passions. The tattered bikini was now a symbol of their relationship gone sour and a sign of Christy's rage at the governor. At least, that was the way I saw it.

I fingered the pieces of material and wanted more than anything to get into that kitchen. But I had to lure Danny out of there first.

I returned to the nightstand and retrieved the frame. I looked one last time at Christy as a little girl.

"Danny, you doin' okay?" I called out to him from the hallway. "There's something back here I think you should see. Come here for a minute."

I heard the sounds of the refrigerator opening and of another beer bottle's breathy exhale. Danny emerged from around the corner and walked unsteadily down the hall.

"What you got there?" Danny asked, gesturing with his bottle. His eyes narrowed at the frame in my hands, as he ran his free hand along the wall to keep steady.

"Something for you, Danny," I said. "Come here and look at it. It's something I think Christy would have wanted you to have."

He met me in the doorway, snatched the frame, and swept into the bedroom. He plopped down on the bed but never took his eyes off the picture of him and his sister. As he sat there, he didn't even raise the full beer bottle to his mouth, an act that I was sure had become as involuntary as breathing for him by now. He was frozen by that moment in time from Hersheypark.

I left the statue of Danny Denza on his sister's bed and headed for the kitchen.

The counters were clear, except for the freshly drained beer bottles Danny had left behind. There were no dishes in the sink. A couple of bottles of wine, along with some scotch, tequila, rum, and bourbon, were lined up on a shelf. A magnet shaped like a chocolate bar clung to the refrigerator door.

I went immediately for the freezer.

The frosty air spat at me over a high-rise stack of frozen dinners, the low-calorie kind. There was also a barricade of frozen veggie bags. A couple of beer mugs were frosting in back. A frozen pizza created the foundation for the stack of food.

I reached in a hand and moved some of the items. Way in back, I noticed a freezer bag. I grasped it, but it was anchored by frost buildup on the freezer's floor. I didn't want to tear the bag, so I slowly worked it free. It was the single-serving size, the kind that would protect a sandwich nicely, and it contained what looked like frozen milk. A tablespoon or two at the most. The clear plastic had a white label that had been marked with a single letter: W.

I fingered the frozen substance through the bag and smiled. The pieces were coming together fast now, but time was growing short. I returned the bag to the freezer. I didn't want this carefully preserved piece of evidence to spoil.

I took a quick peek in the fridge, immediately smelling soured milk. Aside from that, there were about eight bottles of Yuengling, a wilted salad in a clear plastic container, and not much else.

I pulled a few nearby drawers and checked the cupboard, but the hot pads, silverware, plates, and coffee mugs offered me nothing. I was running out of places to look, but I didn't care. I imagined the clock back at the *Herald* ticking down toward deadline and felt time slipping away. I had so much to do and so much more to investigate, and the answers seemed only to lead to more questions. But I felt the sudden overriding urge to get back to the paper. My first obligation was to write the story of Christy's murder and retract my false report of her suicide.

I practically ran down Christy's hall to retrieve Danny. I wasn't prepared for what I found. Danny, the beefy construction guy, was reduced to a fetal position atop Christy's double bed. He clutched the framed photo to his chest and was crying so hard he was red faced. I wasn't sure how to approach him.

As he rocked himself and sobbed, I rested a hand on his shoulder.

"I knew it," he murmured. "I knew she was good. She stayed true."

"Of course, Danny. Christy was good."

"She loved me," he insisted. "She thought of me. She didn't forget."

I glanced back at the nightstand and saw the clean spot among the fresh-fallen dust. The whole thing, all of it, was beginning to rip at me, too. I had to get out of there.

"Danny, I think we should go," I said as soft and sympathetic as I could.

"My sister was good," he said, his voice rising through his sobs. "She loved me, and somebody took her away. I'll kill 'em." In an instant, his sorrow mutated into anger. "I'll kill whoever hurt her. I couldn't help her before, but I can even the score."

Danny bolted upright, his face red, raw, and wet. He turned away, trying to collect himself, a bit embarrassed by his display of emotion. I turned, too, giving him privacy.

After a minute, he coughed. I turned to him. The streaks of wetness were gone from his face, but his eyes remained red and puffy.

"Whoever did this to her, I want to know," he said. "I want some time alone with him. He and I, we need to talk." The way Danny said this, it was clear that conversation wasn't all he had in mind. In the state he was in, I dared not tell Danny all my suspicions about Governor Winters. I dared not show him the other photo I happened to have of his little sister.

"Why don't you keep that picture?" I said, gesturing to the framed photo in his lap. "I'm sure Christy would want you to have it."

He looked up at me, searching my face for reassurance.

"She loved her brother," I said.

Danny smiled through his pain.

• • •

On the way out, I retrieved the Baggie from the freezer and deposited it in a thermos I found in one of the cupboards. I dropped in a few ice cubes from the freezer and hoped it would keep.

"That should hold it," I said to myself.

I met Danny, who was milling by the door, still looking at the picture.

"Thanks for doing this," I said, opening the door.

"Did it help?"

"I think so. We'll see."

I downplayed things to Danny, but I could feel the sharp edges of the Polaroid scratching at my leg from inside my pants pocket, as if the photo was itching for me to show it to the world. I badly wanted to do that very thing. The governor was a married man with three kids. Soon, he'd be running for the highest office in the land. And there he was on a Mexican beach, kissing a young staff member. It sure seemed damning to me. But, maybe, in the post-Monica world in which a president walked away with a blow job and even higher approval ratings, my evidence might not mean all that much.

In this case, however, the girl happened to be dead. Murdered. That changed everything.

As for me? I had convinced myself that I was the only one who could solve this mystery and tell Christy's story. I would trust no one else with this sacred task, not the police, not the D.A., and certainly not Abe Braxton. I'd do whatever it took to find the facts, obtain the evidence, and print the truth. I was naive enough to think that was the only thing that mattered.

"We'll see," I muttered again to Danny, as I shut the door to Christy's apartment.

21

I DROPPED DANNY OFF AT HIS PARENTS' PLACE, THEN RACED TO the paper. By the time I arrived, it was nearing five o'clock. All the major players in the story would have been informed of the change in the case by now. I was sure Jack had talked to the D.A., and as per my instructions, Braxton would have taken the matter to Governor Winters for comment. The story would be all there, waiting for me to write.

I strode into the newsroom like a man possessed. I walked directly to my cubicle, and colleagues respected my air of authority. Jack Towers spotted me and rushed to intercept me at my desk.

"Where the hell have you been?" she hissed in an urgent whisper.

I was out of breath again. "At Christy's apartment," I managed, glancing at her as I went about the task of settling in at my desk to write.

"Her apartment?" She kept her voice hushed, but she was clearly annoyed that I had left her behind again. "Isn't that a crime scene?"

"Not yet, it isn't." I booted up my computer. "Police had it a suicide. They impounded her car, but they never sealed her apartment. Takes a while for the police and D.A. to mobilize when there's a change in a case like this. I'm sure they're over there by now, or soon will be."

"Whatcha get?" she prodded, hungrily.

"Not much. Nothing for tomorrow, anyway. What about you? Talk to the D.A.?"

"Yeah, got some quotes. Already shipped them to you on the computer," she said. "I'll tell you, Nash didn't like the fact that we knew about the coroner's ruling before his office did. He was none too pleasant."

"Tough shit. He shoulda dragged his ass to the morgue if he wanted to know so damn quick. You don't see him doin' that now, do ya?"

"No reason for Nash to go down there," Jack said. "Dead people don't vote."

"Right." I chuckled, then changed subjects. "Speaking of none too pleasant, did Braxton talk to the governor?"

She nodded.

"Damn, I'da loved to have seen Winters's face when Braxton asked him about Christy's murder." I smiled for the first time all day. "Pity we didn't get the satisfaction ourselves. Burns my ass that we have to keep going through Braxton to get anything out of Winters."

"Tell me about it," Jack agreed. "Braxton got something, all right. But I don't think you're gonna like it. Just Winters's usual horseshit. I'm sure Braxton didn't press him any, either."

"That's our ace reporter you're talking about," I joked. I could afford to, knowing I'd be pressing Winters soon enough with the other evidence I'd gathered.

"Yeah, right, forgot. Silly me. So, need any help with the story?"

"No, I want to do this." I locked eyes with Jack. "I still feel bad about the obit."

"What about that other information you promised

me?" Jack was not one to let go of things, and she looked at me so adorably, I could not deny her.

"Let me take care of Christy first," I said. "Then, I'll take care of you."

"Hmmmm, sounds kinky." Jack smiled, and I blushed.

"You know what I mean," I said, flustered. "Soon as I'm off deadline, we'll go somewhere to talk." My fingers were already working the keyboard.

"Okay," she allowed, "but not one of your cheesy, depressing dives. I'll pick the place. You buy the drinks. From the smell of it, you already had a head start, Budweiser breath."

I looked in surprise. I had one beer more than three hours ago. She'd make a very demanding wife someday, I thought.

I watched her walk away, swinging her perfect hips across the newsroom. Then, I thought of Christy Denza. In my mind's eye, I watched the men pull her ashen body from the river. I let the image go and glanced at the blaring headline on today's story—my story—about her suicide. Anger breathed its fire within me. Then, I wrote:

CORONER: WINTERS AIDE MURDERED, BODY DUMPED IN RIVER

By Lenny Holcomb and Jacquelyn Towers

In a stunning turn of events that could have major political implications for Gov. Lowell Winters, the death of Christy Denza, the governor's press secretary, has been ruled a homicide by County Coroner Harold "Buzz" Swanson.

Authorities are now working on the scenario that an unconscious Denza was dumped in the Susque-

hanna River sometime in the wee hours of Wednesday morning. District Attorney Earl Nash has promised a full-scale investigation, and Governor Winters, himself, may be questioned in the probe . . .

Of course, I couldn't put in everything that I knew. In my mind, the trail of Christy's murderer would lead right to Winters himself. But I couldn't write that, not yet. What I had was strong enough.

After I filed the story, some of the editors on the city desk were debating whether to tone it down, bleed out some of the choice adjectives, and lose some of the more inflammatory quotes, mostly from Danny Denza. Well, if the desk wanted to change it, so be it. But I couldn't write it soft. I had to write that one angry.

Christy's story told, I looked for Jack. It was time to let her in on all that I had learned about Christy and the governor. I walked over to her desk and found her reading a copy of my story on her computer, nodding in appreciation as she did. I felt good and waited anxiously for her to finish. Yes, I wanted to hear her positive review of my work, but an even more pressing matter was Happy Hour. I yearned for a drink.

"Another fine piece of American journalism, Holcomb," she concluded, clicking off her computer. "Thanks for the byline."

"Hey, we're a team now."

"Then how come you get to go to all the cool places yourself?" she protested. "First, her autopsy and then her apartment. You gotta tell me everything."

"Ply me with alcohol," I deadpanned. "It's the only way to get me to reveal my secrets."

"Let's go." She moved like a whirlwind, which I followed out of the newsroom.

22

Jacquelyn Towers drove me in her nearly new car. It was a sporty foreign model, though I wasn't sure which one. I knew enough to realize that a sizable chunk of her monthly income was being eaten by car payments. Unless of course she came from money, and the car was a gift from Daddy, though I did not suspect this.

The car's speakers belted out a driving beat, and Jack's head bobbed from side to side with the music. Smiling as she watched the road, Jack seemed completely happy, and her mood was infectious.

I didn't try to speak over the music, though I felt somewhat uncomfortable sitting so quietly in her leather bucket seat. She quickly and effectively navigated the agile car through evening traffic, gassing and braking her way across town to North Second Street and its row of trendy bars and restaurants. It was the after-hours playground for the governor's young crowd of aides, a bevy of state lawmakers, and a dozen or so top lobbyists—not to mention the many women that this concentration of wealth and power attracted.

Skillfully, Jack swung the car into a tight parking space. She popped out, flattened her spring skirt, and glided toward Scottie's, a drinking spot where state senators were said to cavort with women who were not their wives. I walked behind, laboring to keep pace. As we neared, I saw the outside deck populated with smartly dressed young women and men in shirt-sleeves, cuff links, and neckties, all sucking on massively fat cigars. Immediately, I felt out of place. Jack turned and winked at me. Through a devilish grin, she said, "Come on, old man, you're my date tonight. You'll make all those other greasy guys jealous."

I quickened my pace until I was at her side. We walked up a set of steps, crossed the deck, and I held the door for her as we went in.

A wave of music, cigar smoke, and loud conversation hit me as we crossed the threshold. The bar was packed, and I felt instantly claustrophobic. Every seat was taken and people were standing three deep at the bar, waving twenty-dollar bills at bartenders who always seemed to be looking the other way. Jack grabbed my hand, pulled me away from the bar, and up some steps to another section of tables, where still more people were gathered to smoke and talk. Jack hunted a table while I scanned the room. I recognized faces from photographs in the paper: lawmakers, staffers, lawyers. The place was thick with suits. I hated it.

I noticed a portrait on the wall. It was dimly lit by a little lamp that hung over the painting, as if it were a museum piece. I instantly recognized the broad, fleshy face as Herb Bucher, his gluttonous mouth contorted into a smile and every one of his multiple chins memorialized in the artist's rendering. Underneath the framed portrait was a gold plaque embossed with these words: "In Loving Tribute To Herbie, A Scottie's Regular For All Eternity."

I nearly laughed out loud. No doubt every bar and restaurant downtown sorely missed Herb Bucher.

Profits would be down all over town now that he and his largesse were six feet under.

In my distraction, I nearly lost Jack. My head swiveled nervously until I spotted her across the room. She waved at me impatiently from a small table in back. A waiter was taking her order, and a short, young fellow in a blue suit was standing over her. The waiter departed just as I arrived, but the small fellow remained.

"So what story are you working on now?" I heard the young man ask Jack. "Going to drag Winters's name through any more shit, or what?"

"Hi, Lenny," she said, ignoring the man. "Have a seat. I ordered you a scotch."

"Who's this?" the short fellow asked, referring to me.

"This, dear George, is Lenny Holcomb," Jack said, waving a hand toward me. "He's the fine reporter who's been ripping your precious governor a new asshole. Lenny, this is George Procter. Works for the governor, not sure what he does." To George: "What do you do again?"

"Economic policy." He was red faced and annoyed, and his voice did not disguise this.

"Guess you're too far down the food chain to know the latest bomb to rock Winters's world, eh, George?" Jack needled.

"What?" he asked insecurely, knowing full well that Jack was right and his lack of knowledge represented the considerable distance at which he was held from the governor's coveted inner circle.

"Christy Denza was murdered, Georgie boy. Winters got the bad news late this afternoon. It'll be front-page tomorrow." Jack watched for his reaction, relishing breaking the bad news. It was a task all reporters secretly enjoyed. Hell, the privilege of ruining someone's day was one of the reasons people became reporters in the first place.

"Once again, you and the governor can thank this gentleman right here for exposing yet another scandal in that beehive you call an administration." Jack nodded at me respectfully. "Before it's all over, Winters may be doing a term, all right, but it won't be as president. I wouldn't be looking for any apartments in D.C., if I were you."

George Procter looked totally offended, but didn't seem to know what to say. "Says you," he spat.

Jack laughed in his face.

"Leave us alone now." She shooed him. "Lenny and I have to talk about other ways we can catch the governor fucking up."

"I thought you were supposed to be biased," George protested.

"Don't you mean *un*biased?" Jack pointed out, not even looking at him anymore.

A wave of confusion swept his face, and he turned and walked away.

"Jesus, Jack," I said as soon as we were alone. "That's baring the teeth a little, isn't it?"

"You heard what he said, we're supposed to be biased. And that simple mind devises economic policy for the governor of the fucking state?"

Maybe Jack was more jaded than I thought. It wasn't something I'd hold against anyone, but Jack always seemed so damn optimistic. Of course, this job will cure most anyone of that.

She reached into her bag and pulled out a pack of cigarettes, just as our drinks arrived. Her hand returned to her bag, and she slipped a credit card to the waiter.

"Run us a tab, will you, kind sir?" The waiter took the card, nodded, then walked away. Jack lit a cigarette.

"Thought you were some kind of athlete," I said, as

she enjoyed her first drag. "Didn't I read in the company newsletter that you ran a marathon or something?"

"You read that shit?" She puffed smoke and smiled. "I'm healthy. I only smoke when I drink, and drink when I smoke."

"Glad we got that straight."

"Yeah, and I'm sure your daytime trips to the bar are for medicinal purposes?"

"Works better than therapy," I said. "Cheaper, too."

"Especially when someone else is buying," she pointed out. "And since I'm the one pouring single malt scotch down your throat, I expect to hear all about these secrets you've been keeping from me. I have a feeling that Christy's homicide is just for openers."

"Did I hear you say single malt?" I asked. "Why are you spending your money on that? I'm a cheap date. Plain ol' Dewar's or Johnnie Walker Red's good enough for me."

"That ain't so cheap, either," she said. "Not in this place. Come on, Lenny, enough stalling. Dish."

"Okay, all right." I took a deep drink of the single malt, which I found delicious, and began. "Christy Denza was a secretive person," I said, putting together for the first time all that I had learned. "That's one of the things that made her good at her job and truly valuable to the governor. She was absolutely loyal. But that loyalty may have helped her killer hide certain things, even the circumstances of her death."

Jack was rapt. Her eyes were locked on me as she absently sipped a fruity-looking concoction through a straw that dangled from her mouth.

"Basically what I think is, Christy and the governor were having a relationship that went well beyond professional." I punctuated these words with a sip of scotch.

"He was fucking her!" Jack yelled loud enough for half the place to hear. "Get out!"

I winced at her reaction, and she turned down the volume to a breathy whisper. "How the hell do you know?"

"Well, this for starters." I freed the Polaroid from my pants pocket and flung it across the table to Jack. Her hands pounced on it with the quickness of a cat. She turned it over and gasped.

"Holy shit," she said. "Nice bathing suit, too. The governor sure seems to like it."

Her hungry eyes practically devoured the image. "He's gettin' some tongue, too. Looks like Mexico. Must have been that junket they took last winter. I'll be fucked—hard!"

"Not you," I corrected. "Christy."

"Nice snapshot," she admired, "but I think we're going to need a little more if we're going to start the next Monica-Chandra scandal."

"That's just it," I lamented. "She was so damn secretive, I don't think she told anybody. We could try working her friends, but I'm doubtful. Even if she did spill it, most of her friends are in the administration, and their loyalty goes to Winters. They're not going to fuck him."

"So to speak." Jack laughed. "Where'd you get the picture, then?"

"Sorry, gotta protect my source."

"Come on," she prodded.

"Can't do it." Jack had no idea how true that statement really was. Finally, she relented.

"Do you think this source can get you anything more?"

"Doubt it, but I got this at her apartment," I said, pulling out the printout of Christy's E-mail. I slid the still-folded piece of paper across the table to Jack. She smoothed out the paper, and her eyes raced over the printed lines.

"She had a habit of sending these E-mails to herself," I explained. "This one reads like she was having a tough time of it."

"Whiney type, isn't she?" Jack said. "Doesn't mean much, though. I mean, I go through days of hating myself, my job, and practically every fucking person on the planet. Happens at least a couple of times a month. I don't write E-mails about it, but it's normal. Probably was her time of the month."

I shrugged, realizing Jack was probably right. She handed back the paper, and useless or not, I kept it.

Jack considered the Polaroid again. "What's this mean? Says *Freezer*."

"Shit, almost forgot. I found something rather odd in a bag in Christy's freezer. I'd like you to take a look and test my theory." I moved to get up, but Jack stopped me.

"Wait. You think there's more." She studied my face. "You think he did it. You think Winters killed her, don't you?"

I paused for a long time, debating how to answer. I drained the rest of the scotch, which had mixed perfectly with the melting ice. Then, I picked up the photo of Christy and the governor.

"Yes I do. I think he killed her, or he had her killed, somehow. I think the bastard did it." My eyes never left hers.

"I can't fucking believe this. The governor of Pennsylvania—the odds-on favorite for president—involved in killing his press secretary? Christ. *New York Times*, here I come."

I smiled at her, couldn't help it. I returned the Polaroid to the safety of my pocket, then turned the same question on her.

"Whadda you think?" I reached out and gripped her wrists so she'd know I required a serious answer.

"I think he did it, too," she said, evenly. "I think the bastard thinks he can get away with it, too. And he probably has a better than even chance of doing just that, if we don't get more." She paused, her mind going a hundred miles an hour. "So where's this freezer bag of yours."

"In your car. It's safe and sound in a thermos in my bag."

"Let's go see." She was already standing.

"What about your tab?"

"Let it run. I may need a drink later. The night's young."

Her heels clicked on the sidewalk as I followed her back to the car. The adrenaline must have been pumping, because she was nearly running.

We both got inside, and she sat impatiently as I pulled my bag to my lap, rooting through the notebooks and the paperback books to find the thermos. I unscrewed the lid and withdrew the bag. It was dripping wet from the melted ice. Inside, the substance that once looked like frozen milk had turned to goo.

I passed it to Jack, who inspected it closely, squeezing the oozing liquid through the plastic. Carefully, she opened the Baggie and raised it to her nose.

"It's cum," she promptly declared, confirming my own suspicions. "Sperm. Semen. I know cum when I smell it."

I looked at her, realizing all the implications. There was no longer any doubt of a relationship between Christy and the governor.

"Lenny, I think I'm sitting here with a bag full of the governor's love juice in my hand. Looks like good ol' Christy did Monica one better. To hell with a stained dress, our girl collected her own semen sample. We gotta get this tested, and we have to find out why she did it."

I knew immediately where we should take this precious piece of evidence.

23

It was after seven, but I suspected Buzz Swanson could still be found in his cluttered basement office. The way I figured it, Buzz would have taken his time getting Christy's body ready for release. Watching him earlier in the day, I sensed it would be difficult, maybe even painful, for him to finally let her go. The emptiness would have driven Buzz to his collection of bones and skulls. He could spend hours with those skulls, trying to fill in the long-dead faces with clay. Plus, I was sure old Buzz had a couple of bottles of his choice stashed away, probably on the same shelves with all those jars of tissue samples and pieces of organs floating in yellow liquid that lined the walls of his office. Those white cabinets were like morbid trophy cases memorializing Buzz's most interesting cases. Not a bad hiding place for one's favorite booze, either.

When I told Jack where we were going, she was predictably excited. She'd get to see the grim quarters of the morgue and the coroner's office, but she sounded like a kid who'd just got a free ticket to the North Pole for Christmas. I wondered if I was once so irrepressibly curious about such things. I imagined I was, until this business drained that, along with everything else, right out of me.

It was with secret delight that I watched Jack's excitement dissipate considerably once we arrived at the basement of the county home and walked through that cluttered garage. We peeked into the operating room window, where seven hours earlier Christy's body lay. The table was empty now, but Buzz hadn't gotten around to cleaning up yet. Bloodstained instruments were strewn on a tray, and the tree branch that had impaled Christy lay discarded on the floor.

When Jack stuck her face in that window, the frankness of what she saw shocked her. She snapped her head away and began breathing deeply, repressing the reflex to retch. She would not have lasted long inside that room, where the smells would have combined with the sights to further confirm the reality and finality of death. Jack Towers wasn't as weary, worldly, and grizzled as she thought. I was tremendously happy about this, but I said nothing. I pretended not to notice.

We moved along quickly down the hallway. I peeked through the window of the second door, Buzz's office. He was perched on a tall stool, his back to the door. He worked under a hanging fluorescent light. His worktable was a scatter of bones, and he was staring lovingly at a skull molded with clay. Next to him was a mountainous pile of the modeling clay he used in his macabre facial reconstruction projects and, nearby, a water bowl to better work the clay.

The walls of his office were lined with those white, official-looking medical cabinets, the many samples visible through the glass doors. I noticed that Buzz had already removed his secret stash from one of those cabinets. The bottle of Johnnie Walker Black rested on his cluttered desk. No doubt, the original copy of Christy Denza's official autopsy report lay at the top of the pile of papers.

I tapped lightly on the glass, not wanting to startle him. I knew all too well the force of any interruption when you were zoned out on your work. His body jerked with the sound, but he collected himself before turning to the door. When he saw Jack and me, he smiled. He swiveled off the stool, picked up his clay-smeared glass of amber liquid, and proceeded to the door. It'd been locked, which I found odd.

"Well, if it ain't Lenny Holcomb," Buzz said as the door swung open. Then to Jack, "You should be careful about the company you keep, young lady."

Jack smiled, and Buzz felt encouraged.

"Is this your idea of entertaining a pretty young woman, Holcomb?" He pretended to scold me.

"Hope we're not interrupting, Buzz," I said, worried that my feelings about Jack were somehow apparent to others. "We're here on business," I felt the need to point out. "This is Jacqueline Towers. She's with the paper, too."

Jack extended a hand, and Buzz touched it gently, not wanting to dirty her palm with the remnants of clay.

"Pleasure," he said, smiling. Then to me, "What brings you down to my humble dungeon two times in one day? I must be popular and don't know it."

"I wanted to thank you again for your help today," I said, moving inside the room as Buzz locked the door behind us. His eyes were glassy, and he was a little unsteady. But Buzz was a professional drinker. "Just wondered whether there were any more surprises in the report."

"Ahh, the report, the report," Buzz said, as if it had somehow slipped his mind. "Everyone is interested in my report. A very hot case, indeed. The D.A. is calling. The governor's office is calling. The police." Buzz did a two-step around the office, waving his now empty glass in the air as he talked. He poured himself another two fingers before proceeding to his stool.

"I'm a popular man committing a very public political suicide," he added bitterly, after a sip. "And you media guys will make sure of it, won't you? Counting your lovely sidekick here, it makes three reporters from the goddamn *Herald* sniffing around on this story, all in one day. It's turnin' out to be one big bag of shit, and it's right here in my lap."

"Wait a minute." Jack ceased looking around the cluttered, shabby office and spoke. "What do you mean the *third* reporter, counting me? I thought it was just Lenny."

"Oh, no, not on this case. Hell, everybody's interested. A few hours after Lenny left, I got a visit from none other than A. Abraham Braxton. That's one hell of a byline he has, sounds so damn journalistic, like he should be working for *The New York Times* with R. W. Apple, Jr., and all his friends." Buzz chuckled and drank. "It's a lot better sounding than Lenny Holcomb. Although, reading Braxton's byline all this time, I'da never made him for a young black kid. Always had him pegged as some professor type, favoring sweater vests and half-rim glasses and such."

Buzz was about to laugh again when he must have noticed our serious faces. Jack turned to me. "The son of a bitch knows something," she said.

"I always suspected he did," I said. "He's been talking to the brother, too. Danny Denza had Braxton's name and number when I visited him today. Yes, Braxton's been right behind us all the time."

"What's he looking for?" Jack stared at me.

"I think we should ask Buzz that one." I nodded toward him. "Well?"

"Braxton's a smart man," Buzz surmised. "But I don't think he has the stomach for this part of the business." He waved a hand proudly about the office. "He's used to hobnobbing with the governor and sitting in those leather chairs behind those big wooden desks they've got at the capitol. He had no interest in taking a look at our guest of honor. But he was interested in one thing. Kinda strange, I thought."

"He wanted to know if Christy Denza had had recent intercourse," I interjected, everything making sense now. "He wanted to know if you found semen."

Buzz nodded, swinging his index finger to the tip of his nose. "Yepper," he said. "I was sorry to disappoint him. I didn't find any. But your man, he didn't seem too disappointed by that."

"He knows about the affair," Jack said in gotcha fashion. "He knows, and he's trying to scoop it. He wants the story."

"He knows of or suspects an affair," I agreed. "But I don't know what his interests are."

"What affair?" Buzz stood up, his bushy brow furrowed with intrigue. "Wait a minute, you think the governor was fucking her?" He pointed his glass at me. "Ho-ly shit." Then, suddenly embarrassed, looking at Jack: "Oh, dear, excuse my language."

"Don't worry about it," she said. "I think he was fuckin' her, too." This put Buzz at ease.

"You think more than that, the both of you," Buzz said. "Damn, this case just gets shittier and shittier." Buzz shook his head and reached for his bottle. "It'll ruin me. I'll be out on my ass."

"Whadda you mean?" I asked him.

Buzz glared at me like I was stupid. "This is a political town, and it's a Republican county. You guys are fuckin' with a popular Republican governor, and you're usin' me to do it. That's how political careers get squashed. That's how little old coroners who are happy in their shitty little offices lose everything. I don't even have my funeral home to fall back on anymore. What the hell would I do? This is my life, my work."

"That's right, it's your work," I said. "And you're good at it, too. That's why you're gonna do your job. You're gonna speak for Christy Denza, and you're gonna help us tell her story. You're not gonna let her down, politics or not."

"Yeah, easy for you to say." Buzz drank.

"What did you really find?" I asked him.

"Nothing. I wasn't holdin' out on your man, Braxton. No semen. She was as clean as a whistle down there. I've taken this case as far as I can. I made it a murder. That's my ruling, and I'm not backing off of it. But you'll have to make the case against the governor yourselves. I'm out."

"I found something in Christy's apartment." I raised the thermos in my left hand.

"A thermos?" Buzz asked, confused.

"Semen," I said.

"I was hopin' for Irish coffee, myself." Buzz looked pathetically unhappy.

I began unscrewing the lid to retrieve the freezer bag. "I want you to test this, document it, and treat it as evidence in this case. This could be the only proof there is of a sexual relationship between Christy and the governor. And we both know that a proven affair would put Winters right at the top of the list of suspects."

"Evidence?" Buzz boomed. "I don't call that evidence, not after you've been carrying it around all day. Since when are you the police? Jesus Christ, this is gonna make me look like I'm in bed with the goddamn newspaper. That'll finish me for sure."

"I found this in her apartment," I said, presenting the freezer bag. "Her place wasn't a crime scene at the time, and I was there at the invitation of her brother. In fact, I had another key piece of evidence that led me directly to that bag in her freezer."

I pulled the Polaroid from my pocket, and Buzz looked at it glumly.

"Shit," he said.

"Buzz, I need you to test the semen, do up a report, and keep it on file with the other forensic evidence in this case. I know you can do that. Put everything in the report about how it was obtained, whatever you need to do. But we need this sample made part of the official coroner's file."

"Exactly what do you expect to prove with that?" he asked.

"That the governor was fucking her," Jack Towers chimed in.

"It don't work like that, honey," he said. "I can get a blood type, and we can match it with the governor's type, which is in his public medical file. But to get an ironclad DNA match, which I think is what you're lookin' for, I'll need a sample from Winters. And where are you gonna get that?"

"Not to worry, I have a plan," I said. "Just work up a blood type, and let's see if it matches. If it does, I'll get you your sample. Just make sure that semen is part of this case file. Guard it with your life."

"I'll keep it under my pillow," he said, not amused that I was telling him his business. "Will that work for you?"

I smiled at him. "Buzz, you're doing the right thing, and you know it. This here isn't politics anymore. It's murder. You treat your patients too well not to stand up for them."

"I like them better than I like you. They don't talk back, for one. And they don't tell me my job. And they don't usually try to get the Republican Party to throw my ass out of office."

There was a long silence, and Buzz looked both angry and perplexed. Then, abruptly, he grabbed the Baggie from me. "Give me that," he said. "That's evidence, don'tcha know?"

Jack and I both smiled at him.

"How 'bout leavin' me be," he said, pretending to be more irritated than he was. If Christy's story led to the governor, I knew Buzz would not hesitate to help bring him down. "Got a ton a paperwork to record that evidence of yours. And I have to get a sample down to the hospital lab, if you want that blood type. I'll be here most of the night."

"When will you have the results?" I asked, sounding almost as impatient as Jack.

"A few hours," he said. "I'll call over now for a courier and have them put a rush on it at the hospital. Check back here later tonight. I'll be around. 'Til then, I'm sure a nice couple such as yourselves can figure a way to keep occupied."

Buzz shot me a shitty grin, and embarrassment heated my face. Jack just smiled.

"We know what to do, don't we, Lenny?" she said.

24

THE NEXT THING JACK SAID MADE MY PULSE RACE.

"Let's go to my place for a while," she said, as casually as could be, as we exited the county nursing home, leaving Buzz Swanson to his bones and his bottle. Those things would occupy Buzz until the test results came back.

I had no idea what Jack had in mind for us. I dared not ask.

She zipped her sporty car around the streets of Harrisburg en route to her riverfront apartment building. As she did, she shouted over her car stereo, telling me that this was the most exciting story she'd ever reported on. She gushed in thanking me for making her my partner. "I just don't know what to say, Lenny," she said. "I mean, there are no words."

We reached her place in no time. She slid a parking card into a machine, and a wooden bar lifted, granting us admittance to the controlled lot. She parked and popped out of her bucket seat. Keys jingled as she tucked them away in her purse. Jack used a second key card to gain entry to the lobby of her building, where a few people were milling about. If Jack was concerned with what people might think of her bringing me up to her apartment, she didn't show it. She checked her mailbox and strode confidently to the elevator, me in tow. She even grinned at a young woman who waved hello from across the lobby.

Finally, the elevator swallowed us and transported us to Jack's floor. I followed her as she fumbled with keys. She ushered me inside and dead-bolted the door behind us.

"What a day, Lenny," she sighed as she plopped keys back into her bag and flung it on the nearest chair. "You really know how to show a girl a good time. And Buzz is just the sweetest. I really think we're gonna do it. We're gonna nail Winters's ass."

Jack talked as she flitted about the small place, doing the little things one does after arriving home from a long day. She pouted at the answering machine, which advertised with a big red zero that no one had called. And she frowned at some bills before flinging them, along with the rest of her mail, on a table.

I remained by the door, trying desperately not to look nervous. The furniture was mostly secondhand but looked comfortable. There were art prints and framed pictures on the wall. The air smelled sweet.

She glared at me from across the living room. "You *can* come in, Lenny," she mocked. "I'm not going to rape you or anything, if that's what you're worried about."

My face turned red at the remark, but I forced myself to move deeper into the room.

"Sit down, make yourself comfortable. I'll get us a drink. Just gotta use the little girls' room first."

Jack disappeared around the corner, and I did as I was told. I settled into the couch, adjusting the multitude of cushions and throw pillows that overpopulated it. Then, I heard sounds echoing from the bathroom. It was the soft, delicate tinkling of Jack's urine stream. That's when it dawned on me. The two of us were alone together in this beautiful young woman's apartment. The spell was broken by the gurgling of the toilet flush. Jack zipped from the bathroom to the kitchen. I heard the distant rattling of ice in glasses and the clanging of bottles. She returned with two glasses of scotch. She handed me one, then plopped on the soft couch, right next to me.

"To us," she said, raising her glass. "The best damn reporters we know."

I met her glass with mine, sipped the scotch, and felt the burn of the alcohol. Jack twitched her nose and blinked hard after her swallow. She recovered but placed her glass on the table. I stole another sip from mine, then followed suit.

Jack pivoted to face me squarely. "Okay," she said. "Get it out."

My heart chugged like a freight train. I gulped but couldn't speak.

"I want to boot up and check something out," she went on. "C'mon, Lenny, we gotta do it. We have to find out."

"Yes," I coughed. It was all I could manage.

"Okay, give it to me, then." Jack held out her hand.

I reached for her awkwardly, but her outstretched hand stopped me.

"The paper," she insisted. "Christy's E-mail. Give it here. I want to check something. I'll boot up my computer and see if we can hack into Christy's account."

I was bewildered but tried to follow her instructions. I retrieved the printout, and Jack plucked it from my hands as she shot from the couch. "C'mon, let's try it. Computer's in the dining room. It doubles as an office."

I was caught in the quicksand grip of those deep

cushions and had to fight my way out. Once on my feet, I stole a glance at my crotch, just to make sure there was no protruding evidence of my misunderstanding of Jack's intentions. There wasn't.

I joined Jack in the next room. Seated in front of a glowing screen, she was already tapping keys and navigating some far-off region of the Web. I stood behind her, watching over her shoulder.

"The one interesting thing we discovered about Christy's E-mail, aside from all her bitching and complaining, is she kept two accounts." Jack talked to her computer screen. "When you think about it, I guess most of us do the same thing. An account at work and one at home. The personal account is the one I'm interested in."

Her fingers raced over the keyboard until she brought up the entry screen for MailNow.com. She typed Denza2010 into the top space, which asked for the screen name. But to tap into Christy's on-line E-mail service, we would also need her password. The space that demanded this code remained blank, as Jack studied the screen.

"We know Christy liked to write herself E-mails," Jack began. "It was her way of sorting out her thoughts and dealing with her insecurities, which were many, apparently. I'm thinking, if it was a regular habit, there might be more of those messages in there. Maybe even something that she wrote in the days leading up to her murder. If we're really lucky, there could be something to tell us what she was afraid of, even a clue to why she was stockpiling Winters's semen."

Jack's fingers came to life. "Let's see," she said as she typed in "WINTERS" and hit the return key. The Web site spat back an error message: "Password Incorrect."

"Too obvious," Jack scolded herself. "Come on, Holcomb, you were in her apartment, sniffin' her undies. Give me something."

"Try Danny or Daniel, the brother."

"I know, I know. But it's too easy. We're only gonna get a couple more cracks at this before the Web site kicks us off. Something else. A favorite movie, a book, an author? Something you saw in the apartment, maybe a sports team? Or how 'bout the name of the street she grew up on, the parents' house?"

"I'll have to check that. I don't remember right off."

"Later. Try something else. Anything." Jack's tone was urgent, and my mind raced. It ran all the way back to Christy's obit.

"That singer," I said. "James Taylor. Try that."

"Why?"

"I don't know, just try it."

She did, running all the letters together.

Denied again.

"Damn," I said.

"I know." Jack's fingers typed one last attempt: BABYJAMES.

A tiny hourglass appeared on the screen. We had picked the lock of Christy's E-mail.

Jack swiveled to face me. "How'd you know?"

Before I could make up an answer, she pointed an accusing finger.

"Wait a minute, that's what you wrote in her obit. The song 'Mexico', written by who? James Taylor. Since then, we've found out that Mexico was where Christy and Winters were fucking around. It was the setting for the picture you found. And now we know that 'Sweet Baby James,' another Taylor song, just happens to be her password. But the question is, how in the hell did you know all of that way back on Wednesday, when this case was nothing more than a local girl who took a swan dive into the river?"

I didn't know what to say, so I told the truth. "I didn't know. I didn't know any of it."

I tried to hold Jack's skeptical eyes until I could no longer stand their scrutiny. That's when I noticed that Christy's E-mails had appeared on Jack's screen.

I pointed. "Why don't we take a look at those?"

Jack turned and manipulated the mouse, running the computer arrow over the list of electronic dispatches. There were dozens, some already read, some not. Jack sorted through them quickly. A surprising number were junk mail, what Jack called spam. There were a few postings from friends and several from Christy to herself. Jack focused on these. She sifted through Christy's complaints about work and her memos about speeches and press releases until she encountered Christy's final dispatch.

It was filed at 9:16 P.M. on Tuesday, the day she'd been fired. The last full day of her young life. The E-mail, sent from and to Christy's personal account, had remained unopened. The subject line contained a single word: "Winnie."

Jack clicked on it, and the following puzzling message filled the screen. Christy spoke from her grave, but Jack and I didn't know what to make of it.

To: Denza2010@mailnow.com
From: Denza2010@mailnow.com
Subject: Winnie

I can't believe this. A letter! He cans you with a letter!

At least now you know you're not paranoid. Damn right, you're not. You knew something was up—something that's been in the works for a while. But it still doesn't seem real. A fucking letter!

You should have known Winnie could never face you. He's too chicken shit. Probably thinks you're pissed about the relationship. He would, the egotistical bastard. Can't conceive of anyone NOT falling in love with him.

What relationship? There was no relationship. There was sex. But you knew he'd never leave his honey pot. Hell, it never even entered the equation. His thinking that you ever dreamed of a life with him, that's the real pisser. Pisses me off. He's the one who couldn't keep it in perspective. Couldn't separate it.

So he cuts you loose at the first sign of trouble. Plans have changed, he says. Unforeseen events. Shifting circumstances. Bullshit! That was the plan all along. Had to be. Too much is already in place. It's too smooth. And that fucking Tigger has been bouncing around here far too much lately. I wonder when they hatched it. It's fucking brilliant, have to give them that. But they didn't have to fuck you in the process.

News flash: you've made a few contingency plans of your own. A girl's got to have a little security. A little safety deposit in case things go sour. Winnie and Tigger can banish you from the tree house. They can team up and think they have a shot at the big prize. But you must be taken care of, first. You get references and recommendations, and you get calls made on your behalf. And you land wherever you choose.

Otherwise, Winnie is going to have to learn the hard way to be more careful where he drips his honey.

He better realize that you'd do it, too. Don't let

them back you down. You've put him first for damn near three years. Time to think about yourself.

And you never, ever tell yourself again that you're paranoid. You did the right thing. You're learning, girl. You're playing hardball with the big boys. You'll be okay, you'll see. In fact, you'll be fucking great. Now, go clean out your desk before that fucking Tigger comes skulking around. Couldn't take seeing that smug bastard right now. It'll be hard enough seeing him on TV for the next year. Just pray they don't win. Please, God! Every time there's a press conference at the White House, you'll be eating your liver, thinking it could have—should have—been you.

Too cruel. Anything but that. Fire me, sure. But don't torture me.

Winnie can't win.

Jack finished reading before me, and she started right in with the jokes.

"The hell kind of childhood did this girl have? Doesn't she know Winnie the Pooh is sacred?"

Jack turned and smiled, but I didn't respond. My eyes were locked on Christy's words.

"Despite the juvenile nature of her code, I think I can decipher what she's saying. It's sure as hell no fairy tale, either." Jack continued being a sarcastic wiseass. "Winnie is Winters, of course, and our Christy knows she's gettin' the boot. Seems to have known it for some time. Ergo, she puts a sample of the governor's love juice in the deep freeze, just in case. A safety deposit, to use her wording."

I nodded, still going over the words, again and again.

"The interesting thing is this Tigger person," Jack continued, unable to contain her smirk. "Tigger was always my favorite, actually, but Christy seems not to trust him. Has good reason, too. Sounds like he's takin' her job. Whoever this is, he's the person the campaign has been talkin' about. He's the savior, the guy who's supposed to come in and right the sinking ship that is the Winters campaign, gallantly leading the governor on to the White House—or the tree house. After this E-mail, I can't decide which."

I wasn't about to react to any of Jack's jokes. Christy's words were turning in my mind. I could hear her voice inside my head.

"Don'tcha see?" I said. "It's all there. The motive for her murder. It's right there. She had the governor's sperm, and she was going to use it. He killed her for it."

Jack shook her head. "Not smart, not with Winters's semen still floating around. Think about it. She was getting canned, and she may have threatened to blow the whistle, take the affair public. May have even hinted about some kind of evidence. But Winters, ever the politician, would have tried to soothe her, give her what she wanted. By the sound of it, she wasn't askin' for much. Just wanted to land on her feet."

"Then why kill her?" I asked.

"Can you say crime of passion? Christy and the governor were fucking. She gets fired. The governor has someone lined up to take her job, someone she despises. That can lead to quite a tussle. She's pissed that Winters cans her with a letter, so she calls him and makes some threats. He has no choice but to meet her somewhere, someplace private. They argue. She gets bumped on the head, gets knocked out. Hell, maybe she even looks dead. At this point, she's a major problem, dead or alive. So better dead. Better for Winters. That way, she doesn't end up in the hospital, battered and beaten at the hands of the governor. Can you imagine the Barbara Walters interview, right from her hospital bed? Winters can. So he panics and dumps her, or has someone do it. Safer that she's found floatin' in the river. Better still, make it look like a suicide."

"That's it," I agreed. "That's how it happened."

"Too bad this E-mail isn't going to be much help with our story."

"Why not?"

Jack looked at me pathetically, like I was irredeemably stupid. "Can you imagine quoting her little story of 'Winnie the Pooh and Tigger, Too' in the paper? I mean, come on, our readers would laugh us right out of journalism. This is serious shit, calling the governor a murderer. We can't do it on the strength of a note about Winnie."

My mouth drooped in defeat, but I wasn't letting go. "Print it out, anyway," I instructed.

"I am, I am. Could make a nice bedtime story, at the very least. Except for the part where she talks about Winnie fuckin' her." The printer spat out the E-mail, and Jack held up the page. I grabbed it from her and studied it again.

Jack shrugged, marked Christy's E-mail as unread, then signed off the computer. She glanced at the clock on the wall. "Time for one more," she announced, and got up.

She returned with freshened glasses. "Here, drink this."

I took the glass reluctantly.

"Sorry, Lenny," Jack soothed. "So maybe the E-mail isn't that much help, but we are getting closer. And that freezer bag down at the lab is a different story. I'm gonna go apeshit waiting for the results."

Along with the drinks, Jack had retrieved a pack of cigarettes and a lighter. "Usually don't smoke in here, but I'm a little antsy," she explained.

She tried to relax, she really did. But nothing worked.

With every deep inhalation of carcinogen there was another question about the case and another glance at her watch. Jack's restless impatience was making me nervous as well, despite the soothing properties of the scotch.

As the minutes stretched out, Jack became more and more like a caged animal. Her need to know the results of the blood-type test became an overwhelming ache. At Jack's insistence, we headed back to Buzz's office early. She reasoned that the wait would be more bearable there. At least we'd be in the same room when the hospital lab called with the results.

25

Buzz acted as if he'd been expecting our early return all along. "Well, if it isn't Woodward and Bernstein," he joked. "No news yet."

He offered us a drink, and we both accepted. I watched as he pulled the tumblers from the back of a cabinet filled with specimen jars, and I felt my stomach turn. As he poured the drinks and passed them, first to Jack, and then to me, I half expected the whiskey to taste like formaldehyde. It didn't, thank God. And in time, as the liquid warmed my throat and eased my mind, I relaxed in the momentary lull of a long day that wasn't over yet.

Meanwhile, Jack provided an eager audience for Buzz's ramblings. I watched her from behind Buzz's desk, her young face revealing unquenchable curiosity. Slowly, the conversation between the two of them grew more distant as my mind preferred equally distant fantasies starring Jack. It was all very pleasant. Then came the rude interruption of Buzz's ringing phone.

I jumped at the sound, and Buzz stepped quickly to his desk to take the call. Jack wore a look of horrible anticipation.

As he listened to what the lab had discovered, Buzz

masked any expression with his best poker face. "Thanks," was all he said before carefully replacing the receiver.

He glanced up, his eyes finding Jack, then me. In the silence, I could hear the hum of the fluorescent lights above us.

"AB negative," he announced.

"What does that mean?" I asked, my voice a whisper.

"It's a match. According to the lab, the sample was mixed with saliva, probably Christy's. They'll test that, too, just to be sure."

"Ah," Jack said in appreciation. "Christy was a spitter. Crafty little devil, wasn't she? I always say, spittin' and swallowin' are the difference between like and love."

So it was true, I thought, the governor and Christy were lovers. Hell, Winters was regularly enjoying the pleasures of oral sex. With suspicions confirmed, I went from hating the governor to feeling jealous of him.

"Like I said," Buzz interjected. "That's just a blood-type match, which doesn't really get you very far. You need a DNA match to be conclusive, and the only way to get that is with a sample from the governor. Not exactly the kind of thing you can just walk up and ask him for."

"Yes it is," I corrected. "At the right moment, that's exactly what you do."

Buzz and Jack turned to me as I rose from Buzz's chair.

"Buzz, I don't know how to thank you," I said, reaching to shake his hand.

"Don't thank me," Buzz said sourly. "I'll add the paperwork about the semen as an appendix to my official report, but that's as far as I go. It will contain nothing about your suspicions of the governor, just an evidentiary report and a blood type. Sure, the clues will be there in black and white for the cops or the D.A. to follow up, just don't hold your breath. Whatever happens from here, I think it's up to you two."

"I understand," I said, fully believing that only Jack and I—not the police, not the state, not even Buzz—could see this case through. When the time came, of course we'd turn over what we had to the D.A., just like I'd come to Buzz with the semen sample. For now, though, I liked the newspaper's chances best when it came to toppling a governor. I gestured to Jack that we should go.

She approached Buzz and shook hands, too. "We'll take it from here, damn right we will."

As we left Buzz for the final time that night, all of Jack's nervous anticipation from before had turned to energy. She was ready to start our investigation right then. But I wasn't.

Instead of a reporter's high from all that we had learned, I simply felt drained. Jack was kind enough to offer to drop me by my row house. My beat-up car would bed down in the newspaper's lot, and I'd walk to work in the morning. We pulled up to my place. Jack was tapping the steering wheel to the beat of music on her car stereo.

"Sure you won't come back to the bar with me?" Jack said. "We could have a couple more drinks and talk about the story. Maybe you could fill me in on how you're gonna get Winters to give us a blood sample?"

"Can't, Jack," I said. "I'd love to, but no. This old man's ready for bed."

"Okay," she said, mischievously, her tone making it clear that I'd be second-guessing this decision for the rest of my life. Jack had a wild look in her eye, and I felt unease over what she might do or say when she returned to the bar. I needed her to promise to keep quiet about our story. After all, secrecy, crucial in any investigative reporting, was a necessary element in my plan for obtaining a genetic sample from Winters.

I asked for her vow of silence, and Jack took instant offense. "Whadda ya take me for?" she scolded. "Some kinda damn rookie who wets her pants over a story? I can keep my lips shut."

"I shouldn't have brought it up," I backpedaled. "It's just that we're so damn close. And I saw how much you enjoyed baiting that guy at the bar tonight. We just can't afford to let the governor know there's a freezer bag of his cum floating around Harrisburg."

"George?" She laughed. "I was just bustin' his balls, small as they are. He's harmless."

"Jack, I'm sorry. I really enjoy working with you." I looked down.

"All right, Lenny. You're forgiven. What's the plan from here?"

"We get our facts together, along with the picture of Christy and the governor, and we go to Bill Sharps in the morning. Then, we'll see how big the paper's balls are."

"Coooool!" Jack purred. "I can't wait. I just want to scream it to everybody."

"You're scarin' me again, Jack." It was true. The urge to tell a secret was often overwhelming, and it was that much worse for reporters, whose job it was to gather secrets but print only the ones they could verify. Holding big news—or dish, as Jack would call it—wasn't in our nature.

"I'll be fine," she said, unconvincingly.

"You say that now, but what happens after you get a few more drinks in you down at Scottie's?"

"Why don't you come and find out?"

"Not exactly my crowd."

"Well, don't worry, then," she said. "Our secret's safe, but my virtue's not. Wanna know what happens after a few drinks? I get a little—uninhibited, shall we say. That's the polite term, anyway."

I smiled and reached for the door handle. Surely, she was playing with me again. Baiting me, getting the old guy worked up.

"Well, have fun," I said.

"I will, but you should worry about yourself in that regard."

"I'm okay."

"You don't sound too convincing to me," she said. "Here, lemme make it better."

Before I could react, Jack Towers reached across the bucket seats and pressed her mouth to mine. Her lips were full and sweet and moist. I felt my heart pound—flutter, really. Actually, I thought I was having a heart attack. Then, I felt the incredible sensation as her lips parted slightly and her slippery tongue swept over my mouth, ever so gently. Just as suddenly, she pulled away.

My face was an inferno.

"Feel better?" she asked, back behind the wheel as if nothing had happened. I, meanwhile, had been cast into a dream state. My limbs were weak, and I felt as if my body were floating. I had zoned out many times in my life, but never like this.

"Yeah," I mumbled. "Thanks."

"I've had stronger reviews. Well, Lenny, gotta go."

It was my signal to get out of the car, but I didn't move. More to the point, I couldn't move.

"Lenny," she said.

"Uh," I sputtered.

"Gotta go."

"Oh."

I reached for the door handle but couldn't seem to find it. Jack reached across me. Her breasts pressed against my chest as she grabbed the latch and cracked open my door.

"See ya tomorrow, big guy," she teased.

I managed to get out of the car, but I must have fumbled with my house keys for five minutes outside my door. When I finally made it inside, I got as far as the living room couch, where I plopped down and stared blankly at the ceiling.

Originally, I'd gone home with the intention of thinking about Christy Denza and Governor Winters until my mind was tired and I drifted to sleep. I didn't think of them once. Instead, I couldn't erase the image of Jack's beautiful, smiling face from my starstruck eyes. The urgency I once felt about this story had been replaced by the simple, boyish longing to see a girl. I couldn't wait to see Jack Towers again. To smell her. To feel her standing over me. To be close to her.

26

THE NEXT MORNING, IT WAS THE SAME DAMN THING. I FELT like a fucking school kid with a crush. Then, the phone rang.

Jack, I thought immediately. Probably checking to make sure I was up so we could meet with Sharps before the ten-o'clock editors' meeting. I rushed to the phone.

"Hello," I said in my deepest, most commanding voice.

"Is this the right number?" The voice was like a cold shower, one that I guess I needed. "Leonard, is that you? You sound weird."

"Yeah, Maddie, it's me," I answered my wife in the bored, unexcited, uninterested tone to which she'd become accustomed in our long years together. "I'm on my way to work."

"Work? You never go to work this early. What're you up to? Are you drinkin' in the mornings again? You know you're too old for that anymore. Your system can't handle it. You're asleep by eleven when you have a nip in the mornin'. You'll be snoozin' at your desk, and they'll fire you. Then where will we be?"

"Well, *we* won't be in Orlando anymore. That's one

thing I can tell you." It was my favorite weapon in our dirty little quarrels. She loved that Florida condo, and I loved threatening to take it away from her. "But, no, to answer your question, I haven't been tippin' it in the mornings again."

"Well, you *were* out boozin' last night," she countered. "I know that for a fact."

Shit, I thought. How in the hell did she know that? She was twelve hundred miles away, and she was still riding my ass.

"I called last night," she went on. "Left you a message. Don't you check the machine? What time you get in?"

"Nobody calls. Why would I check it?"

"I call," she shouted back. "Ain't I somebody?"

"Yes, you sure are," I agreed. "If you must know, I was workin' last night."

"Workin'? Ha," she spat. "Last I checked, the paper don't pay overtime to obituary writers. Our bank account sure doesn't show any evidence of overtime, now does it?"

"Our bank account would be a lot healthier if it wasn't for a certain condo I know," I pointed out. "Certainly isn't me puttin' a dent in the account. Long as I have a few twenties in my pocket every week for the bars, I'm happy. That's all I need."

"That's what's wrong with you." She lunched into the same diatribe she'd been reciting for years, ever since Eddie Moore left the paper and landed one cushy job after another. "You don't want nuthin', so you have no ambition. No get-up-and-go. That's why you're still in that crappy job, makin' shitty money. We should have a house down here by now, not just a little condo."

"We don't even own that," I pointed out. "Bank does. Anyway, I gotta go. Any particular reason you called, other than to brighten my day?"

"As if someone needs a reason to call her husband?" She tried to sound innocent. It didn't work.

"You usually do need a reason. Long as I keep the cash turned on up here, you'd never give one thought to callin' me."

"I called to congratulate you, Leonard," she said, playing hurt now. "You take a person's best intentions and turn them all around. I swear."

"Congratulate me? For what?"

"Bea sent down some of your articles. Seems you've been on the front page quite a bit up there. I was wonderin', you know, if you got a promotion, or something? Lord knows, after all these years, you're due."

I was onto her now. "No, I'll tell you what you were wonderin'. You saw those bylines, and you're wonderin' if there's any money in it for you. You wanna know if you can increase your weekly draw, you know, drain a little bit more from the account. That it?"

"Well, it crossed my mind," she confessed. "I mean, a wife should partake in her husband's success."

"Partakin's one thing. You've been suckin' me dry for years. And to answer your question, no. There's not more money, and there's no promotion. I'm just fillin' in. So, if you overspend down there, the condo payment doesn't get made. Then, the bank'll be kickin' your ass outta there real quick."

"Hmm," she snorted. "Shoulda known. Well, if there's no extra money comin' in, I better get the hell off the phone. I'm runnin' up the bill, and what you're makin' can hardly cover me down here as it is."

"I hear Wal-Mart's hirin'," I suggested.

"Good-bye."

There was a click as she hung up, and I noticed then that my armpits were soggy and my face hot.

She could still do it to me. She could still get my blood boiling for all the wrong reasons.

At least she got my mind off Jack Towers, who had my blood pumping for totally different reasons. I just hoped it would stay that way. I wasn't much good when I was thinking about her. It was even worse than the times when my brain checked out and went to la-la land someplace.

I coached myself in the mirror as I shaved gray stubble from my face. "It has to stop." I said the words out loud, trying to convince my reflection. "It all has to stop before you make a damn fool outta yourself."

I repeated those words like a mantra as I walked along the river to work. I wished then that I had the river's relentless resolve to just keep moving forward.

27

I ARRIVED AT THE PAPER AT A QUARTER TO NINE THAT FRIDAY, more than an hour before the editors' first story meeting. I felt it was plenty of time to meet with Jack, settle on our pitch, and go to Sharps. Jack apparently disagreed. She was waiting impatiently at my desk, her fine rear making a seat out of a pile of old obits.

"Damn it, Lenny, where've you been?" She scolded me the moment I was in earshot. "What do we tell Sharps?"

"Everything," I said. Make that everything, except how Buzz Swanson received the semen sample, I thought. All Sharps needed to know is that the coroner had tested the sample.

"We show him the picture and tell him about the blood-type results and the implication that the homicide investigation, at least preliminarily, may focus on a possible sexual relationship between Christy and Winters," I continued. "To pull this off, we'll have to share the photo with the D.A. 'Course, that's after we make a duplicate to run with our story."

Just then, I noticed Abe Braxton spying on us from behind his cubicle wall. A wave of fear swept me, as I hoped I hadn't been talking too loudly. I shot him a glance, but he didn't break his stare.

"Sounds good to me." Jack swung her head, looking for Sharps. Her sweet-smelling hair flew temptingly close to my face. "Looks like we're up." She gestured to Bill Sharps, walking toward us with a mug full of black coffee and a stack of morning papers. We intercepted him at his computer, which was just clicking to life.

"You guys are in bright and early," Sharps admired, doing most of the looking at Jack Towers. Who could blame him?

"What's up?" Sharps asked the question of Jack, but she deferred to me.

"Well Bill, it looks like there's another development out of the Denza autopsy." Sharps's gaze was now locked on me. Jack may have been better eye candy, but what really got Sharps hard was a good story. "A semen sample has been recovered, and it's the same blood type as the governor's," I said.

"Same type? How conclusive's that?"

"The first step to a match," I said. "Buzz would need a blood sample from the governor to get a complete DNA match."

"I see." Sharps nodded. "Why do we think it's the governor?"

"There's this." I handed him the Polaroid of a bikini-clad Christy Denza French-kissing the governor.

"Jesus, Lenny, where'd you get this?" Then to Jack: "Looks like Mexico, musta been that midwinter trade junket."

"Yeah," Jack smiled. She loved this as much as Sharps.

"Picture came through a source," I said. "Given the Polaroid, which I suspect we'll have to turn over to the D.A., and the semen, I think we're safe in saying the governor's alleged relationship with his press secretary will be explored as part of the homicide investigation."

"This has the potential to be a colossal scandal," Sharps said. "It's national news and tabloid time here. You've got all the ingredients: sex, murder, and a presidential candidate."

"And we can break the story," Jack enthused.

"There's nothing I'd like more," Sharps said, already debating things behind his eyes. "But how strong's our stuff? What do we have?"

"I see your point," I said, picking up on his reservations. I knew all along that this story would prove a tough sell. It took Monica's story months to hit the papers, as editors wrung their hands over its merits. In the end, it was some Internet hack who broke it, forcing the hands of the more respectable news organizations.

"Obviously, we can't run a story saying Governor Winters was having an affair with Christy Denza," I continued. "The only way we say that is with a DNA match. But I don't think we'll ever get to that point unless we run something to put a little pressure on. I say we write it soft. It's a follow on the Denza case. We mention the semen sample. We run the picture. And we say investigators are looking into a *possible* relationship, the key word being *possible.*"

One thing I did love was the way we journalists could hedge stories and say things without ever really saying them. I knew I could write a story that would have everyone in Harrisburg concluding that Governor Winters was giving it to his press secretary, and I wouldn't need to come anywhere close to writing those exact words.

Bill Sharps held a hand to his chin and bobbed his head thoughtfully. Jack Towers looked on expectantly. I wasn't sure whether she was even breathing, frozen as she was with anticipation.

"I think we can do that," Sharps said finally. "Get

the photo over to the art department so we can scan it, then call the D.A. Without the photo, the semen sample doesn't necessarily link things to Winters. If we're going to say this investigation is probing a possible relationship between these two, we better be goddamn sure it is. And we're going to have to give Winters every opportunity to comment."

Jack beamed, but I had one last concern.

"Sounds good," I said, "but there's just one more thing, Bill. I'd like to call Winters myself. Up till now, we've been feeding everything through Braxton. But on this, I'd like to have a go."

"Don't see why not," Sharps said. "But go easy," he cautioned. "No calling him a cocksucker. Let him have his say."

He smiled.

"I will." I smiled, too.

28

Everything went as planned. Hell, it went better than planned. Jack called the D.A., then went to the courthouse to personally deliver what she billed as "highly sensitive evidence germane to the Denza case." Filling me in later, she said Earl Nash practically fell out of his leather chair when he got a look at the Polaroid, which was tucked discreetly inside an envelope marked with the newspaper's logo.

"Where'd you get that?" Nash sputtered at Jack.

"Sources," she said. "We thought you should have it. Thought it could be helpful in the investigation."

Nash just stared at the image. Like Buzz Swanson, Nash was a Republican. And it was becoming increasingly clear to county officials that success with the investigation was inversely proportional to their political welfare.

Nash already had a copy of the preliminary test results on the sperm sample. So when Jack noted that the blood type of the semen matched the governor's, Nash turned even paler and drier of mouth. Still, she managed to extract a few useful quotes from his tongue-tied mouth.

"Given the romantic nature of the photo and the presence of semen that matches the governor's blood type, do you foresee this possible sexual link being a part of the investigation?" she asked him.

After some stammering, which we kindly dropped from the quotation, Nash said: "Everything will be investigated thoroughly. All aspects of the case and all possible leads will be pursued fully."

Bingo. We had Earl Nash, the district attorney of the county, more or less saying he was going to look into whether the governor was fucking a former press secretary who had the indifference to Winters's political career to end up dead. Murdered, yet.

With that, we made our story. We had our official hook. We could bring in the photo, which would run on the front page, above the fold, in full color, I might add. Even with the paper's poor photo reproduction, one would be able to make out Christy's left nipple poking against her swimsuit. And anyone could see her tongue in the governor's mouth. That's all people in Harrisburg would need.

I insisted upon the honor of questioning the governor myself but had forgotten what a pain in the ass it was getting top officials on the phone.

"Governor's office," answered the snooty secretary in a tone that instantly communicated there were a million more important things for her to be doing than talking to me.

"Hi, governor's office," I said to be smart. "How're you doin'?"

"May I help you?"

"Yes, the governor, please," I said, as if it were a casual thing, calling the governor.

"May I say who's calling?"

"Sure, go ahead. I'll wait."

"Your name, please, sir." The woman was stern, not amused in the least.

"Of course. Lenny Holcomb, with the *Herald.*"

"I don't think the governor is taking calls from the press, Mr. Holbrick. Did you try the press office?"

"Last I checked, your press secretary was dead," I pointed out. "In fact, that's why I'm calling. I'm working on a major story on the Christy Denza murder investigation. There's some significant new evidence that involves the governor. I'm sure he'll want to comment. Just let him know the subject matter, and tell him my name—that's Holcomb, by the way. I'm sure he'll take the call. We had quite the cordial conversation at Herb Bucher's funeral, don'tcha know."

The woman sighed audibly, as if my request were impossible. "I'll check," she said doubtfully. "Hold, please."

There was an interminable pause. Finally, the snooty woman came back on, "Hold for the governor."

Winters's voice boomed, "All right, Holcomb, what is it now?"

"Governor, thanks for taking the time."

"What choice do I have?" he said. "You seem determined to attack me, so I have to defend myself."

"Interesting choice of words, considering there's a murder investigation on."

"What are you implying, Holcomb?" Winters's voice battled to restrain what I was sure was rising anger. "I don't like the way you talk to me. You ambushed me at a funeral, and now you call with implied accusations. I need to ask you right now whether you are recording this conversation. I must point out, recording someone over the phone without their full knowledge and consent is a felony in this state. And I sure as hell do not give my permission, do I make myself clear?"

"What are you worried about, Governor?" I expected more finesse, more confidence. Instead, I had him on the run.

"You didn't answer the question, Holcomb. I'll terminate this interview right now unless you declare that you're not recording this conversation."

"I'm not, okay? I don't use tape recorders, never did. Just pen and paper. Governor, I am not recording you, but we are on the record. Is that clear?"

"On the record, that's a joke," he scoffed, his bitter sarcasm freed by my assurance there was no recorder. "I know about your record, Holcomb, your track record at the paper. I found out all about you. You're a washed-up obituary writer, is all you are. What I can't figure is what you're up to."

"I'm trying to ask you a question or two, is all," I said innocently. "There's been another development in the Christy Denza investigation, and I'd like a comment."

"I assure you, I know nothing to be of help in the matter."

"Seems you might know something, sir," I said. "Seems you might be able to explain a few things, some evidence that's been found."

"I'm waiting. You take a long time to get to the point."

"The new direction in the investigation? It involves you, Governor."

"Oh, yeah?" He sounded intrigued but not at all nervous.

"Recent evidence points to some kind of, well, deeper relationship between you and Christy."

"I don't know what you think you've discovered, but I'm very close to my staff, all my staff. That included Christy, when she was in my employ. She was a wonderful woman, vital to this office."

"Perhaps I should make myself clear," I said. "The evidence suggests a relationship of a sexual nature, an inappropriate sexual nature."

"What evidence?" he bellowed. "No doubt you had something to do with this evidence, Holcomb. All this so-called evidence that's been popping up lately has your greasy fingerprints all over it. I find that strange. Who's feeding you, Holcomb? Who's pulling your strings? You're just a front man. There's someone behind you, whispering in your ear to come after me."

"I have sources, sir," I said.

"Who?"

"You wouldn't believe me if I told you."

"Try me."

"How 'bout answering my questions, Governor?" I said. "How 'bout you answer for the picture we have. You remember, Christy in a blue bikini? She's all over you, her tongue in your mouth. Did you have a nice time in Mexico, Governor?"

There was a long silence.

"I'm an affectionate person," he answered at last, his voice as feeble as his explanation. "I'm huggy—I like to hug."

"Well, it looked like more than a hug to me. Guess we'll let the public decide. We're running the picture in tomorrow's paper."

A seething silence from the other end of the line.

"The D.A. already thinks something of it," I went on. "I believe he'll have some questions for you. Then, there's the matter of the semen that's been recovered."

"Impossible."

"It matches your blood type. It also contains Christy's saliva."

"Impossible, I tell you. It's a setup. Someone is setting me up, and you're helping them."

"You haven't answered the questions," I pressed. "How do you refute this evidence?"

"You want a statement? Write this down." His tone

was low and even, but it was just window dressing for ugly, naked rage. "I'm a family man. I'll do everything in my power to defend my honor and my family's honor in the face of these salacious, politically motivated attacks. You are doing a disservice to yourself, your paper, and your readers if you insist on printing your lies. I must warn you, Holcomb. I will do everything to defend my honor."

"Governor, you haven't answered the question," I repeated, trying not to let on how much I was loving this. It was an old journalistic maxim that the more a politician threatened a reporter, the more one could depend on the accuracy of the information. And the more determined one became to print it. So, I swung for the fences, rolling out my words slowly, as if I were talking to a dumb child.

"Were you having an affair, a sexual affair, sexual relations, oral sex—whatever you politicians call it these days—with Christy Denza? Were you, Governor?"

There was a long, pregnant pause. I thought I heard a click.

"Governor?"

"You make me sick," he seethed. "You're bottom-feeding scum and you sicken me. I refuse to waste another second of my time and the people's time talking to the likes of you. Good day."

Winters punctuated his brush-off with a loud, forceful slam of the receiver. There was no doubt this time—we were disconnected in every sense of the word. But I had my quotes, and I had my story.

I raced through the writing feverishly, my fingers dancing over the keys. I could barely contain the euphoria of my adrenaline-fueled reporter's high.

Engrossed by my story, it was some time before I

noticed Abe Braxton's animated discussion with Bill Sharps in a glass-enclosed newsroom office. The door was shut, but the action inside played like a silent movie. Braxton waved his hands as if conducting an orchestra, and rage inflated the veins of his head and neck to the point of bursting. It was a full-blown argument, and it wasn't going Braxton's way. Sharps shook his head. Whatever it was, the answer was no.

I just smiled and went back to the story:

D.A. TO PROBE GOVERNOR'S RELATIONSHIP WITH MURDERED AIDE

By Lenny Holcomb and Jacquelyn Towers

The discovery of two key pieces of evidence has authorities investigating the murder of Christy Denza asking a politically explosive question: Was Gov. Lowell Winters having a sexual affair with his 26-year-old press secretary?

Officially, police say they have no suspects in the case. And for his part, Winters has vowed to cooperate with the investigation. But he became agitated with a reporter seeking comment on the latest developments, labeling the reporter's questions "trash" and abruptly hanging up . . .

I smiled as I wrote that part, knowing it would needle Winters for me to report that he'd lost his cool. Fuck him. If you slam a phone in a reporter's ear, you better expect to read about it in print. We get the last word. Always.

Pleased with my efforts, I shipped the story to Jack Towers, in what had become our custom.

"Looks like you did it again, Lenny," she said later

from her usual perch on my cubicle wall. "Nice lead, too. And just think, you didn't even need your afternoon drink."

"You're half right," I corrected. "I may not have *had* a drink today, but that doesn't mean I didn't *need* it. I was just stuck at my desk all day tryin' to get through to Winters, which is like tryin' to talk to the president."

"If you ask him, it's the same thing," she jested. "But the poor guy just keeps getting further and further away. How does it feel to be burying him?"

"Pretty damn good, actually."

"He's not the only one you're throwin' dirt on," Jack whispered shamelessly, in full dish mode now. "Braxton got his pressed-and-starched boxers all in a knot over our story. Did you hear about his big blowup?"

"I saw him and Sharps goin' at it in the fishbowl. I thought Braxton was gonna stroke out, the way his veins were poppin'."

"Word is Braxton was dishin' dirt on you, claiming there's something wrong with the story and tellin' Sharps to hold it. Of course, he was bitchin' that you pulled an end run by calling the governor directly, trampling all over his beat. Rumor has it that Winters is so pissed, he's planning to complain formally to the publisher. All in all, not a bad day's work, Holcomb."

I smiled. "Sounds like Winters doth protest too much, if you ask me. 'Sides, the governor's the one who called me a washed-up obituary writer. That hurt my feelings," I joked.

"He said that?"

"Yeah, you can add that to the office gossip."

"What can I say? You *are* the hot topic around here, Holcomb. Now everyone's waiting to see who Sharps'll back. My guess is he's goin' over our story right now, debating whether to run it."

"Don't see why he wouldn't," I said. "We have it nailed down pretty good."

Just then, I glimpsed Bill Sharps walking toward us. He looked solemn. Then again, he always did.

"Just read the story," he announced from the entry to my cubicle. "Looks good, but I want to be absolutely sure on this one. Are there any doubts?"

I looked at Jack, and she at me. We both shook our heads. "No," we said, almost in unison.

"Obviously, the governor's irate," Sharps went on. "He called Braxton right after he got off the phone with you, Lenny. Says you have a vendetta against him, that you're working with a political foe who's feeding you information."

"Bullshit," I said. "I have sources, yeah, but they're not political. 'Sides, all my information has been solid."

"True," Sharps said. "That's why I'm inclined to go with the story. There's just a few things. I think we need to point out that the photo was originally obtained by the *Herald,* but we later turned it over to the D.A. I want us up-front about our role."

"No problem," I agreed.

"Braxton's also raised some concerns about the semen sample," Sharps went on. "Says he checked with the coroner about recent intercourse, but Buzz had told him no."

"Shows you the kinda reporter he is," I shot back, knowing Sharps had not seen the amended autopsy report. "He didn't ask the right question. The sample wasn't found vaginally. So, he's right, no intercourse. But there was semen."

Once again, I did not inform Sharps of my very direct—many would say overzealous—role in obtaining the sample. I didn't want him to have any doubts about the story. I told myself that I was doing this for

Christy, but truthfully, I was after Winters now. Winters and Abe Braxton.

"The real question is, what's Braxton know that has him sniffing around the coroner's office, asking about intercourse?" I pointed out as Sharps considered every possibility. "Maybe he suspected the same damn thing. And you've got to wonder why he always takes the governor's side over the interests of his own paper. Remember, Bill, he's the one who wanted to put the brakes on the Bucher story. Now, he wants to kill this one."

"Says he's lookin' out for the paper," Sharps responded. "Says we could blow our credibility if we're wrong."

"Funny, we didn't blow our credibility on the Bucher story," I said, indignant now. "And we didn't blow it when the Denza case was ruled a homicide. Fact, we gained credibility. We've been out in front on all these stories, leading every paper in the state. Now, we can break another one, or we can hold off and let some other paper or the TV break it for us."

"I don't want that. You know that, Lenny," Sharps said. "I'm as proud as anyone at the work we've been doing—at the work you and Jacquelyn have done. But I don't want us to be wrong on something this important. If we're vulnerable on any aspect of the story, I'd rather hold it."

"We're not wrong, Bill," I said.

"All I needed to hear. We run it, then," Sharps declared. "Good work, you two."

Sharps walked away, and as he did, a grinning Jack Towers jumped from behind my cubicle wall, swooped down, and hugged me in my chair.

"Good job with the boss," she whispered in my ear, her hot breath sending a thrill down my spine.

"Uh, thanks," I said, reaching awkwardly to ease

her away. "But I don't think this is a good idea. Look what happened to the governor. Says all he is is a huggy guy, and tomorrow we're runnin' his picture on the front page."

Jack grinned. "I don't think you have anything to worry about. Nobody'll ever accuse you of being huggy."

She laughed, and I smiled, embarrassed again.

"Just so there's no danger of us being seen together on a Friday night, why don't you take me to your dive bar? Your turn to buy, anyway."

The offer took me off guard. I hadn't realized our hanging out together was becoming a regular thing. I was elated at the thought.

"Sure," I said. "How's The Passway sound?"

"Cheap, sleazy, and just right. Let's go."

29

THAT NIGHT, WE SAT AND DRANK AT THAT CLEAN BAR, UNDER those dim lights, with Jack Towers's leg touching mine and her smiling face shining upon me like the moon. I had no inkling that it would be my last happy evening for a long, long time.

But forces were at work—had been at work for some time. I just never realized it. I never put it together. I'd been too busy chasing little bits of information. I'd been too blinded thinking about Jack. I never saw the big picture.

At least I had that last night at The Passway. It was a busy Friday night, but it felt like Jack and I had the place to ourselves. We guzzled beers from the bottle, and she played the jukebox. I watched her laughing and dancing, and my old man's fantasies flourished. I felt wonderful and foolish, all at the same time. I was a reporter again, drinking in the old reporters' bar. And I was sharing drinks with a beautiful woman who was way, way too young for me. And one who I knew had wowed more than a few men to get a story. Okay, so I managed to delude myself into thinking Jack and I were having some kind of half-assed relationship, even if it was the story that she really loved. But we *were* going for drinks on a regular basis, and she *was* kissing me good night. It was enough to fill this old guy's sail.

Jack's kiss to cap that last wonderful night was real enough. Maybe, it was the only thing that was. At least I was alive again, and I was livin' life. I was light-years away from that half-comatose obit writer who'd walk around like the ghost of the newsroom, farting at his chair as the faxes about dead people piled up on his desk. I got my second chance. I had my reporter's instinct back.

In the end, it wasn't enough, nowhere near. But that weekend, it felt like everything.

We broke the story of Winters's alleged relationship in Saturday's paper, and major papers around the state, as well as the wire services, followed with their own versions on Sunday. They extracted similar quotes from Nash and ran the now famous picture of Winters and Christy, which was syndicated nationwide. The image also popped up on weekend television reports and later appeared on the front page of one of those supermarket tabloids. It was a huge story, and every media outlet in Pennsylvania wanted in on it. That kind of pack mentality is the best barometer of a story's newsworthiness and accuracy. I had no reason to feel anything but confident as I strode into work the following Monday morning.

In the end, however, maybe I was too damn overconfident about everything. Either that, or just stupid. A stupid old fool, or worse—worse even than my reputation as a once burned-out obituary writer.

It was early that Monday when I arrived at work, way too early to find Bill Sharps already at his desk and on the phone. I made it the whole way to my cubicle before he caught sight of me. While still engaged in his phone conversation, he motioned for me to come over.

Out of habit, I grabbed a pen and a reporter's notebook.

Sharps nodded his head vigorously, agreeing with whoever was on the other end of the line. "I—I understand your point," he said, trying to get in a word amid the barrage from the other end.

There was a long pause and more nodding by Sharps.

"All we're saying is that there's an investigation—" He talked quickly to make his point. "We're not investigating his private life," he snapped. "The D.A. is. I can assure you we have no political agenda. We're just covering a murder investiga—"

Another pause. More nodding.

"I'm sorry you feel that way," Sharps said. "Yes, we'll cover anything the governor has to say."

Another pause. "Well, you won't be able to read what we print if you cancel the paper, but it's your choice."

Sharps frowned. He had lost. "No, I can't do it. You'll have to call customer service to stop your paper."

Sharps pulled the dead receiver from his ear and stared at it a second.

"Seems like every Republican in the county's calling," he said. "We sure put our hand in a beehive on this one. Can't wait to see the letters to the editor. People will say we're printing tabloid trash and picking apart a man's personal life. But Winters is the one who was fucking a girl who turned up dead. Where's the outrage about that?"

I nodded, still unsure of why he had summoned me.

"Least no one has stepped up to say the story is factually wrong," Sharps said.

"Thank God." I exhaled, feeling instant relief.

"But we did get an interesting call from the governor himself," Sharps added, looking to catch my surprise. "Well, I didn't get the call, the publisher did—at 5:30 Sunday morning."

Sharps paused for effect, communicating quite clearly that our fearless leader, the buttoned-down Angus Merrin, wasn't amused.

"The governor tells Angus that the paper might be interested in a press conference he's holding today. Winters says he has some clarifications to our report. He personally invited us to cover it."

I noted the caution and concern in Sharps's voice. He searched my face, as if I should have known what the governor was up to.

"Clarifications?" I asked.

"Yes."

"So he's still not denying it, then," I pointed out.

"No, but this worries me. He's got something."

"I'm sure he asked for Braxton to cover it," I said, referring to the press conference. "I'm sure that's part of the reason Winters called the publisher. He thinks I'm out to get him."

"He may think that very thing," Sharps said, looking puzzled. "But he asked for you personally, Lenny. Says you'll get the first question. He tells Angus to send however many reporters and photographers he wants, but make sure Lenny Holcomb's there."

"I'll be damned," I said with appreciation. "Least the guy has some balls."

"What's your play, Lenny?"

"I go at him," I said with conviction. "I ask him to do the one thing that will settle this whole affair. I ask him to give a DNA sample so it can be tested against the semen. That's been my plan all along. He's giving us the perfect forum—a full-blown press conference that's gonna be covered by every news organization in the state. There's no way he can get out of there without agreeing to turn over a sample for a DNA test. It's perfect for us."

Sharps nodded. "That'd be my play, too. We can't back down now, not even for the governor and half the angry Republicans in the county. Angus stands by our story, and I stand by it, too. You ask your questions, Lenny, but be careful. We don't want to make it look like we're on a crusade. This bastard's getting enough sympathy as is. Let's not make it easier for him by showing our fangs, know what I'm saying?"

"Yep, just sit back and ask the questions. Put the pressure on him. Let *him* get ugly."

"You do that, Lenny. Press conference is at eleven. Every paper and TV station in the state will be there. It'll probably be on goddamned CNN."

"Can I take Towers?" I asked.

"Sure. Braxton will be there, too, but don't worry. I told him you're the lead guy. You get first question. Right now, you're the reporter with the hottest byline and the highest profile in the goddamn state." Sharps smiled with more than a hint of amazement at the words he had just spoken to his former obit writer.

"Give 'em hell, Lenny," he said. "We own this town, remember?"

"Damn right."

30

The Capitol Rotunda, the most recognizable and prestigious location in Harrisburg, not to mention its premier architectural showpiece, was jammed with reporters and photographers. The horde had gathered in front of the grand staircase. On the first landing of the stairs, a podium emblazoned with the governor's seal had been arranged. Folding chairs fanned out in front of the podium, each chair with a white card on the seat designating the reporter or the news organization assigned to sit there. Jack and I were shown to seats in the front row, center.

"Boy, do we rate," Jack whispered to me as we sat down. "Break the governor's balls and get the best seats in the house. Not bad."

Other reporters filled the remaining seats quickly. Unlike many press briefings, there were no handout materials or press packets. Veteran capitol reporters, accustomed to such accommodations, seemed severely put out that they would actually have to take notes, instead of merely rewriting a press release.

The governor was late, as usual. I amused myself by looking up at the ornate dome, which was speckled with gold leaf, decorated with elaborate artwork, and featured all manner of lifelike statutes watching from above. It was eerily like an old cathedral, and it reminded me of the history that was almost alive here. I could sense the faded presence of long-dead governors and lawmakers who once roamed these marbled halls. As my thoughts wandered, it seemed like only a few moments passed before an aide made the formal introduction.

"Ladies and gentlemen of the press, the governor of Pennsylvania, the honorable Lowell Winters."

The governor strode in from the rear of the rotunda and skipped up the first set of marble steps to reach the podium. He looked as confident as ever. His white hair was perfectly combed, his suit was gorgeous, and his blue eyes were bright. If he had agonized over my story all weekend—my secret hope—he sure didn't look it.

"Good morning," he said enthusiastically, as if leading a self-help seminar, instead of opening a press conference about his alleged affair. The gathered journalists grumbled an inaudible response.

"I think you know why I'm here today," the governor said, locking eyes with various reporters as he scanned the room. "My personal life has been called into question, and my integrity has been attacked. And I think I know what brings all of you out today, too. I don't want to get into a long discussion about the nature of the media, so let's just put it this way. I never saw this much interest when I talked about the education budget or proposed tax reform."

There was a brief smattering of laughter.

"Unfortunately, I don't have any more jokes today," Winters said, setting an earnest tone. "There hasn't been much to laugh about around here, lately. We've suffered tragedies, and we've grieved. There were questions raised about the use of some campaign funds, and we responded in a quick, efficient and, most importantly, an open manner. I'll be the first to say that no administration is perfect. That's why I am the first to react when problems are pointed out. I won't defend us when we're wrong. Instead, I'll work to make it right. That's as honest and open as I can be."

Winters paused and seemed to summon himself. He looked down at his notes, and when his eyes returned to the assembled media, they burned.

"But a different situation is being played out now." His voice was halting, as if holding back a deep reservoir of anger. "Last week, we had a dear friend and former colleague die. It was a great and painful loss to my staff and to me, personally. We all knew Christy Denza and had great affection for her. We were shocked to learn that authorities had ruled her unfortunate death a murder. Immediately, we promised full cooperation with the investigation. It was no time for politics, even though these unfortunate events could not have come at a more awkward time for me and my political career. The last thing on my mind was campaigns, stump speeches, polls, and approval ratings."

He stopped, summoned still more indignation, then continued.

"But my political enemies did not see it that way. They didn't get the message. Either that, or they don't care, and they have no decency. I say this because those who would stand against me have chosen this unfortunate time and these tragic circumstances to attack me. How do they attack me? They float stories in the press. They pass pictures to reporters. They come dangerously close to manufacturing evidence. In short, they will stop at nothing to destroy me. Well, I am here to declare that I'm fighting back. I will challenge these preposterous allegations. I will defend my honor. I will uphold my family values. And make no mistake, I will be fully exonerated with my integrity intact."

Winters stopped on a high note, reached under the podium for a glass of water, and took a slow but shallow drink.

"I think I've said enough for you to know where I stand." His stern face softened into a comfortable campaign smile. "I'm sure you have questions of your own, and I plan to entertain every one of them."

At once, the press corps erupted in shouts. "Governor! Governor!" Reporters strained their arms like overanxious students in an elementary classroom.

Winters smiled, took another shallow drink, then pointed with presidential flair right at me. "Let's start right down front," Winters said, quieting the press. "Mr. Lenny Holcomb of the *Herald*."

Bill Sharps had been right. I got the first question, all right, but I still managed to be taken by surprise. I remained in my seat as the eyes of the press corps focused on me. Jack gave me an elbow to the ribs, and I finally stood. I looked down nervously at the questions I had scribbled in my notebook, only to be horrified to discover that I couldn't read a word of my piss-poor handwriting. I'd have to do this cold.

I glanced up and nodded at Winters. "Thank you, Governor."

He smiled back—a full, cheesy campaign smile. I knew he hated my guts, and that fake fucking smile of his kicked my brain into gear.

"Governor, I guess the question I have, after listening to your speech about all your political enemies and these malicious attacks, is why don't you just settle the matter once and for all? There is a certain sample that's been found. It would be easy enough to determine, through a DNA test, whether it's yours or not. What I'm asking, Governor, is why don't you roll up your sleeve, provide a blood sample, and end this, rather than go on talking about political attacks? Either it's your semen that's been found, or it's not. Either you were having a sexual relationship with Christy Denza, or you weren't. A simple test would settle everything."

The governor fought hard to maintain a semblance of a smile. "I don't think that will be necessary," he said as evenly as he could through gritted teeth and a plastic grin. Winters could afford to lose his temper on the phone, but not at a press conference. Not with all those cameras and the live video feed going out to the entire state and the rest of the country on cable news.

"I suppose we should just take your word for it?" I shot back, still on my feet and feeling more confident. "I suppose the police, the D.A., and the people of Pennsylvania should just leave it at that?"

"The district attorney is right here." Winters pointed to his left, where a group of staffers and officials stood. District Attorney Earl Nash, wearing a sharp blue suit, took a step forward. "The chief is here, too. We had long talks over the weekend. They asked me all kinds of questions, and I told them everything. They seem satisfied, and they see no reason for any kind of DNA test. Mr. Nash, would you care to address the question?"

Winters stood aside as Nash, the loyal Republican, stepped to the podium. Nash had the subdued look of someone who'd been taken to the woodshed and was now being forced to make amends. He was paying the political price for his quotes in our story. Winters, meanwhile, wouldn't have to deny a thing. He could look on with cool confidence as the goddamn D.A. did it for him.

"That's correct, Governor," Nash leaned toward the

microphone but was reluctant to assume the vacant position directly behind the podium. "The DNA issue has become irrelevant and even unreliable at this point in the investigation."

A murmur swept the room.

"That is the determination of my office, in conjunction with the police, in light of certain facts that have come to us over the weekend," Nash concluded.

I was stunned. How could the police and the D.A. just roll over like that? It was a Republican county, but this wasn't ordinary party politics. This was murder.

"How's that possible?" I managed. "There's a murder investigation going on here, and the semen sample is the biggest lead in the case. A match could lead you right to a suspect."

Winters nodded at Nash, who reluctantly leaned toward the microphone once more. "It seems the reliability of that particular sample has been called into question."

Reporters scribbled furiously and flashbulbs popped all around me. I had an inkling of what was coming next, but I could barely hear Nash's words. Nothing seemed real. It wasn't happening.

"The final coroner's report has changed my office's opinion about the evidentiary value of that sample," he went on, more sure of himself now. "In your story, you implied that Coroner Buzz Swanson obtained the sample, but that's not true, is it? You brought it to Mr. Swanson, and you convinced him to test it. Didn't you?"

I looked down at Jack. Her face was red and she was shrinking in her seat, hoping to slip through a crack in the floor. Overzealous reporting had done in many a good scribe before me. I was about to become the latest victim.

"I have Mr. Swanson right here, if you'd like to ask

him." Nash pointed to the same group officials. My head turned with the rest of the press in time to see Buzz step forward.

Looking very sober and very uncomfortable, Buzz wore an uneasy smile as he baby-stepped toward the podium that Nash was only too happy to yield.

"That's right," Buzz said, his voice scratchy at first until he coughed to clear his throat. "The sample in question was brought to me by Mr. Holcomb. I did not recover it from the body of Ms. Denza. That's the way I have it in the final report."

With that, Buzz sank me—and my story. I didn't hold it against him. Hell, I should have known it would come to this, but I never thought it through. Up until that very moment, I had no idea of the damage I had unwittingly done to Christy Denza's case or of the colossal favor I'd performed for Winters. I'd been blinded by the story.

Wearing a perplexed look, Winters leaned toward the microphone. "Correct me if I'm wrong, Mr. Swanson and Mr. Nash, but that's a little unusual, isn't it? I mean, for a reporter to be obtaining forensic evidence and then ordering the coroner to test it and make it an official part of the case file?" Winters feigned confusion, as if his question were purely academic, having nothing whatsoever to do with saving his own ass.

"Highly unusual, yes, Governor." Nash was right on cue. "Unless Mr. Holcomb is a detective or something, and we don't know about it."

The crowd of reporters chuckled.

"I didn't think so," Nash went on, liking the fact that he had warmed up the room.

I had to respond. I had to say something. I had no choice.

"I found that evidence in Christy Denza's apartment, where I presume she kept it in case something ever happened to her!" I shouted. "The governor was having an affair with her, and she was smart enough to keep the goods. You're caught, Governor!"

"The police sure didn't find anything like that when they searched the woman's apartment," Nash shot back.

Pleased that Nash was warming to the task of discrediting me, Winters simply raised his chin in a show of confidence and defiance.

"I was invited to that apartment by Christy Denza's brother," I continued, sounding like a desperate defendant at my own murder trial. "We went there before the case was ruled a homicide. The apartment was not a crime scene at that point. While there, I found a freezer bag containing the sample, and I turned it over to the coroner the same day."

"But at the time of your little search, you knew the apartment would be treated as a possible crime scene and be thoroughly searched by police." Nash pointed a finger, accusing me with a prosecutorial air. "Because of a breach of procedure, you were informed before my own office that this case was being ruled a homicide. You had the jump, and for some reason, you thought it better to remove what you believed could be vital evidence, yourself."

There was nothing I could say to that. He had me. The prosecutor got his man, and now he was going for the conviction. All the while, Winters watched.

"You must know that investigators go through a great deal of trouble to establish a chain of custody with regard to evidence," Nash lectured. "You must also know that an interruption in that chain, even the smallest tracking or custodial error, can result in said evidence being considered tainted and challenged in court. Yet, here you were, walking around with what you're calling vital evidence practically in your pocket for an entire afternoon."

In his courtroom rhythm now, Nash let that one hang for a moment. Had to give the jury some time to digest his best stuff.

"Where I went to law school, we don't call that evidence, Mr. Holcomb." Nash sounded disgusted and indignant. "We call that very strange. We call that pretty damn close to manufacturing evidence. What we don't call it is proof. Even if the governor gave a DNA sample, it wouldn't mean anything. That sample of yours has no credibility as evidence. It would be laughed right out of court."

"If it's the governor's semen, where'd I get it, then?" I shouted, the TV cameras and their lights now trained on me. I had become part of the show, the malicious accuser being revealed a fraud.

"You're attacking the evidence, you're not refuting it," I pleaded. "And neither is the governor. He's never once denied an affair with Christy Denza. He hasn't even denied that the semen is his. A lot of things have been said here today, but not that."

My throat felt dry, and my voice sounded strange to me. My armpits were a river, and my bowels were rumbling. I promised myself I wouldn't fart, not in the middle of the Capitol Rotunda with all the state's press there, and the governor himself staring me down. Oh, no, I wouldn't.

Winters examined me with a look of complete contempt and total arrogance.

There was only one question left to ask.

"Governor," I commanded, with all the authority I could muster. "Where were you on the night Christy Denza was murdered? The people may not have the right to know if their governor was having an affair.

But I think even you'll agree that the people have a right to know whcther their governor is a killer."

The air went out of the room. Every single person in that packed rotunda was holding his breath.

For a second, I thought Winters would lose it. A wave of anger flashed across his face, but he dialed it back. When he spoke, his tone was soft. There was pity in his voice.

"Is there no end to your attacks, to your wild accusations, to your hatred of me?" He shook his head pathetically.

But everyone was waiting for an answer to my question, and he knew it. Hell, he counted on it.

"I knew there would be attacks, unsupported, reckless attacks, like yours," Winters went on. "That's why I found it necessary to make a call to our good district attorney and our fine city chief of police. I called *them*." He smiled over at the officials.

"I want it on the record. I was never a suspect. But I felt the need to clear my name in face of these wild accusations. Bright and early Saturday, the day the false story came out, we had a meeting. And numerous good and honest people have given statements on my behalf. Where was I the night and early morning when Christy Denza so unfortunately lost her life? The district attorney can tell you. He has a file of witness statements four inches thick on that very subject."

Winters nodded to Nash one last time, the signal for the district attorney to issue Winters a clean bill of legal health.

"That's correct," he said. "We've taken statements from a variety of people, all of whom support the governor's account of his whereabouts on the night and early morning in question. These witnesses include House Minority Leader Art Paulis; Mimi Watson, head of the governor's wait staff; Dave Lange, chief of information services; and Commander Lou Pena, chief of the governor's security detail."

Nash raised a thick stack of documents. "Through these statements, we are able to establish an uninterrupted timeline for the governor's whereabouts from eight-thirty last Tuesday evening until six A.M. Wednesday. In other words, ladies and gentlemen, Governor Winters has an airtight, witness-supported alibi."

Winters nodded proudly, and why wouldn't he? He was managing to reverse the worst press anyone could get.

"The entire file of witness statements will be made available to all of you following the briefing," Nash continued. "In addition, all of the witnesses are here this morning, if there are any questions." Nash gestured to his left, as several of the gathered officials nodded acknowledgment.

Winters beamed at the assembled group that personified his alibi, then leaned toward the microphone. "Sorry to bore everyone with the mundane details of my uneventful evening, but I felt I had to put everything on the record. How 'bout it, Art?" Winters nodded to Democrat Art Paulis, who smiled back. "We get along well enough for leaders from opposite political parties, but, no offense, you're not the first guy I'd count on to set me up with an alibi."

Winters got a good rise out of the gathered press. But Nash had more ground to cover and seemed annoyed at the governor's unscripted interruption. Eager to finish, he launched the final assault.

"In addition to the witness statements, Governor Winters volunteered to sit for a polygraph test, which was controlled and conducted by the police and my office. I personally observed the questioning."

Nash paused for effect.

"I'm pleased to report that the governor passed every question regarding Christy Denza's death. The media will get complete copies of the results, of course." Nash glanced up at the glaring television lights in what seemed like relief. "In short, ladies and gentlemen, Governor Winters has been unequivocally and irrefutably cleared of any suspicion, whatsoever, regarding Christy Denza's death. He is not a suspect in this case. Period."

By this time, the assembled media were growing restless. But before they could fire their questions, Winters leaned in for the capper.

"That's quite a difference from what you read in the paper this weekend," he said, sounding fully vindicated. "Now that we've taken these unprecedented steps to clear things up, I'm hoping you, the press, will treat us fairly. That's all I've ever asked. I pray that the ugly politics of this case are over."

Winters took one last sip of water. "Christy Denza's death is a police matter now. This administration will move on, as it must. But before you in the media turn the page, you might want to ask just one more question. You might want to ask Lenny Holcomb and his newspaper why they tried to set me up. That sounds like a pretty good question to me. Thank you for your time and attention."

Winters smiled broadly and then gestured to an aide: "Can we pass out those materials?"

At once, reporters clawed for the documents, as the papers floated down the rows of assembled media.

I just stood there, watching it all. I really think I was in shock. I was a statue.

Winters stepped away from the podium, prompting several reporters to launch themselves toward him, tape recorders and microphones aimed at his face. Sure, the hungry media hollered out more questions about Christy Denza, but the worst was over for Governor Winters. The mountain of evidence he produced would bury the story under an avalanche of mostly useless facts. I wondered if Nash had had the balls to ask about the affair when he had Winters hooked up to that lie detector. I doubted it. Despite everything, I was sure Winters couldn't have passed that question. There was probably some kind of deal to avoid the issue. But all that didn't seem to matter now. Winters had passed the big question. He didn't kill her. That would be the headline: "GOVERNOR CLEARED IN DENZA MURDER." The accusations of an affair might hang in the air for a while, but eventually, they'd get buried, too, right alongside Christy.

But if Winters didn't kill her, who did? The first lady, perhaps, in some wild, jealous rage? Now I really was grasping at straws. I mean, the governor's wife was a grandmotherly woman whose main mission in life seemed to be urging women to get regular mammograms. Worse still, I had no time to think about other suspects just then. To my surprise, another group of shouting reporters had surrounded me. Microphones and tape recorders were in *my* face.

"How 'bout it, Holcomb, where'd you get the sample?" asked one. "Why'd you do it? What's your motive?" shouted another. "Who're you working with? What political party do you belong to?" they wanted to know. "How long were you an obit writer? And how did you get on this story, Holcomb?"

I felt everything closing in—the noise, the lights, the cameras, the microphones, and the shouting. I couldn't breathe. I pushed through the outstretched microphones and the intrusive cameras. I heard my name but didn't look back. Then, I felt someone pulling on my arm. I was about to jerk it away, when I recognized the voice.

"Lenny." It was Jack Towers. "What are you going to do?"

My world had just collapsed, but I felt serene, like it was all happening to someone else. I was merely watching. But that look—that sad, pathetic look on Jack Towers's face—brought it all home. She was defeated. And worse, she was disappointed—in me.

"I don't know," I said, wearily. "I'll take the fall, I guess."

She looked like a little girl about to cry. A little girl who had skinned her knee, and the tears were welling up against her will. She moved to hug me, but I raised a hand.

"No, Jack." It was my clearest statement all day. "You stay away from me now, you hear? Just stay away. I'll take the fall. You have a life and a career. I don't. Just ignore me like all the rest will."

Jack halted, saw the determination in my eyes, and knew I was right.

She turned away.

I pushed through the crowd and headed for the revolving doors that would take me away from this madness. My chest hurt, and I was panting for air. I feared I'd never reach those doors. The world was in slow motion.

I couldn't see any of the people trying to talk to me. But in the back of the room, I recognized a familiar face. Abe Braxton, looking fantastic in a perfectly tailored suit, was watching me. He watched, and then he smiled.

It was a terrible, hateful grin.

PART III

ISLAND

31

I BURST THROUGH THE ROTUNDA'S REVOLVING DOOR, SENDING me out onto an ocean of steps leading away from the capitol and the governor's press conference. The noon sun was blinding, and I didn't think I'd have the energy to walk down all those steps. Where was I going, anyway? I couldn't go back to the paper. Not today. Tomorrow would be bad enough. I'd walk into the newsroom, and no one would look at me. I'd wander back to my desk, and waiting for me would be the obits. Waiting for me would be the rest of my life.

No, damn it, tomorrow was soon enough.

What I needed now was a drink. A whole damn bottle. But not at The Passway. Never again at the old reporters' bar. I was just an obit writer now. Any old dive would do.

I escaped the sun in the dark, stale confines of a small bar. The crowd was thin, just the hardcore drunks, who mostly kept to themselves. I liked the place already. So, I sat and I drank. And my mind faded away. It all went away: Christy Denza, Governor Winters, and Jack Towers. But the scotch was real, and I drank it.

Already, I dreaded the morning.

• • •

I slipped into the paper well after 10:00 A.M. the next day. I was suffering from a queen bitch of a hangover, and I couldn't shake the feeling that I'd throw up at any minute. I walked back to my desk, feeling invisible. But I guess that wasn't exactly true, because people did see me. They'd look for an instant, then turn away. I much preferred my former incarnation as the ghost of the newsroom. But now I was something even viler. I was a leper, a source of horror, scorn, and revulsion to all who cast eyes on me.

I walked past Bill Sharps, seated at his computer. He took no notice of me and didn't utter a word. He didn't have to. The stack of fresh obit faxes on my chair said it all. So did the copy of the morning paper, which had been deposited haphazardly on my messy desk. The headline trumpeted Winters's victory and my defeat: "*GOVERNOR CLEARED IN MURDER INVESTIGATION; WINTERS SAYS, 'TIME TO MOVE ON.'*"

A. Abraham Braxton had the byline, of course. I noticed him at his cubicle as I sat down. He never so much as turned around. He needn't worry about spying on me anymore.

Under the main story was a subhead: "*PAPER INVESTIGATES REPORTER'S ACTIONS IN CASE.*" It was a full disclosure statement, signed by the publisher himself, explaining my role in gathering certain evidence from Christy's apartment. The piece cited "inappropriate interference with an official investigation" in describing my actions.

The statement innocently pointed out that "these facts were not known by the newspaper's management at the time of publication." Then, the publisher sounded a full retreat: "We now agree that the evidence cited in the newspaper's original account could legitimately be viewed as tainted, due to the unusual handling by a reporter." What's more, he said, the paper's allegations were proven "irrelevant" to the murder probe, since investigators subsequently ruled out Winters as a suspect. Finally, the statement noted that Lenny Holcomb, the lead reporter on the story, had been disciplined and demoted. It ended by apologizing "to our readers and to Gov. Lowell Winters."

My need to retch became an overwhelming urge. I fought it, balling my fists and squeezing shut my eyes.

I opened them to see Jacquelyn Towers walking across the newsroom. She looked as beautiful as ever, but everything had changed. She was just halfway across the newsroom, but she might as well have been in another time zone. She didn't look over, and I didn't blame her. My heart sank, and I felt even sicker.

For some unearthly reason, my queasiness passed when I glanced at the stack of death notices. I felt strangely comforted by them. I realized that I could type them, one by one, and let everything else go. I wouldn't have to think anymore, and I'd no longer have to hurt like this. I couldn't be defeated again, if I didn't try. There was no risk for an obit writer. Well, almost none. One did risk his sanity, but for me, it wasn't a high-stakes wager.

I took the fax from the top of the pile: Marjorie Burma, age eighty-seven.

"Hi there, Marjorie," I said. "Welcome to obitland. I've been away for a while, but I'm back now. Glad you waited. Then again, you weren't going anywhere, were you now, old gal?"

I began typing, and I didn't stop for the rest of the morning.

Perhaps in honor of my return, there was a steady stream of death notices that day. I was being welcomed back with a vengeance. Hell, the dead were practically lining up to say hello. One person, a Mrs. Glenda Jackson, had a bit more to say:

> *Glenda L. Jackson, 68, of Harrisburg, died Monday at Sunset Hospice, following a long bout with liver cancer.*
>
> *She was a lifelong resident of the city and worked for 30 years in the Pennsylvania Department of Revenue. She volunteered in the community and was a life member of Zion Bible Baptist Church.*
>
> *OOOOOOHHHHH, IT HURRRRRTS. GIVE ME MY OXY. I WANT MY OXY!*
>
> *Friends may call Wednesday evening at the Ben Johnson Funeral Home. Burial will be Thursday morning in Amber Waves Cemetery. In lieu of flowers, mourners are asked to make memorial contributions in Jackson's name to the American Cancer Society or Sunset Hospice.*
>
> *DON'T GIVE THEM HOSPICE BASTARDS A DIME. THE NURSE IS SWITCHIN' PILLS. SHE TOOK MY OXY AND GAVE ME SOME DAMN THING THAT DOESN'T WORK. IT DON'T DO SHIT FOR THE PAIN. I CAN'T STAND THE PAIN.*

The added words caught my eye immediately. Everyone and everything had deserted me, but not my instincts. The dead stuck by me.

Despite my fresh defeat at the hands of the governor, I felt a familiar rage welling up as I thought of Glenda Jackson dying in unimaginable pain. All because some nurse realized the street value of OxyContin, the latest prescription drug that dope fiends were perverting into a quick and easy high. Some soulless person who called herself a caregiver had it figured that a bunch of half-dead and mostly unconscious cancer patients marking their last minutes at a hospice center wouldn't miss their daily doses. No, it would be far more profitable to switch the Oxy with a couple of Extra Strength Tylenol. After all, why waste such a valuable painkiller and such a good high on the old and dying?

If I was right, it was one sick plan, so fucked up that it may just be working. Perhaps not for much longer, if I had anything to say about it.

Newsroom leper or not, I could still stand up for the dead. I was the obit writer, after all. It was my job to tell their final stories. The paper couldn't hold me down, not as long as I had my instincts, it couldn't. I could still do some good. I could do something for Glenda Jackson, who went off to die in peace only to be robbed of her final comfort.

It'd be a hell of a story, too. Maybe even Jack Towers would want a piece. Either way, I wasn't done. Not by a long shot.

I was about to plot my investigation of Sunset Hospice, when the phone rang.

Instinct or not, I was still the obit writer. Figuring it was an undertaker calling in another one, I was poised to take dictation.

"Obituaries, this is Holcomb," I said, the receiver cradled under my chin and my fingers positioned over the keyboard. My first day back and it was already like I'd never left. Funny the way it worked like that.

"You blew it, Holcomb," said the loud, sloppy voice. I knew that voice. "You held out on me, and you let him beat you. You let him outsmart you."

It was Danny Denza, and he was drunk over the moon. I suspected he had traded in his bottles of Bud for some harder stuff. And it wasn't even noon.

"Danny, I'm sorry," I said. "I tried my best. I tried for Christy."

"You shoulda told me everything," he said, the alcohol exaggerating the inflection in his voice. "I coulda helped."

"You did. You got me into her place. We had some good evidence, but Winters is a powerful man. Smart and powerful, with a lot of friends. He turned everything around. He made it about me. What can I say, Danny? I made too many mistakes."

"And that's it? You just walk away?"

"You don't want me on your side. Not now. I'm a liability. I'm just some crazy bastard, had it out for the governor. That's what everyone thinks after yesterday. Hell, I'm an embarrassment, even at my own damn paper. Especially at the paper."

"You were the only one who had the balls to go toe to toe with him," Danny said. "You looked him in the eye, and you asked him if he killed my sister. You were the only one who'd do that."

"Lot of good it did. After yesterday, no one's going to be asking Winters any more questions. He passed the lie detector. He got the cops and the D.A. to sign off on everything. And he scared the press half to death with the way he roasted my ass. No one's gonna touch this case. He won."

"You're wrong." Danny's voice was full of hatred and purpose. "He's got to answer for my sister. He's gotta answer to me and my family. I'll make him talk."

"Danny, you need to let it go. Winters may have beaten me, but this thing is always going to be there, hauntin' him. Just like Ted Kennedy and Chappaquiddick."

"What?" Danny said, bewildered.

I realized the futility of trying to reason with a drunk, but I went on, giving it my best shot.

"Danny, don't you see? Christy's death may never be solved, but in everyone's mind, Winter's is always going to have something to do with it. That alone's probably enough to keep him outta the White House. I'm afraid that'll have to do as punishment."

"It's not enough, not for me," Danny snapped. "Fuck that smug bastard. I saw him on TV. He thinks nothing can touch him. You can walk away, but I can't. She was my little sister. Winters is gonna answer, just you wait and see. Just make sure you write it. You write it for Christy."

"What are you talking about, Danny?" I could no longer mask the concern in my voice. "The governor isn't going to talk to you. If you try something stupid, you'll end up in jail. Then how will you feel, knowing it was Winters who put you there? Sleep it off, Danny. Sleep it off and move on."

"I can't," he shouted. His voice sounded desperately out of control. "I can't sleep it off. I can't drink it off. I can't do anything. I just keep seeing Christy's face. I see her sweet, beautiful face. Then, I see his face, Winters's. I see his smiling, smug face, and he's laughing. He's laughing at all of us. He's laughing at Christy."

There was a long silence. I didn't know what to say. When Danny continued, his voice was cold, matter-of-fact, and full of purpose. "I'm going to make him stop laughing," he said.

"No, Danny, wait," I shouted, but the line was dead. The dial tone raged in my ear, its flat line contrasting with my racing pulse.

Danny Denza would never let it go, I realized then. Suddenly, I had the strangest feeling about him—about what he might do and what he might already have done. All his drinking and emotion—was it rage over his sister's death?

Or was it guilt?

As much as I despised him, Winters had passed the polygraph on the big question. So, if the governor didn't do it, if he really didn't kill Christy, I had to begin to consider who might have. Could Danny fit the bill?

They say nine times out of ten, the murderer is family. And Danny had good reason to be jealous of Christy. She had her yuppie life in Harrisburg and a list of friends that read like a Who's Who. What did Danny have? A room in his parents' rancher and his demolition job? She had left him there, forgotten about him. Danny's little sister didn't need him anymore. More to the point, she didn't want him. The very thought could have eaten away at Danny with every Bud he drank. I had to consider it.

Then I had another thought: Abe Braxton had been calling Danny all along. I had seen Braxton's number on the Denzas' fridge. What if he suspected Danny, too? What if he were developing a story that would blow the case wide open? Braxton had been up to something this whole time. Maybe that was it.

These thoughts raced through my head as the hum of the dial tone bored into my brain. Danny's call had left me cold. I had the horrible feeling of impending tragedy, along with the sickly weak realization that I couldn't do a damn thing about it. Danny was going to come at Winters. I just knew it. But I was impotent. No one would believe a word I said. If I called the governor's office to try to warn them, they'd probably have me arrested. I sure as hell couldn't do anything, but maybe—

I stood up at my desk, my eyes nervously scanning the newsroom. People scurried about doing their work. They were oblivious, oblivious to the danger that I was sure was coming. As my eyes roved, I spotted Abe Braxton, his head raised above his cubicle wall to just above eye level. He looked at me and seemed to sense my torment. Not only sensed it, but enjoyed it. His eyes were smiling.

I shifted focus to Jack Towers's cubicle, located far across the open newsroom. I couldn't see her, but I knew she was there. I sat down abruptly, and my fingers rushed over the keyboard:

To: jtowers
From: lholcomb

Hi Jack.

I guess I screwed things up pretty good, huh? I hope I managed to keep you out of the worst of it.

As long as you're okay, I was content to go back to writing my obits. It's what I do best, I guess. And I still have my ways of getting a story or two, from time to time.

That was my plan, honest. But then I got this call. No, not another source. It was Danny Denza, drunk off his ass and half out of his mind. He thinks Winters is getting away with murdering his sister. Or at least that's what he wants everyone to think. I just don't know anymore. Denza's been acting strange, and I think he could be dangerous.

Danny was talking a lot of shit about how he's

going to make Winters answer for the murder. He didn't make any threats, not really, but he's up to something. I just know it. But who the hell's going to believe me?

I could only think of you.

I know I have no right asking you to get involved, but I think this guy's going after the governor. I don't know how. I don't even know when. But he's coming. The editors and the governor's office might listen to you if you warned them. I know it's sticking your neck out, but I got a bad feeling. Otherwise, I never would have asked.

Yours,

Lenny

I really didn't know what I expected Jack Towers to do. I didn't know what she could do, really. But I sent that E-mail anyway. Thinking back on it, it wasn't out of concern for Winters, or even Danny Denza. I reached out to Jack because I was longing for her. I could handle losing everything else; I could be a ghost in everyone's eyes, but not hers.

I sat paralyzed, staring at the computer screen for what seemed like forever. Then suddenly, Jack's E-mail appeared. For a long time, I just looked at the mail announcement: "From jtowers."

I was terrified to open it. I feared the finality of the end.

I guided my mouse, slowly. The computer arrow took position over the unopened mail. My finger was poised over the click button for the longest time. Finally, I took a deep breath and lowered my finger. The tiny hourglass icon appeared, but it seemed like an eternity before that E-mail finally opened:

To: lholcomb
From: jtowers

People can (and do) say a lot of things about you, Lenny. But one thing they can never accuse you of is being boring. You'll always make me smile because you put yourself out there. You're not a fake. If I learned anything from you, I hope it's how to be more like that.

I'll always be indebted to you for taking the heat. It was my name on that story, too, but you protected me. Thank you.

They have me doing harmless little features, now. They say it's not a demotion, but I think they're testing me, seeing how I'll react. I'll show 'em. I'm going to do every damn thing they say, and do it well. Somehow, I'll write my way back to the capitol. That's the plan.

But I can't give them anything to hang me with, Lenny. You, above all, should realize that.

You have to know it's over. The Denza case will fade away, or maybe there'll be a break. Either way, I can't afford to care.

Winters has already moved on. He'll bring on his new image maker, and he'll announce his run for president. I don't think he'll make it, but that's another story. As a matter of fact, it's Braxton's story. Our favorite reporter is back as the number-one man at the capitol. He'll go on giving the governor his usual front-page blow jobs, and you and I will bite our tongues and eat our livers.

That's the way it has to be. I can't get caught up in this again. Danny Denza is an angry drunk. He's hurt, and he's powerless. The only thing he can do is work his mouth, make some idle comments and try to stir up that crazy reporter down at the Herald.

No offense, Lenny, but that's what he's thinking. He wants to get you going again. He won't let it go, and neither will you.

But I have to. I have no choice. You were right, I'm young. I have a career to think about. That's what I'm doing.

It doesn't mean we can't have a drink sometime, when all this has been replaced by some other scandal of the moment. We'll go back to that sleazy place you like.

Meanwhile, don't knock back too many during the day. You're a good reporter, you just care too much. On this one, you just cared too much.

Well, Lenny, gotta go. Got a big feature on some lady who collects refrigerator magnets. Supposedly, she has the largest collection in the world—or at least Pennsylvania. Big fucking deal. I go from covering the governor to writing about fat housewives with too much time on their hands. But I'll survive. Don't you worry about me. I do wonder about you, though. Take care of yourself, Lenny.

Always,
Jack

I read it, and I read it again. The first time, I damn near cried. The second time, I smiled. Jack was a smart, wonderful woman, and I was lucky to have had the time we shared.

Maybe she was right about everything, but I still didn't think so. She said Danny Denza was powerless. I knew better. Grief, anger, revenge, and guilt were a powerful cocktail, and he'd been drinking a lot of it since his sister's death. I was sure I hadn't heard the last of him.

I, on the other hand, was the powerless one. I was a reporter who couldn't be trusted. In my business, there was no use for such a creature.

Governor Winters had stripped me of everything. I could not help him.

32

THE RELENTLESSNESS OF THE OBITS CAPTURED ME ONCE AGAIN that afternoon. My mind and everything that had consumed it in recent days were far away from me as I worked my way down the endless list of the dead. I had to type at a steady clip to keep pace. After all, Bronski would be coming over for the afternoon count soon enough.

My brain was about to slip away for good, when the crackle of the police scanner reached out to find it. The emergency tones blared, and their echoes struck a familiar chord deep in my mind. It was the sound of news—a fire, a police call, an accident on one of the interstates surrounding Harrisburg. Though it wasn't my job anymore to write such news, I was never completely able to retrain my brain to ignore those sounds.

The pulsating tones grew louder as my attention returned. It sounded like a goddamn symphony of emergency tones. They must be bringing out every piece of equipment in the county, I thought. I saw other reporters and editors begin to gather around the black box on the cluttered police desk.

The tones were finally silenced, and a voice came

over the air with an emergency bulletin. The words stripped away twenty-five years in an instant.

"Middletown Communications dispatching all county emergency services. Three Mile Island security reports an incident at the plant. Repeat. Three Mile Island security reports incident at the plant. This is not a drill."

The hair on the back of my neck stood at attention. Abe Braxton dashed over to the scanner. Bill Sharps rose quietly from his spot on the city desk and drew near in disbelief. Instead of his usual excitement in the face of major news, Sharps looked sober and scared. Jacquelyn Towers was there, too, along with so many others, all huddled around the police desk, girding themselves for an instant replay of 1979. Or was it?

The voice returned.

"Three Mile Island security has informed county control of a security breach at the plant. This is not a reactor malfunction; this is a security situation."

The transmission was cut off by static, and it seemed as if the whole newsroom held its breath, waiting for more. Finally, the voice broke through the radio clutter.

"Unknown perpetrator driving a truck . . . (crackle) . . . stormed gates and gained entry. Subject parked . . . (static) . . . near reactor. Claims . . . (white noise) . . . has explosives. Dispatching Code Red terrorism response, including SWAT and negotiator."

With that, the emergency went from being a replay of '79 to an eerie epilogue to September 11th. Someone was threatening to blow up Three Mile Island, the most notorious nuclear plant in America.

Phones all over the newsroom began ringing, but the group of fifteen or so top reporters and editors didn't budge from the scanner.

"Jesus Christ, we've got a terrorist," muttered one catatonic editor. Others simply looked on, stunned into silence. Braxton appeared to be the only one actually working the story, jotting notes each time the voices spoke from the scanner.

Gathering himself, Bill Sharps tapped the police reporter, Robert Macy, motioning for him to go. Macy sprinted out of the newsroom, almost losing it while navigating a cluster of desks in the features department. In that same instant, the photo editor dashed back to the darkroom to round up as many photographers as he could. The newspaper was mobilizing. And no doubt, the television stations were, as well.

In minutes, the threat at that famous nuclear plant would be reported all across America, jolting an already shell-shocked nation with the latest terror. The images would be broadcast live on all the networks. The television news anchors would need only to mention the deadly combination of Three Mile Island and a bomb, and the fear of '79 and the terror of September 11th would come rushing back.

As the scanner crackled with more beeps, tones, and chirps, my mind was flooded with images of Three Mile Island. I could see the mass of media stomping through the spring mud after the near-meltdown back in '79. Some carried their own personal Geiger counters, along with their notebooks and tape recorders, as if the unusual equipment were standard issue. But most of all, I just kept seeing those cooling towers. Then, I imagined it all blowing up. I saw those towers crumbling down, finally setting free the nuclear fury they had managed to vent all these years.

The rush of memories was overwhelming. But I had a nagging feeling that I was missing something—something that I should have pieced together.

I forced myself to focus. Radio banter was picking up again as police and emergency crews began arriving on scene. With cops and crews from all over central Pennsylvania responding, police had to hold off from switching to scrambled channels. Their dialogue played like old-time radio theater. It was *The War of the Worlds* all over again.

"This guy just bulldozed his way in . . . (dead air) . . . blew the gates. All that security didn't do a damn thing. Timed it during a shift change."

The voice sounded like a young local officer, one of the first on scene. His words were flush with adrenaline, that strange mix of excitement and fear.

"Sure wasn't any pickup truck did this," the excited officer said, closer now and seeing more. "Had to be one of those big construction trucks . . . Real heavy-duty. Hate to think if he really has that truck filled with explosives."

"Easy, 32," came a controlled, authoritative voice. "This is open air. Essential communications only." More tones announced a multiple-channel transmission: "All units be advised that state police command is en route, along with FBI, ATF, NRC, and the National Guard. We're gonna need them . . . Had the first conversation with our visitor . . . (a loud burst of static) . . . He wants to talk to Gray Fox."

My eyes rose from the scanner and found Braxton. The light of realization ignited his eyes. He knew something. I should have known it, too. I should have known it right then and there.

An older editor lunged for a black binder on the cluttered police desk. It was a glossary of police codes. It included the standard numerical ones, used nationwide, as well as special codes that referred to local police units, places, and people. Over the years, the paper's police reporters had deciphered these codes, dutifully recording the corresponding definitions in that book.

The editor thumbed the wrinkled, coffee-stained pages and ran a finger down the lists of words. Eventually his finger stopped, and he looked up.

"Gray Fox is the governor," he said to no one in particular. "It's the code name they've been using for Winters since the inauguration. This nut at Three Mile Island is demanding to talk to the governor."

For a moment, Sharps and the others simply stared at the older editor's ghost-white face. His frozen finger still marked Winters's code name in the binder. Then came the scanner.

"I see the truck," the young cop yelped. "A big dumper. Looks like it has a company name on it . . . can't make it out . . . (crackle) . . . Shit . . . It's loaded with barrels, big ones . . . connected with wires. Maybe, it's that fertilizer stuff . . . (loud static) . . . like Oklahoma City."

"Okay," the command voice said. "We know he's serious."

"Serious," the young cop said, "but about what?"

"Our boy wants an audience with Gray Fox," the commander repeated amid the radio static, his voice sounding so far away. "And he may just get it."

My heart fluttered in a rush of realization. I had to fight for my air, fight for it so I could speak.

"This ain't some Mid-East towel-head terrorist bastard," I shouted. "It's the Denza kid. It's Danny Denza. He's trying to make Winters answer for his sister, damn fool kid."

All eyes were on me now. I found Jack's eyes first. She looked at me with a combination of sympathy and fear. Fear that I was right, perhaps. I nodded to her almost invisibly, and I could have sworn she mouthed the word "sorry." She didn't have to be.

"What're you talking about, Lenny?" Bill Sharps

asked, stepping toward me as if for closer inspection.

"It's the Denza kid, Bill," I repeated, finding his eyes. "He called me this morning, all drunk and angry, talking shit. Said he was gonna make Winters answer for his sister, for Christy. Maybe he still thinks Winters killed her."

"And I wonder where he got that idea?" Abe Braxton shouted from the newsroom crowd. He moved with catlike efficiency to take position next to Sharps. I watched Jack's eyes burn a hole through the back of Braxton's monogrammed broadcloth shirt.

"You've been the one making the wild accusations, Holcomb," Braxton continued, his face contorted to register disgust. "So what happened? You get your ass handed to you at that press conference, so you decide to stir up the crazy brother? Get him to go after the governor, after you couldn't?"

Sharps reached for Braxton's arm. "How 'bout it, Lenny?" Sharps asked. "What was the nature of this conversation?"

"Told you, he just called. Out of the blue. Sounded drunk and angry, but that wasn't new for him. He was like that the first day I met him, the day he took me to Christy's apartment."

Braxton grimaced at this, wordlessly pointing out how that had been my undoing.

"I kept it all from him," I added. "I didn't tell him anything, none of my suspicions. Didn't want to set him off. But now this. I'd forgotten that he worked with explosives."

"What?" Sharps demanded, surprised.

"Yeah, when I was doing Christy's obit I looked up the whole family," I explained. "Danny works with some demolition outfit. He brings down buildings. Hell, he helped rig the charges when they imploded the old transportation building. We quoted him in a story, for crissakes. Knows what he's doing, and I expect if he wants to, he could have all of Harrisburg glowin' in the dark."

"Jesus," Sharps mouthed.

"I'm going out there," I said. It was a demand, not a request.

"No way," Braxton shot back, drawing a look from Sharps. It wasn't Braxton's call to make.

"I know him," I pleaded. "He called me. He came to me with the warning. He trusts me. Reporters will be falling all over themselves, thinking it's another terrorist strike. We'll be the only news outfit that knows who's really in there. We know because of me. I deserve this, Bill. I know Danny Denza. I know his family, and I know what there is to know about his past. He *wants* me to cover it."

Sharps studied me. I may have fucked up that press conference, but Bill Sharps had a good gut. He believed me about Denza, and he knew I should be there. He hesitated only because of how sending me, Lenny Holcomb, the old-new obit writer, would look to the rest of the staff.

After a long pause, he spoke. "Okay, Lenny, you made me a believer. You go and cover the Denza angle. I want as much background as we can get on this guy."

From over Sharps's shoulder, I saw Jack smiling, looking proud.

"No!" Braxton shouted, turning to Sharps like a spurned child. "Maybe I missed something, but I thought this guy was back on obits. I mean, didn't we just spend an entire day cleaning up after his last mess? He says the wrong thing this time, the mess could be nuclear. I should go. From the sound of it, they're bringing in the governor, and I cover the governor. It's my story."

The newsroom's focus had shifted now. The police scanner had quieted, as police switched to scrambled channels and commanders ordered radio silence. Instead, a new drama was being acted out by three of the newsroom's own: Sharps, Braxton, and myself. It was the final showdown, the big fight to cover the biggest story in America that day.

Braxton's angry eyes bored into Sharps, whose face had gone completely red. Even the bald spot on the crown of Sharps's head turned purple. His hands shook with the rush of emotion we'd all experienced over the last ten minutes, but he meted out his words calmly and deliberately.

"This is a major terrorist act at a nuclear facility, the most famous nuclear plant there is. The one that happens to be in our backyard. We may have the governor of Pennsylvania en route to the scene. National media will be all over the story in minutes. But we're the only news organization who knows the suspect's name, identity, and motive. Yet, here we are arguing over who will cover the damn thing. Is something fucked up here, or is it me?"

Sharps scowled at the both of us.

"You'll both go," he declared, swiveling his head between Braxton and me as if he were watching a tennis match. "You'll go together, and you'll work together. And I don't want to hear another fucking word about it. Do you understand?"

No response.

"Abe?" Sharps insisted.

Softly, looking at his shoes, Braxton mouthed, "Yes."

"Lenny?" Sharps turned to me.

"Yes."

"Then get the fuck out of my sight and over to the plant right now."

Braxton and I looked at each other. He was tall, lean, and young, and he made me feel old. This is what I'm up against, I thought. He's like Tiger Fucking Woods at The Masters, always strokes ahead of the old white guys.

We both had words on our tongues, but we thought better of crossing Bill Sharps, who was still studying each of us for any trace of insubordination.

"I'll get my jacket," Braxton said, quickly moving for his desk. I grabbed a fresh notebook and a hand-held scanner from the police desk.

Braxton raced by my cubicle, slipping on his suit jacket and pocketing his cell phone and his silver mini tape recorder as he moved. "Let's go, old man," he said.

I followed right behind him, trotting to keep up with his long-legged strides. I looked back to see Jack Towers watching us leave, no doubt wishing she was going, too. I was glad she wasn't.

"Hope you know where we're going," Braxton said, without so much as turning to look at me. "I've never been."

"Don't worry," I said, as we neared the elevator. "I know the way."

33

As Abe Braxton deftly navigated his BMW toward Three Mile Island, he repeatedly thumb-dialed a cell phone. Each time, he'd promptly get someone's voice mail, or worse, a busy signal, and he'd look like a frustrated kid.

"Shit," he said under his breath. I didn't think he was actually talking to me. Why would he? "Can't get any of the governor's staff. They all must be on their fucking cells."

I, on the other hand, was completely relaxed. The combination of the symphony music playing low on the car's expensive speakers, those plush leather seats, and Braxton's skillful driving was actually making me a little drowsy. The adrenaline of a good story lasted but for the moment in an old reporter such as me. I probably could have drifted off, but I was too busy watching Braxton, the perfect reporter. His long fingers clawed at the leather-wrapped steering wheel as his bright eyes, which seemed illuminated in the darkness, anticipated the road. He couldn't wait to get there. His need to be right in the middle of whatever was going to happen was palpable. It was leaking right out of his coffee-and-cream-colored pores.

"How we doing?" he asked me, perhaps sensing my eyes on him. "We almost there?"

"Yeah, we're in Middletown, so we're almost there. We'll see the towers soon. I just don't know how close we're going to get. I know they won't let us on the island. They'll probably hold us at the gate, like they did in '79."

"Oh yeah, '79," Braxton said, as if it were ancient history. "What'd they call it, the China syndrome? You old guys still talk about that? Reliving the glory days, I guess."

"*China Syndrome* was the movie," I corrected. "Three Mile Island was a partial meltdown, and for three days, the eyes of the world were right here. Half of the population was evacuated, and President Carter had to come in personally to calm nerves."

"And the goddamn newspaper couldn't even turn it into a Pulitzer," Braxton pointed out, sounding disgusted.

"No, the Philly *Inquirer* grabbed it out from under us, I guess."

"And what did you get out of it?" Braxton looked at me. His eyes glowed, then sharpened.

"I got the satisfaction of doing my job," I answered spontaneously, having never really thought about it before. "I really wasn't looking for much else. Some guys rode the story, sure. Friend of mine, he went to work for the state and then on from there. He's a big executive now, wears those nice suits, like you. But I wasn't thinking about anything like that. Being a reporter was enough for me."

"Not for me," Braxton smiled. "No way. You're not going to see me put in forty years and have them shit on me like they did you. Got bigger career plans for myself. Writing obits? What's that?" He chuckled at the absurdity of the very thought. Then, his tone grew serious. "Did I ever tell you that I've never written a single obit in all the time that I've been a reporter? I consider it a matter of pride. I don't plan on breaking my streak, ever."

"Well, good for you," I said, not really knowing how to respond. I should have been offended. He had just trashed my life, my career, and my current occupation. But I wasn't. I could see the big white cooling towers rising up over the freshly leafed trees. The tops of the towers blinked red to warn away aircraft.

"Looks like I won't be writing any more obits, today," I announced, nodding ahead. "Take the lot across the street."

The road ahead was thick with fire trucks, cop cars, and ambulances. Flares and wooden barricades blocked further access. A man in an orange vest waved a flashlight, and Braxton rolled down his window.

"Press," he said. "We're with the *Herald.*"

Braxton flashed a press pass, but it didn't impress the old fire cop.

"No media on the island," he said. "Take it in the lot with the rest of them."

Braxton turned left, and as he did, we both saw the television vans, their satellite dishes already erect and reaching into the dusky sky. Reporters stood in front of live cameras and gestured to the backdrop of Three Mile Island, which looked somehow fake in the fading sun, like a movie prop. The service road leading to the island was an artery of activity. Men dressed in blue jump suits, wearing body armor, and carrying rifles trotted toward the island marked by those four cooling towers. Way in the distance, I could see harsh spotlights trained on a big red dump truck. The large vehicle was parked haphazardly, half on a barrier, and very near a flat concrete building. But not just any building, the reactor and containment building, the most sensitive building on the island.

They called it simply Unit One. Its twin had once been the scene of its own drama, but Unit Two was sterile now. It took years after the '79 accident, but it was cleaned up as best as was possible, closed, and sealed. Unit One remained hot. Its twin cooling towers still breathed steam. Now it, too, was being threatened. Science and physics and all those precision calculations that helped rule the day twenty-five years ago meant nothing now. This time, one desperate and angry man would decide the fates.

I should have been afraid, but I wasn't.

Braxton's eyes were wide as he looked out at the island in amazement. He jumped a bit when a helicopter swooped over us from behind. It flew low, hovering over the island. At first, I thought it was a TV chopper swooping in for video. But airspace directly over the island had been closed since September 11th in yet another security precaution. It was a state police chopper, and it trained another spotlight on the dump truck. A man leaned out from the side of the chopper and sighted a rifle. With all those sharpshooters and all their firepower, Danny Denza wouldn't get more than two steps if he left the cab of that truck. They'd drop him in an instant. A head shot, just to be sure.

Braxton walked with authority toward the gathering of reporters near the parking lot's gate.

"Is the governor coming?" he asked someone carrying television cables.

The production assistant, the lowest link of the television food chain, just stared at him. These people knew lighting and sound and cables, but they rarely had any idea of what was actually going on with a story.

"Goddamn, nobody knows anything," I heard Braxton say as I tried to keep pace.

Just then, we heard the sirens. Braxton swung around to see the line of state police cars screaming up the highway. I took one look and knew. They were escorting Governor Winters. The big guy—Gray Fox—had arrived.

Cameramen rushed to the street to get the shot. The story was a natural: a terrorist was threatening a nuclear facility and the governor of Pennsylvania was coming to defuse the situation. High stakes, to say the least.

I looked over at Braxton. His eyes examined each car as it whisked by and made the right turn onto the island. He thumb-dialed his cell phone again, but still couldn't raise anyone.

"Okay, this line of police cars is believed to be escorting Governor Lowell Winters to the scene," I overheard a blond, good-looking reporter say, as she narrated the live video feed for the folks at home. "The ugly face of terrorism has come to central Pennsylvania, and now Governor Winters, himself, has come to Three Mile Island to try to stop it.

"Negotiators have been talking to the suspect for about thirty minutes over a cellular phone," the reporter went on. "I must repeat, however, that we do not know the identity of this man or what he wants. Police won't even say if he has a foreign accent. And I must stress that we do not know if this act is related to any past terrorist strikes. Authorities are releasing very few details at this hour.

"The drama will be played out about a half mile away from here on Three Mile Island, itself. That's where the suspect is holed up in the cab of a dump truck, which he has told authorities contains explosives. You can see the governor's caravan now making its way onto the island. That road leads directly to the nuclear facility.

"In the wake of national events, TMI increased its security precautions to try to prevent something like this, but obviously, no security system is foolproof," the TV newswoman continued. "This is the very nightmare that authorities and the public have long feared. In this shot, you can see the twisted gates that this heavy truck crashed right through to make it onto the island. Presumably, the governor will now try to talk to the suspect and resolve this situation. That's what we are all praying for."

The pretty blonde finished her recap, and I could tell that she was excited by the story, the biggest of her life. But she was also scared. Scared enough that her microphone hand was shaking. Watching her made me think that reporters are either very brave or very stupid. Or maybe we're neither. Maybe we just need to be there, right in the middle of the action. We need to see. I could smell that need coming off of Braxton on the drive out. And now I could see it on the pretty blonde's young face. We were drawn to power, danger, and death, because that's where things happened. That's where the news happened.

I strained to see onto the island as dusk faded. The spotlights on the truck were bright, but it was like watching an out-of-focus movie. There was no detail. I remembered back to those tense but frustrating days in '79 when they kept the reporters at bay, too. There were long waits for plant officials to come out with their statements. Often for a little diversion, I visited the men at the security station located just across from the island's entrance. It consisted of a trailer stocked with swivel chairs and a bank of video monitors. Back then, I'd gotten to know the gate man pretty well. Po Jacoby was his name. Never knew his real first name, he just went by Po. I wondered if he still worked there.

I glanced over at Braxton. He was thumbing his cell phone again. This guy just wouldn't give up. I had half a mind to leave him, but I knew how badly he wanted to see. And I would enjoy watching him watch.

"Doesn't look like we're gonna get much here," I said.

"Huh?" He looked at me as if I were a distraction, an irritant.

"You just gonna keep playin' with that toy phone, or do you wanna try to get this story?" I said, summoning the weight and wisdom of a veteran reporter who may actually know a few people out there.

"The hell do you think I'm doing? I'm trying to get the governor's people."

"You ain't gonna get shit, okay? You want to go somewhere where we can actually see what the fuck's goin' on?"

"How do we do that?" he scoffed, his eyes returning to the phone. "We can't get on the island."

"Yeah, but we can have the next best thing. Come on."

"Where?"

"To see an old buddy, or as you'd call him, a source."

I led a skeptical Abe Braxton out of the media-jammed parking lot to the security trailer located a couple hundred feet down the road. I rapped a knuckle on the plastic-covered door, emblazoned with Three Mile Island's official logo. I was surprised that no one else was around. Everyone must be on the island, I thought. I heard footsteps, and my hopes rose.

The door opened, and Po Jacoby looked distracted.

He kept turning his head, keeping an eye on the video monitors behind him. He hadn't taken a full look at me.

"The hell you want?" he said, talking to the back of the trailer. "I got a situation here."

If I had encountered Po on the street, anywhere away from the context of the plant, I probably wouldn't have recognized him. He had grown fat behind that bank of video monitors. He had an alcoholic's nose and a deeply rutted red face. But his eyes were the same—clear, penetrating, and trusting.

"Po," I said, "it's me. Lenny, from the *Herald*. You did me a few good turns back in '79. Since you got another show tonight, I thought you might let us have a front-row seat. I brought the popcorn."

I smiled, trying to prop up my attempt at a joke, as Po tore his eyes away from the bank of monitors long enough to give me the once-over. He brightened with recognition.

"Lenny," he said, smiling. "Lenny Holcomb!"

"Can we take a peek at the show? The view isn't too good out here."

He motioned frantically. "Get in here, but don't let anyone else see. I don't want a line of media at my door."

I hurried in, and Braxton followed.

"Who's this?" Po asked suspiciously.

"He's with me," I said. "A rookie. I'm showing him the ropes."

Braxton scowled but didn't say a word. He wanted to see, had to.

"All right," Po said. "But just the two of you."

"That's all we got," I said. "So what's been happening?"

"The Big Cheese just arrived." Po's voice was thick with sarcasm. "I feel safer already, don't you?"

We moved deeper into the trailer. An entire wall was stacked with monitors, which featured color images from every conceivable external location around the plant. Another security station, located on the island, monitored both interior and exterior locations.

Five of the monitors inside Po Jacoby's trailer showed various angles of the dump truck. I could just make out the silhouette of a man inside. Better keep your head down, Danny, I thought. If you want to keep it, that is.

Several other monitors showed groups of armed men huddled behind police vans and large walls of sandbags and mattresses, which the bomb squad was using as barricades. A slight man with striking white hair stepping into a protective suit. It was Winters. I glanced at Braxton.

"You see that?" I said. "Looks like your guy."

Braxton's eyes were already on it.

"I feel safer already," Po joked again, punctuating his statement with a burst of derisive laughter.

There was a time when such a remark would have gotten a rise out of Abe Braxton, but he didn't even flinch. He never took his eyes off those monitors showing Governor Lowell Winters stepping into an antibomb suit for his unscheduled, no-appointment-necessary meeting with Danny Denza.

34

"WHY DON'T WE TURN UP THE VOLUME ON THIS SHOW?" PO Jacoby spoke to no one in particular. "No reason this has to be a silent movie. Just had it turned down to see who was at the door."

Po reached for his desk and fiddled with the knob of a handheld police radio. "I get all the good channels on this. They haven't been saying too much, just the state cops and the city police pissin' each other off and waitin' for the FBI to take it away from the both of them. But now that the Big Cheese is here, it might get good. Oh, by the way, he likes to be called Gray Fox." Po let loose another wicked chuckle.

Abe Braxton continued to ignore the fat security guard in the white shirt and blue pants. His attention was on the video monitor showing Governor Winters getting his briefing from the state police commander and the chief negotiator.

Po finished fussing with the radio, and it came to life.

"Gray Fox is in the suit," said the voice. "We're trying to reestablish contact with the suspect now."

"Hope they got one of those built-in bathrooms in that antibomb suit," Po said. "Winters don't look like he can hold his bowels. I think I liked my chances better back in '79. Maybe we better pop the potassium iodide right now? I have a bad feeling we all may be glowing before this night's over. How 'bout you, Lenny?"

"I don't know," I said. "That was touch-and-go back then, too. And I'm still not sure what this guy wants. Either he's feeling desperate and won't care about taking us all with him, or, he truly believes Winters did it. Maybe it's like he said, he wants Winters to answer for his sister."

I decided I'd let Po in on Danny Denza's mission here. After all, the security guard was kind enough to give us front-row seats to the action.

"You act like you know this bastard." Po looked at me like I was on the other team. The bad team.

"Well, I think I do. We think we know who's in there." I gestured at Braxton, who couldn't have cared less about the acknowledgment. He was held rapt by those monitors. "I got a call from the guy earlier today. Said he was gonna make the governor answer to him. At the time, I didn't know what he meant."

"Well, don't hold out on me," Po insisted.

"We think the guy's name is Denza, Danny Denza. Has there been any mention of that name on the police channels?"

"No, not that I've heard," Po said. "But those assholes like to use code names for everything. I think they're callin' the guy Demolition Man. Apparently the truck he's in belongs to some local demolition company."

"That's him," I said. "Denza does building demolition—rigs explosives and blows up buildings."

"Christ," Po said. "They don't pay me enough to stick around here and watch my flesh melt off."

"Cops must know the background if they brought in the governor," I said, thinking out loud. "It's a very personal score that Denza's out to settle."

"This is that girl's brother?" Po announced, finally piecing it all together. "The girl that was fuckin' the governor and got herself murdered? I'll be a son of a bitch. You boys got a hell of a story here. Hot damn! What's the guy want?"

"Wish I knew," I said.

"Holy shit," Po said. "Maybe the kid's right, maybe the governor was fucking her, and maybe he killed her, too."

"Or maybe the nut job brother killed her himself," Braxton interjected, finally tearing his eyes from the monitor to leap to Winters's defense. "Maybe he's some whackjob who hears an old, reckless reporter makin' some wild accusations, and the kid gets some crazy ideas. The governor passed a polygraph, remember. He didn't kill anybody."

So, Braxton did think Denza killed her, I thought. That's why he'd been calling Danny, trying to smoke him out and get the story for himself.

Po paused and squinted at me, calling something to mind. "That's right. I saw you on TV, Lenny. You think the same thing as the Denza kid. You think the governor did it. I couldn't believe that was you there on the TV, asking questions of the governor like you owned the goddamn capitol. Only thing is, you let the bastard talk himself out of it. You let him weasel out."

No one was going to let me forget that I had accused the governor of murder on national television and actually improved his image. I couldn't think about that now. I was wondering what Danny would say to the governor, and more importantly, what Winters would say back.

A voice came over the radio, and all of our eyes darted to the monitors.

"We have Demolition Man on the line," said the

commanding voice. "We've informed him that Gray Fox is on the island, and we've told him that we're willing to put Fox on the line."

We watched as the commander briefed the governor one last time. Another cop ran up with a cell phone, handing it to Winters.

"All officers check your target," said a radio voice.

On the monitors, Winters raised the phone to his ear and talked. He waved his free hand as if he were making a point at a press conference. Always the politician.

"This guy's pretty angry," said another voice over the radio. In the trailer, we could not hear the actual conversation between Winters and Danny Denza. But the two of them were on a party line. The cops and the FBI were listening in, and someone was giving the play-by-play over a scrambled channel. A police psychologist, I thought.

"He's directing his anger toward the governor," this softer psychologist voice continued. "He doesn't want to be here, but feels he has to in order to get the governor's attention. This is all about the subject wanting satisfaction from the governor."

On the monitor, the commanders and agents huddling around Winters were flashing hand gestures and mouthing various responses for the governor to repeat to Danny. One even had a legal pad and was writing cue cards.

"No, no, no. The governor's being too defensive," the play-by-play voice advised. "This guy doesn't want political answers. He wants straight talk. He's asking whether the governor slept with his sister. My read is this is an older brother who feels he didn't do enough to protect his little sister. He's trying to make up for that now. He's going to have to get some satisfaction here, or he will take action."

The commander waved his arms at the governor, directing Winters to go further in his explanation, to reveal more to Danny Denza.

On the other monitors, I could see images of the lopsided dump truck. Spotlight beams rained down on it from all directions. Every once in a while, I saw the silhouette of a head pop up in the truck's passenger window. Danny taking a peek. But the snipers didn't have a clear shot, and they couldn't risk a miss.

"The governor has to talk to him man-to-man," the psychologist urged. "His sister was very attractive. A man is drawn to a woman like that. Danny can understand that. Winters needs to connect here. He's losin' him."

More conducting from the commander, but Winters appeared reluctant. He stood silently for a long moment. Then, finally, I could see his lips moving. He was talking to Danny Denza man-to-man.

"That's good," the play-by-play voice said. "He's doing well. He's sounding real. He's connecting. He's telling the brother that he was human, that he made a mistake. He gave the apology, and he established some trust, some honesty. Now, the governor can ask Danny for something in return. See if he can get him out of the truck."

Winters, along with the scene commanders, remained behind the barricade of police vans, sandbags, and bomb mattresses. They had no direct sight lines to Danny. Instead, cops and agents watched on video monitors pointed out the rear of another police van. At least two agents monitored these screens at all times.

"Okay, we have another problem," the play-by-play psychologist announced. "The brother isn't letting go of his sister's death. He thinks Winters is responsible. He's trying to use his position, his threat here, to get Winters to make an admission. But I also sense a great deal of guilt on the part of the brother. He's highly unstable at this point. He feels his life is useless because he allowed his sister to die."

There was a moment of radio static, then another voice came over the air.

"The governor's not going to cop to a murder," the voice said, indignant. "I don't care who this guy is, or what he's threatening."

I wondered if it was a Winters aide listening in on a state police radio. The asshole talked as if he were still over at the capitol and the only fallout to worry about was political.

"Clear this channel," the command voice boomed. "No unauthorized transmissions. This channel is cleared for the psychologist. Go ahead, Lomax."

The soft psychologist voice returned. "I'm not suggesting that the governor cop to a murder, but he has to sympathize with this man. He can say that he understands how the brother could feel this way. Say that he knows the brother wants the truth, and as easy as it would be for the governor to tell him what he wants to hear, he can't do that. The governor wants to be straight with him. Winters can deny the accusation, but he needs to do it along those lines."

This advice prompted more coaching from the command team huddled around Winters. The governor nodded, then talked into the small phone pressed against his ear.

"That's good," the radio voice said. "Okay, now the brother is going to want some kind of confirmation. A gesture of trust. Something to back up what the governor is saying, so the brother can invest in it. Remember, he doesn't want to be here, but he feels he has no choice. He's looking for a way out now. I think the governor needs to make an offer. He needs to say that he'd like to talk to Danny face-to-face. Keep using his first name, hammer that trust, and get him out of the truck."

On the monitor, I could see a man in a fine blue suit shaking his head vehemently. Probably the head of Winters's security detail, I thought. If Winters gets so much as a scratch, it would be that man's ass. But if this went bad, the governor would get more than a scratch, and so would a lot of other people. The scene commander argued with the well-dressed man. Then, the governor, dressed in that ridiculous antibomb suit, rested a hand on the protesting man's shoulder. He was going to meet Danny Denza.

"It's the right play," the radio voice said. "Have the governor step out from behind the barricades and show himself. Then, he invites Danny to do the same. If anything goes bad, at least police have a target. But as long as they're talking, there's a chance to resolve this peacefully. Remember, this guy wants a way out. Meeting the governor, talking face-to-face, that will be his satisfaction."

"Okay, we do it," the command voice said. "It's a go. All officers at the ready. Green light."

The commander looked like a football coach with his quarterback, Winters nodding as the commander called the play. The governor raised the phone to his ear and told Danny he was coming out to meet him. Then, Winters put on the antibomb headgear, and walked awkwardly, like a man dressed in a bear suit, around the makeshift barricades.

The monitors showed Winters emerge from behind the white police vans. He stood just beyond them, about fifty feet from the lopsided dump truck. He appeared to be talking on the phone the entire time, his free hand outstretched in a show of goodwill.

"He's coming," said the radio voice, excited now. "He's going to come out. It's working."

"Radio silence," admonished the stern command voice. "Hard target, everyone. Green for a hard target."

The radio fell quiet, and the action on the monitors played like a late-night movie. The truck's passenger door opened slowly. A foot reached down uncertainly in search of the truck's step rung. Danny moved cautiously at first, tentatively. Then all at once, he jumped from the cab of the truck. Still, his head and upper torso remained shielded by the truck's open door.

Winters waddled ever closer to the truck. He had the cell phone raised, but I didn't know how he could hear a thing through the headgear. I believed he wasn't doing much listening now, anyway. He was talking, trying to draw Danny out.

A hand, clutching a small box, poked out from behind the truck's opened door. With the glare of the spotlights, it was difficult to see the item in Danny's hand. It looked like a television remote control. Danny was making his entrance now, and he was leading with the detonator that presumably controlled those yellow barrels of explosives in the truck's bed.

Winters motioned with his free hand, urging Danny to keep moving out from behind the truck's door.

Winters nodded as Danny exposed himself further. He was halfway out now, holding the small black box far out from his body. He wanted everyone to see it. It didn't look much more intimidating than a garage door opener, but its frequency controlled something deadly.

Emboldened, Winters moved closer still. He had Danny's trust, and I have to admit, I was amazed at his bravery. If he got out of this one, Winters would be a hero and justifiably so. He would be the governor who went toe-to-toe with a terrorist. The scandals that had come before would be erased, and this single act could catapult him to presidential heights.

Maybe that's why he was risking so much. He was gambling on himself. The prize could well be the White House, and everything he'd always coveted.

The deadly quiet of the security trailer made things all the more tense as this silent movie played toward its climax. I felt my fingernails digging into my sweaty palms. My face was a sheen of cold perspiration. My armpits were a river.

I could hardly tear my eyes away from the monitors, but I did so long enough to glance at Braxton and Po. They were the same as me: Stomachs in knots, bowels cramped, sphincters clenched, hearts pounding, and balls squeezed up to their throats.

Danny Denza was fully visible now. His image on the monitors looked ghostly, illuminated as he was by those powerful spotlights. There were other things aimed at him, as well. Dozens of rifles, with the eyes of the sharpshooters looking through their sights, fingers already weighing on the triggers. The sharpshooters were just waiting for their chance to squeeze those triggers all the way back.

Governor Winters moved closer, his free hand outstretched. The two were in earshot now, so Winters lowered the phone, his thumb clicking it off. Danny mimicked him, as if a mirror image. Winters motioned Danny forward, and he came. The phone was out of Danny's hand, but his left hand still held that control box.

Winters gestured to it, and Danny spoke. Winters responded, and then motioned with his arms for Danny to lower that threatening box to the ground. I could just hear him: "Put it down and it will all be over. You can trust me. I'm the governor everyone can trust."

Danny hesitated. He appeared to be crying. His body was shaking visibly, even on the slightly ill-focused video image.

Finally, Danny bent and lowered his hand to the ground. Softly, ever so softly, he laid the box on the cement. He paused for a long moment in his crouch. Then, Winters seemed to gesture him forward, away from the box. The governor held out a hand to Danny like a father: C'mon, son.

Danny rose and stepped forward toward the governor. And just as he did, Winters dove to the ground.

Instantly, Danny's head sprayed red. He staggered, then fell, collapsing onto the cold, hard concrete.

"It's a hit," the radio crackled to life again as we watched Danny Denza die. "Subject is down. Move in."

The soft psychologist voice was angry now: "He was giving up. You didn't have to shoot him. We had him out of there. It wasn't necessary."

"Negative, negative," the command voice countered. "It was a hard target green light. We don't know if this guy had any other weapons. He was getting too close to Fox."

On the video screen, the image of Danny Denza's bloodied head looked cheap and unreal, like a smashed pumpkin. Cracked. Pulpy. Runny.

Winters remained on the ground, his hands covering his head, as police rushed up, their guns drawn and trained on Danny. In the same instant, bomb experts surrounded the small box that Danny had so carefully deposited. Others drew closer to the dump truck, inspecting its cargo with flashlights, but no one was touching anything. Not yet.

Two black men in suits grasped the governor under either arm, raising him to his feet, then whisking him away. Behind the protection of the barricade now, Winters's legs buckled as his security team released his arms. His face looked as white as his hair. Even on the inferior resolution of the video monitor, Governor Winters appeared confused, frightened, and dazed. But as the running digits at the corner of the monitor screen counted the seconds, I saw Winters gather himself. He shook his head, waving off the confusion. The men helped him out of the baggy suit, and he brushed himself off.

Meanwhile, the bomb squad huddled over the box and surrounded the truck. They were shaking their heads, too.

In the security trailer, the three of us stood silently, staring at the images on the monitors and struggling to comprehend what we had seen.

I recalled my last conversation with Danny Denza, just this morning. He wanted me there. Maybe he was hoping for some grand admission from Winters. Or perhaps he planned to make an admission of his own. Either way, he wanted me to write it. "Write it for Christy," he had said. Well, what should I write now, Danny, I thought. I just watched you get your head blown off. That's all I have to write about. All I can write now is your obit, Danny.

I was angry and confused. I still didn't know who had killed Christy, and I thought then that I might never know. I just stared at the monitor, talking to Danny in my head.

"Jesus," Po said in a breathy release. He was the first of us to break the silence. "I've never seen anything like that."

"Me neither," I said.

"What you saw, gentlemen, was extraordinary," Abe Braxton announced, in full control of himself. "You witnessed an extraordinary man, a great hero in action. The world will be talking about what happened here tonight. A leader for our troubled times has arrived. We have just witnessed the making of a president."

Braxton was smiling. He was looking at the bloody image of Danny Denza, the poor man's brains running all over Three Mile Island, and he was smiling.

35

A CRUSH OF MEDIA GATHERED AT THREE MILE ISLAND'S GATE. I stood next to Abe Braxton and waited with the rest of the press for the grand news conference to begin.

In the background, the island was lit up like a Christmas tree, what with all the cherry tops of the police cars and the fire trucks. It would serve as a perfect photo op for the press conference. A makeshift podium had been set up for officials to address the media. Nearly thirty microphones were duct taped or otherwise attached to the stand.

A half-dozen uniformed officers took position behind the podium, providing still more set decoration, as if the impressive night scene of the island and its cooling towers weren't enough. Then came the big boys, disgorging from the motorcade of police cars that had slowly made its way down the long, narrow drive leading from the island. First came the suit-clad state police commander, then the FBI field commander. Last was the man everyone in the media longed to hear speak, the man of the hour, Governor Lowell Winters. Hero. Presidential candidate. He stood off to the side and allowed the others to talk first.

As the state police commander took position behind the podium, Braxton clicked the button of his slim, silver tape recorder to capture every word.

"Ladies and gentlemen of the press, I have a statement," announced the commander, who was tall, thick, and stiff. "I'd like to update all of you on the latest details of the incident. I'll be brief because I think there's someone else here you'd rather talk to."

There was a low smattering of laughter among the press, but Commander Wiley didn't crack his stern face. Instead, he methodically recounted the official police narrative of events. But the press didn't want facts; they wanted Winters.

Finally, the commander finished and peered up from his script, seeming exhausted but relieved. I got the feeling that facing the press was more uncomfortable for him than squaring off against twenty Danny Denzas.

"I'd like to introduce the real hero in all of this, Governor Lowell Winters. Governor." With that, Commander Wiley quickly vacated the podium, and the governor took his place.

As if on cue, a wave of flashes popped like fireworks in a blinding display. Reporters shouted questions all at once: "Governor, how do you feel? Why did you decide to put yourself in danger? Were you afraid for your life?"

Governor Winters, looking fresh as a daisy in a dark suit, held court at the podium, surveying the clamoring press in confident amusement.

I wondered if he had had to change his underwear after diving to the ground and watching a man's head explode not ten feet away. Whatever he had done, he cleaned up well. He wore none of the fear and confusion that had marked his face earlier, just quiet confidence now. His puff of white hair was perfect.

The governor said nothing, instead waiting for the shouting to stop. He simply smiled and looked presidential. Very presidential.

Finally, Winters raised a hand to quiet things down, and the press took the cue.

"I just want to say one thing, for the record," Winters began. "I have to give credit where credit's due. The law enforcement team that worked here tonight did an outstanding job. They are the real heroes in all of this. I don't want that to be overlooked. It was just outstanding work."

Not interested in the governor's attempt at modesty, the press protested with another chorus of shouts, as everyone attempted to ask their questions at once.

"Okay, okay," Winters said. "Let's do this thing one at a time. Abe, why don't you start us off?"

Braxton smiled broadly. "First, I'd like to say congratulations, Governor. And I'd like to ask you when you plan to announce your next career move—as a state or federal emergency response worker?"

The media chuckled, and Winters smiled.

"No way," he said, gesturing wildly. "Not me. Once was enough. I couldn't do what these guys do. They're wonderful. No career announcements of any kind, not today."

"Seriously, Governor," Braxton resumed. "Everyone is talking about how heroic you were. How you stood up to terrorism. I happened to observe the negotiation between you and the subject on video monitors. To say it was tense is an understatement. Most of us could never imagine doing something like that. Did you set out to be a hero tonight? How did you hold it together?"

"Dealing with the Democrats in the state house and senate has given me lots of practice," Winters deadpanned, the crowd of media laughing in unison. Oh, he was good, I thought. Even better than on the day he nailed my ass.

"No, to answer your question, I didn't set out to be a hero. No one does," he said. "I just felt I had a duty. A danger was posed, a great threat, and this very disturbed man asked for me. Said if I didn't come, he'd do something terrible. How do you walk away from that? That's something I could never do. So I came, worked with the police, listened to what they told me, and I talked to the man. He was very emotional. He had lost his sister in a terrible, terrible tragedy. I just tried to calm him. We did our best. The main thing was to get him out of that truck and get the threat neutralized. We did that. Unfortunately, the young man lost his life, but when you make threats and put yourself in that kind of situation, the police have to do everything they can to preserve life. They did that tonight."

"What did the bomb look like?" a reporter shouted.

"It looked big," the governor said. "Lots of big barrels. It was terrible."

The FBI field commander stepped up and whispered in the governor's ear. Winters yielded the mike with more than a little regret. "Bob can fill you in on that," he said.

"Just to clarify," the FBI field commander stepped in. "The bomb itself was a replica, made to look like a homemade fertilizer bomb. In reality, the containers were filled with sand, ordinary construction-grade sand. Of course, none of us knew it at the time, but this was not a functional explosive device. Even had the situation been otherwise, I want to remind everyone that these particular reactor buildings were constructed to withstand quite a bit of force, the equivalent of an airplane crash. The walls are four feet of solid concrete. I just think it's important that we keep the possible scenarios in perspective."

The Fed relinquished the podium to Winters, but the governor was visibly deflated now that word was out that he had saved the state from a fake bomb.

"I tell you, it looked real enough to me," Winters added. "If someone sticks a gun in your face, are you no less scared if you find out later it was a cap pistol? The threat here was real enough, especially given Denza's background with explosives and in view of our current national and international climate."

The press peppered Winters with more questions, but he never quite recaptured his heroic glow. Even Braxton looked a little less admiring, a little glum.

Personally, I felt a little better knowing Danny Denza had never intended to hurt anyone. Just like the police psychologist had said, Danny hadn't wanted to be there. He wanted answers, yes. He wanted to take a stand for his sister, and he wanted an outlet for his own guilt, whatever the source of it was. But he wasn't out to hurt anyone. I still wondered what on earth had motivated him to push away his Budweiser to come here and create all this mayhem.

"Cheer up," I said to Abe Braxton as we walked back to his car. "Maybe the governor can start saving kids everywhere from their sandboxes."

He swung his head like a cat and stared at me hatefully.

"That's a great man right there," Braxton seethed. "I don't appreciate your remarks. People will remember what he did here for years, for decades. Only jealous nobodies like you and your fat security guard friend would make jokes and try to diminish it."

I felt the heat of his anger, but I didn't care. The whole night—watching Danny Denza out of his mind with desperation, the gut-churning tension, and the cold, hollow ending—had left me feeling sick.

"Well, this jealous nobody has an obit to write tonight, thanks to your governor," I countered as we entered Braxton's shiny black BMW. "The guy has some fucking luck. Everybody around him keeps dying, but he never gets so much as a scratch. Except maybe that time fat ol' Herb Bucher sat on him."

I smiled, but Braxton waved me off, shaking his head and jutting his jaw confidently. "None of that's going to matter now," he said, pulling out of the lot and onto the dark highway leading away from the island and back to Harrisburg. "Nothing matters. He's a motherfucking hero."

I looked at Braxton, who was perfect in profile. He believed what he was saying, and he was proud.

"All people will remember is how this governor risked his ass," Braxton continued. "He put his life on the line for them. They fear terrorism, and they fear this place more than anything. The thought of it blowing up is their worst nightmare. Who saved them from it? Governor Lowell Winters. All he needed was the right occasion to rise to. Events make heroes. The people won't forget."

I studied Braxton for a long time as he drove toward the city. I could see the story that he would write already taking form in his mind. It would be dramatic, suspenseful, and breathtaking. And Winters would be the star.

There were other thoughts, too. It was as if Braxton could see Winters riding this new surge of support to his long-awaited announcement for president. On a dark highway just outside Harrisburg, Braxton could see that banner day, and the many triumphs that lay beyond.

36

Back at the newspaper, Braxton acted as if we hadn't spent the past five hours together. He jumped out of his BMW and strode purposefully across the dark, half-filled parking lot, leaving me behind to struggle with the door handle.

"Well, fuck you," I muttered. "That's the last time I get you in to see the negotiation of the century at Three Mile Island."

But I was anything but offended. I knew Braxton and I were more or less thrust together by events. There was no pretense of our liking one another. And he clearly detested my continued ribbing of Governor Winters. He would not have to put up with it any longer, either. Braxton was in control now. He would write the lead story of Winters's heroics.

I was left with the mop-up job of penning Danny Denza's obituary. As I walked across that lonely parking lot toward the newspaper, I thought of all that had happened. The images rushed at me: the recovery team pulling Christy's body from the river; her lifeless body on the shiny steel autopsy table; Danny crying over the picture of the two of them; Winters dressed in that ridiculous antibomb suit. And, of course, the fresh image of Danny getting his brains blown out. An event that looked so cheap, fake, and pornographic on the poor resolution of the security monitors.

I looked up at the clear, star-filled sky and wished that my mind could be just as clear. I paused for a moment, took a deep breath of cool spring air, then walked into the paper.

Braxton was nowhere to be found in the lobby. I pressed the button and waited for the interminably slow elevator. I was in no rush. I had the confidence of knowing that my story—the details of Danny Denza's life and unexpected death—would come when I sat down at my computer. I could write this story. I never had any doubt about that.

The newsroom was buzzing, even though 10:00 P.M. isn't typically the busiest of times. Usually, most of the stories are in and edited by then, and most of the reporters have gone home, while copy editors stay behind to put the last touches on the pages, getting them ready to go to press.

But the events at Three Mile Island kept most of the staff on duty, including all of the top-level editors, who had convinced themselves that the paper couldn't handle a big story without them. Everyone else in the newsroom knew the staff could have managed fine, if not better, without their ass-picking and over-the-shoulder editing. But that's newspapers for you.

From across the newsroom, I spied Braxton. He was giving Bill Sharps a breathless rundown of the governor's heroics. A wave of bitterness rushed through me, but there was nothing I could say. The damn governor was a hero, like it or not. Sure, Braxton would embellish and dramatize, but the basic facts would support him pretty much any way he wrote it. The revelation that the truck wasn't actually packed with explosives was a minor detail. Danny Denza's messy death could be explained away, too. He'd been branded a terrorist, after all. Any sympathy evaporated with that label.

I passed the two of them on my way to my cubicle. Braxton didn't so much as look at me, but Sharps did. "You got the Denza obit, right, Lenny?" he asked.

"Yeah," I said. "The way I'm going, I'll bury the whole damn family before the month's out."

"Well, if it's any consolation, you were right," Sharps said, sounding glum. "You pieced it together, and it tied right to the Denza girl's death. Make sure you put that in your story. Braxton will deal with the overall crisis and the governor's involvement. You take it from Denza's side. That stuff about him helping to blow the old PennDOT Building would be good color."

"I'm on it," I said, starting to walk away.

Unexpectedly, Braxton stopped me. "Hey, Holcomb."

I turned to look at him, but he didn't hold my eyes.

"Good working with you tonight," he said to the floor.

"Yeah," I said, wondering if this display was just a show for Sharps. "Good luck with your story."

I walked away, leaving Sharps with a surprised smile on his face. He and Braxton had a few more words before Braxton, too, dashed to his desk.

"Okay, guys," Sharps shouted, amplifying his understated personality into coach mode. "Deadline's coming quick. We need these stories in thirty minutes."

I nodded at him, and I saw the top of Braxton's bald head do the same. I booted up the computer, opened a story file, and got right to it. I was typing away when I heard a familiar voice.

"You did it again, Holcomb," Jacquelyn Towers said from her once-familiar perch on my cubicle wall. "I know you're on deadline, but I just wanted to congratulate you," she said, smiling sweetly. "Despite all the shit you've taken, you had enough guts to go with your instincts. Right in the middle of the newsroom, no less. You should be proud. Sometimes, I wish I could be more like you. You know, balls out, newsroom politics be damned. But I guess that's why I'm doing stories about ladies collecting refrigerator magnets on the same day some guy is threatening to blow up Three Mile Island and the governor himself is trying to talk him out of it."

I watched her perfect mouth as she spoke. She was beautiful, but I did not feel the pang for her that I once did. I could no longer delude myself with my old man's fantasies, but that didn't stop me from admiring her a hell of a lot.

"So how'd that story turn out?" I asked.

"It's a piece of shit, but it sings. I wrote the hell out of the damn thing."

"You'll be back on something big in no time," I said. "Anyone who can make a story about refrigerator magnets sing is an unstoppable force in this business."

"Yeah, I guess." She was unconvinced. "Anyway, better let you get back to it. Sharps will be breathing down your neck if you don't make deadline."

"Not to worry, I'm an old hand when it comes to writing about death. It's my business."

She smiled, and I smiled back. The clock was ticking relentlessly toward deadline, but I took the time to watch her walk all the way across the newsroom.

My smile faded when my eyes returned to the computer screen and the grim task that awaited finishing. There was nothing left to do. I allowed my fingers to resume tapping the keys. I wrote about the short life and early death of Danny Denza. My mind was given over to his story:

BROTHER OF MURDERED WINTERS AIDE SHOT DEAD BY COPS AFTER THREATENING TMI; BOMB A FAKE

By Lenny Holcomb

Daniel Denza, the older brother of murdered former gubernatorial Press Secretary Christy Denza, held the entire midstate hostage last night when he threatened to detonate a bomb outside the reactor building of Three Mile Island's Unit One.

The four-hour siege at the world-famous nuclear power plant ended after Governor Winters came to the scene and personally talked Denza from the cab of a construction truck that Denza claimed was packed with explosives.

Denza, 31, a demolition worker experienced with explosives, laid down a suspected detonator device at the governor's urging, but he was shot and killed by a police sharpshooter after authorities say he got too close to the governor, who was only feet away.

Police later determined that the device—materials designed to appear like a dangerous, homemade fertilizer bomb—was not a working explosive, but rather a fake. No other weapons were found.

"Basically, it was a mock-up," said FBI Field Commander Robert Lewis. "He knew what he was doing, and he made it look real. We didn't know it was fake until after the incident was resolved."

HE DIDN'T DRINK. NEVER TRUST SOMEONE WHO DOESN'T DRINK.

During the crisis, authorities treated the threat as very real. Denza had a vast knowledge of explosives from his work rigging building demolitions. He most recently worked for the BA&M Demolition Co. of Carlisle and helped rig explosive charges for the 1997 implosion of the former PennDOT Building in downtown Harrisburg.

HE SAID IT WAS THE ONLY WAY. THE OTHER ONE FUCKED IT ALL UP.

Denza's only demand was an immediate meeting with Governor Winters. After communicating for a time by cellular phones, Winters emerged from behind barricades in order to lure Denza from the truck's cab and convince him to give up. Just as it appeared the crisis would end peacefully, Denza was shot once in the head as he rose from a crouch and appeared to take a step toward the governor.

"The governor was exposed," said State Police Commander Nick Wiley. "We didn't know at the time what other weapons this suspect might have. We couldn't take a chance. I don't question the decision at all."

THE OLD REPORTER FUCKED THINGS UP. THE GOVERNOR WOULD NEVER HAVE TO ANSWER FOR CHRISTY. NOT UNLESS I DID SOMETHING. THAT'S WHAT THE OTHER REPORTER SAID. THE ONE WHO ALWAYS CALLED.

Denza apparently blamed Winters for the death of his sister, Christy Denza, 26, who police say was murdered early last Wednesday in a case that remains unsolved. The governor was cleared of suspicion in the murder by passing a polygraph test, but questions about a possible sexual relationship between the two continue to dog him.

HE WOULDN'T DRINK WITH ME, BUT HE SOUNDED SMART. I TRUSTED HIM. HE EVEN HAD AN HONEST NAME—LIKE LINCOLN.

• • •

I saw the added lines, words and sentences that weren't supposed to be part of the story I wrote, but were there nonetheless. I did not comprehend them for a moment. Then, all at once, the realization washed over me:

Abe Braxton's phone number at the Denzas'. How Braxton watched me from his cubicle. The echoes of Danny's desperation over the phone. "I will make him answer. He will have to answer for Christy."

But they weren't Danny's words. They were planted in his head like seeds. Braxton had been whispering in Danny's ear: "You can make him answer. You can do it."

Braxton didn't suspect Danny of Christy's murder. No, he was stoking Danny's own suspicions of the governor, manipulating him into threatening Winters. Danny was messed up with grief, guilt, and impotence, but he would have stayed right there in his mother's kitchen, drinking his Bud, if it wasn't for Braxton's urging: "Make him answer."

Braxton must have known that deep down, beyond all the booze and the bad feelings, the guy was basically harmless. Sure, Danny hated Winters. He thought the governor murdered his sister. But Danny wasn't a killer. He was a demolition expert, true. But his life's work was all about controlling the charges, making them safe, and bringing down a building just so. He wasn't reckless. He wasn't about blowing things up.

Braxton had to know this. That's what made it all the more perfect. Fucking brilliant. Get Denza, the distraught brother, to make the threat, just the threat. Plant it in his head that it's the only way to get the truth for his sister.

I don't know who picked Three Mile Island, but it was a stroke of genius. It had to have been Braxton.

He knew it would be the perfect showcase for Winters. The governor would have to come.

And what would happen then? The governor would talk. That's something Braxton could count on. He would talk, empathize, connect. And Danny's resolve would grow soft. He could no longer be sure. Winters would admit to sleeping with Christy, but he'd deny everything else. He'd say he loved her, like Danny loved her. And Danny would come to believe him. The goddamn police psychologist was right. Danny didn't want to be there. He didn't want to hurt anyone.

Yes, Braxton could count on that, I agreed with myself. But why do it?

Wait. My mind raced. What did Braxton say after the press conference? Events matter. Heroes need the right situations to emerge. The right occasions to rise to. A new leader for our troubled times has arrived.

Goddamn, Braxton set it up. He set the whole thing up for Winters. He's the image maker, the outside fixer they've been waiting to bring in to turn around Winters's troubled campaign. He's Christy's Tigger, the mystery man who was waiting in the wings to take her job.

Then it hit me: Mexico.

In her obit, Christy said it all started in Mexico. I thought that just meant her affair with the governor, but I was wrong. Another, much more subversive relationship had blossomed in Mexico that winter.

Braxton was down there, too, I was sure of it now. Winters was on a trade mission, and Braxton was the reporter covering him.

I logged on to the newspaper's database and typed in two words: Mexico and Braxton. Three stories came up, all from last January, all with Mexican datelines, and all having something to do with Winters.

Yep, Braxton was down there, all right. And somewhere along the line, maybe over tacos and Mexican beer in Winters's private suite, the two of them hatched the idea of having Braxton come and work for the campaign. He'd make the jump from journalism to head communications for Winters's presidential bid. But it would be a well-timed jump, after Braxton had milked the paper for all the favorable publicity he could send Winters's way.

But this, all this. They could have never conceived of this. Not in their wildest dreams.

Braxton had just created the perfect photo op. He'd made Winters a national hero, transcending politics. Bigger than a war hero, bigger than a Hollywood star. Abe Braxton had practically put his man in the White House with that single event at Three Mile Island.

Perhaps Winters didn't know all the details—the when and the where. But he knew enough to be ready. He knew enough to insist on going to the scene when the state police told him not to. He knew enough to be smooth, cool, and heroic.

But I had seen the strings of their puppet show. I couldn't prove anything, not yet. But I had my source. I could shake things up with that.

And I could start right now.

37

WITH DANNY DENZA'S OBIT—HIS REAL OBIT, THE ONE WITH the secret truth about the reasons behind his death—still glowing on my screen, I dispatched an E-mail to Abe Braxton.

I looked over at his cubicle, just a row away, right before I clicked the mouse button to send it off. Just the top of his bald head was showing. He was hard at work on his story, the story he had created. The one that would complete the transformation of Governor Winters from a scandal-plagued politician and presidential pretender into an American hero.

I thought of the arrogance of it all. The manipulation. The ruining of still more lives. I had to call him out, so I started with an E-mail.

To: abraxton
From: lholcomb
Subject: My Source Says . . .

I think we have a real problem with the story. Nothing we have is wrong, don't worry. It's just that we don't have all of it. I have a source, Abe. A good source. He says Denza didn't act alone. This wasn't just the frustrated ravings of a half-crazy brother out of his mind over his sister's death. This was some kind of fucked-up conspiracy. Can you believe it? My source, my good source, says someone was behind the scenes, talking to Denza. Talking him into it. Someone put him up to it. I know this sounds like a lot of JFK conspiracy crap, but I believe this guy. I trust him. I wanted you to be the first to know. I thought, maybe, we could work on it together. Maybe we should tell Sharps about it, too, just so he knows.

This story is about to take an ugly and unexpected turn. I feel it. Maybe it's the old reporter in me, but so help me, I feel it.

Lenny

Judging by the time it took for Braxton to come storming over, he opened that E-mail as soon as it arrived. Deadline or no, he wanted to see what I had to say. More accurately, he wanted to see what my source had to say. I hooked him.

I pretended I didn't notice as he walked toward me.

"Holcomb," he grunted, trying to hold his rage. He wasn't mad at me, I didn't think. He was furious that his perfect plan might be unraveling.

I jerked as if in surprise, then looked up. He stood at the entrance of my cubicle. His eyes burned.

"Lenny, I mean." He tried to soften himself. He couldn't come off too defensive, had to dial it back. "I should call you Lenny if we're going to be working together." He adopted a casual half-smile. "So what's this about some kind of conspiracy?" I thought I saw his right eye twitch.

"Oh, I didn't mean to bother you with that on deadline," I said. "Just got a call from a source. It's not something we can do anything about tonight, anyway. But it's worth looking into. I figured I should let you know. There's more, of course, but I didn't want to get into everything in the E-mail."

"More?" Braxton said, his eyes flashing confusion and searching me for what I knew, all that I knew.

"Oh, yeah, lots more. This guy told me some wild stuff. I don't know how much of it we'll ever be able to prove, but it sure sounds like one hell of a political conspiracy."

"Political?" Braxton asked. "What's political? This guy, Denza, he was fucking nuts."

"Was he?" I asked pointedly. "I never got that impression. Depressed, yes. A drinker, sure. Torn up with grief and guilt, absolutely. But I never really thought of him as dangerous. When I first met him, I was a little careful with him, careful with what I told him about the case. But looking back on it, I don't think Danny Denza was prepared to do much more about his sister's death than sit in his momma's kitchen and drink. Then again, maybe you got to know him a little better than I did. Maybe that's it."

"Me? What do I have to do with this?"

"You tell me." I never broke my stare.

"I don't like your tone, Holcomb." His features shifted and rearranged, showing his anger and, perhaps, a little fear.

"Maybe we shouldn't be talking about this right now," I said. "You're still on deadline. I didn't mean to interrupt you. We can deal with this tomorrow. We can both sit down with Sharps and talk about this political conspiracy to get Winters into the White House."

"Fuck deadline," Braxton said, his voice rising. "I filed my story. We should talk now. I think you've got something to say to me, but I don't know if you're man enough. You want to bring in Sharps? Fuck Sharps. You say you're working with me, you bring it to me. I want to hear this shit you think you have. I want to hear how this desperate act by the lone, fucked-up brother of a dead girl has anything to do with politics—anything to do with getting Winters into the White House."

"I'll be glad to talk. Have a seat."

"Not here," he said, eyes darting. "Not in the middle of the fucking newsroom. Not at your desk, where you probably have a tape recorder running, trying to get me to say something."

"What?" I laughed. "Now who's the one dreaming up conspiracies?"

"Follow me," he ordered. "I know somewhere we can go, somewhere where no one will be able to eavesdrop and where you won't be able to record a damn thing. This whole fucking newsroom has ears."

Braxton turned and strode toward the back of the newsroom. I followed, watching him as he walked, the muscles moving under his tailored shirt. That's when I noticed the line of wetness running down the center of his back. The man was sweating. I had never seen so much as a bead of sweat on Braxton's forehead, yet he was soaking through his white broadcloth shirt. I had made him nervous.

Braxton assaulted the push bar on the door leading to the fire stairs. Pushed it so hard, in fact, that the door banged off the wall and damn near swung shut in my face.

I protested, but Braxton paid no attention. He was descending the stairs in a trot. Far below, I could hear the rumbling presses. Those old presses were awake and churning out the early edition.

I followed Braxton down the stairs. I had to go. I started this, after all. I had to let it play out.

With each flight, the noise grew louder. I could feel the vibrations traveling up through the metal handrails of the stairs. On the pressroom level, which was literally the basement, Braxton pushed through another door. This time he held it open for me. The noise was intense now. Industrial. Powerful.

Abe Braxton wanted me to go with him into the pressroom. Again, I felt I had no choice but to accept his invitation. It was long past time for this to end.

We had arrived at the ultimate deadline.

The door opened onto a rail-protected platform forty feet off the pressroom floor. The platform ran the length of the large room and opened onto several catwalks that stretched out over the presses below. I looked down at the large blue machinery that spat out thousands of newspapers each night. On one end were large rolls of newsprint that fed the monster. The machine grasped the paper, which looked like giant-size rolls of toilet paper, then sucked it through the webbing of presses. As the newsprint snaked its way through the machine, it was filled up with words and pictures. Then, it was cut and folded. All of this occurred at what seemed like fifty miles an hour, the paper rushing through the machine in a blur, newspapers streaming out the other end.

Even from my perch far above, I could see the banner headlines and the unmistakable image of Three Mile Island's cooling towers. "THREAT AT THREE MILE ISLAND," the headline blared. Of course, later editions containing Braxton's and my stories would tout Winters's heroics in defusing the crisis and report on Danny Denza's death.

Once again I marveled at the brilliance of Braxton's plan. But I couldn't think about that now. Abe Braxton was in my face. He screamed over the loudness of the press.

"Now we can talk, Holcomb. Now we can get down to it." His face looked evil as he shouted at me. The relentless churning of the presses below us matched his rage. "What the fuck have you been trying to say to me? What is it that you think you know?"

The hatred behind his eyes was enough to start backing me up, but I wasn't backing down.

"You really want to know?" I shouted so hard, it felt like my throat was ripping. "Well, how 'bout this? How about that this whole thing tonight was just some kind of fucked-up photo op to make the governor look good. How about that it was you who put Denza up to the whole thing. You were the one calling him, playing with his mind. Christ, I saw your phone number at his house. I'm sure other people, neighbors, saw you. And of course, there'll be phone records. But I have to say, it was brilliant. You gave Winters his situation, his event. You made the image. I know about Mexico, Abe. I know Winters offered you a job. What'd he promise you? A top spot in the campaign and then a plum staff job in the administration? I hope it was at least that."

I'd been screaming so hard, I felt light-headed. I didn't even recognize my own, raw voice. But even as I shouted out everything I knew to be true, the words had no effect on Braxton. His face was empty, blank. Maybe it was all the hopes he had for his grand plan draining out of him. Or maybe he still thought he could beat me.

"You're tired, old man," he said, stepping closer and backing me up farther. I was getting ever nearer to the yellow rails that guarded against a forty-foot drop into those churning presses. "You're too tired for all this," he went on. "Too old and tired, and you drink too much."

Step by step, he walked me back to the railing.

"Maybe you were drinking tonight." He talked right in my face now, leaning down so I could feel the dank warmth of his breath and, occasionally, the light spray of his saliva. "Maybe you had a little too much. Maybe you slip and fall and hurt yourself. It looks like a long drop."

He peeked over the yellow railing at the blur of newsprint being turned into newspapers below us. Instinctively, I looked over, too. It might be a fitting end, I thought. After all, that press—that beast in the basement—had chewed away most of me over these last forty years. Why shouldn't it have the rest?

"What good would it do?" I asked him, showing no fear. "There's the source, Braxton. You forget the source. He knows everything, and he wants to tell. It's in his best interest to tell. He who tells the story, controls the story. Isn't that true?"

I spoke right into Braxton's ear. I didn't want to look at his face. I didn't want to see if there was rage and hate in his eyes. I did not want to know if there was murder on his face. I didn't want to know if he was going to pick me up and throw me into those whirling presses.

"Isn't that how we all think? Control the story." I went on talking low and steady into his ear, as if he were hearing his own thoughts, his own doubts. "It's true in journalism and true in politics. Especially politics. You saw what Winters did to me at the press conference. What do you think he'd do here, if there was even a hint of a setup? Do you really think he'd hesitate even a second before doing the same to you? Do you think you're so different? For all you know, he's already started to spin it, to tell it his way. Right now, there's no real connection between him and you. But the moment he puts you on staff, he's in bed with you. Think about it. If he's gonna make a move, it's gonna be now. If he breaks ties now, he stays out of it. You're just some overaggressive reporter talkin' to the brother of a dead girl. A reporter who wants a story, so he pushes the brother a little too far. The reporter starts talking about makin' threats. Tells the brother to put the governor on the spot, force him to talk? Force him to answer? I can see it playin' that way. It could play that way real good. Be real nice for the governor, huh?"

I pulled back a bit and made myself look into Braxton's eyes. I saw questions there. Doubts.

"Think about it, Abe," I said. "It's going to come out, sooner or later. Questions will arise. Maybe the parents start to wonder about the reporter who kept callin'. Maybe even Danny said something before he went ahead with it. I mean, he called me, didn't he? Nothin's perfect. There are leaks. Secrets don't hold. If we're havin' these doubts, what's Winters thinking? Now that he's ridin' high, why would he risk another scandal? And when he looks at you, Abe, that's exactly what he sees. The stink's on you now, and you can't wash it off. Winters'll do what he does best—save his own ass."

Braxton was thinking, weighing everything. His mind was racing, his emotions building. I felt myself grow tense. I braced for him to heave me over that yellow railing. Then suddenly, his face changed. He reached a conclusion. I could hardly breathe.

"It's him, isn't it?" He said the words in disbelief. "It's him. He's your source. Isn't he?"

I didn't answer.

"That's what you're tryin' to tell me," Abe went on,

the disbelief giving way to realization, and the realization building to anger. "It's Winters. He came to you. He wants to bring me down. He thinks he can fuck me, the way he fucked his whore of a press secretary? The way he screwed over some old obit writer? That's what you're telling me, isn't it, old man?"

Braxton's eyes went wild. He threw his large hands onto my chest, gripped my shirt, and shook me. I looked down and watched the buttons pop, one by one. I was sure I was going to die.

"Who's your source?" he screamed at me. His open, howling mouth was all I could see, assaulting me with a torrent of words, breath, and spit. "Tell me who's the source. It's Winters, isn't it? He thinks he can fuck me. Tell me. Say it. It's Winters, he's the source."

Abe Braxton shook me so violently, my back went numb against the railing and my limbs flailed like those of a rag doll, powered under the might of Braxton's rage. I didn't know what to do. I didn't know what to say. So I uttered one word:

"Yes."

And once I said it, I kept repeating it. "Yes! Yes! Yes!"

He stopped. My head hung to my chest, my legs giving way. I'd accept whatever fate Abe Braxton decided for me.

"He really thinks he can fuck me?" he asked, the anger fading and the disbelief returning. But this time, it was the cynical disbelief of someone who knows he holds a better hand.

"Does he think I'm that ordinary? That I would not have prepared and protected myself? Does he think himself so superior that he can just scrape me off his shoe?"

Braxton smiled at the new plans that were forming in his mind.

Finally, when his eyes returned to me, he seemed startled. He looked down at his own hands, still twisting my shirt in their clutches, and he seemed embarrassed. He quickly released me, reacting as if he'd been touching something unpleasant. He scanned me, up and down. I was rumpled, jostled, weak, and confused. And Braxton appeared shocked by the sight of me. Then, without saying another word, he turned and walked away.

The metal door banged shut in Braxton's wake. I was left alone with those screaming presses. The sounds grew louder, the constant churning and chugging of the press, cranking out paper after paper. The sound exploded in my ears and bored through my skull. But I couldn't move. I hadn't the strength.

I just clamped my hands over my ears and slumped to the concrete floor. I sat there, leaning against the yellow rails of the platform. I tried desperately to hold out the noise—and everything else.

38

The next morning, I entered the newsroom to find most of the early risers huddled around a TV at the city desk. A local newscaster was delivering a breathless account of a late-breaking story.

I glanced at the screen and recognized the setting immediately. The female reporter was standing outside the fence of the governor's mansion. The fence was decorated with yellow police tape, and she was talking about a shooting.

"There are very few details about the altercation at this hour," the good-looking blonde said, gesturing at the mansion behind her. "But the shooting happened right here inside the governor's mansion. Once again, we repeat, the governor and the first lady were not hurt in the late night shooting, though both were in the mansion at the time. But one person was shot and killed by a member of the governor's state police security detail.

"At this hour," the reporter went on, "the police are releasing no details about this person. All we know is the person was shot by security inside the mansion. And he or she had some sort of weapon, a metallic object, as it's being described by officials. Once again, the governor, the first lady, members of the governor's security dctail, and the mansion staff were unhurt in the incident."

The woman went on like that, in the staccato style typical of television reporters, but I had heard enough. I glanced over at Bill Sharps, who was shaking his head.

"I've never seen anything like this," Sharps marveled. "It's like there's a plague on this guy. Death and destruction just follow Winters around. It's biblical. Biblical or Shakespearean. I don't know which."

"Do we know who died?" I asked.

"Not yet," he said, still looking at the screen. "Macy's down there now, but nobody's talkin'. But the mansion's only a couple blocks away from a couple of dicey neighborhoods. It's right on the fringe. Who knows, maybe a homeboy got his Jones up, wanted to take an unscheduled tour of that big ol' mansion by the river."

I stared at the television, then shook my head. "It wasn't any homeboy."

Sharps glanced up, his face begging an explanation.

"You know something, Lenny?" he asked.

"Too much. I know too damn much."

He studied me, his eyes wanting more. But I turned and walked out of the newsroom. I had somewhere to go just then.

"Lenny?" Sharps called after me.

I kept walking. He'd know everything soon enough.

I drove to the old county nursing home and pulled around back. The garage door was open. I walked past the rusty wheelchairs and the old hospital beds to the first basement door. I took a deep breath, steadied myself, and then looked through the glass.

I saw Abe Braxton on the metal table in the small autopsy room. He was stripped naked, except for a towel over his groin. His body looked perfect, and his skin, the rich color of his skin, hadn't yet lost its luster. It was smooth and clean and showed off the ripples of lean muscle underneath. There was just one minor imperfection, a small hole in the center of his chest. Around the dark center of the hole, there was the brownish-red tint of dried blood. It looked like such a small blemish on that grand body of his.

Braxton's face was smooth. He looked calm and relaxed. His eyes were opened, but they had nothing behind them. The fierce intelligence, the unmatched arrogance, and the driving ambition that was Abe Braxton were all gone.

Buzz Swanson and the pathologist hadn't gotten around to Braxton yet, but there would be no surprises this time. The cause of death was as clear and easy to see as that dark hole at the center of Braxton's chest.

The why of it all would be much less clear to everyone but me. I knew why Braxton went to the mansion last night. Why he had to see the governor. And why he got killed. Hell, I practically sent him there with my lie. I might as well have pulled the trigger myself. I wasn't any better than Braxton. He sent Danny Denza to his death, and I had doomed Braxton. The only beneficiary of all this death was Governor Lowell Winters. Everyone who could hurt him was dead now.

Everyone but me.

As I peered through the window of the morgue operating room and my thoughts wandered to the night before, I did not hear the footsteps come up behind me.

"You again," Buzz Swanson whispered. He was standing so close, his breath tickled the hair of my neck, and I could smell the whiskey.

"Got any more cum samples for me?" Buzz laughed, bellowing more whiskey breath my way. So many things had happened, and so many people had died since Christy Denza, I'd nearly forgotten my previous visits to this dark place of death. And I certainly had stopped blaming Buzz for his small role in undermining my investigation of Winters. I had made the mistakes. All he did was tell the truth.

"No," I said to the window, my breath steaming the glass, making Abe Braxton's body disappear behind the fog. "Just came to look this time."

"See anything you like?" he asked devilishly. "You two never did like each other much. Must do you some good to see him on my table."

"Not really."

"Me, either," Buzz agreed. "That there's one black male I'da never expected to come to me dead of a gunshot. Just wasn't the type. Hell, the police won't even release the identity because they can't find the parents up in Boston. Apparently, they jetted off to some island somewhere for a little R and R. I have to hold off on my work until they make the notification. The C of D is obvious, but the D.A. wants a full autopsy, everything by the book on this one. When I finally do get in there, I half expect his blood to be blue and his organs monogrammed."

Buzz laughed at this, but I didn't.

"What happened?" I asked. "What did the police report say?"

"Guy went nuts, made threats, wouldn't leave. Cops say he was shouting all kinds of shit at Winters, making all kinds of accusations. When the police burst in to the private study, he wouldn't obey commands. Wouldn't get down on the floor."

"Cops said he had something," I said, remembering

the TV report. "Some kinda weapon. That's why they shot. What was it?"

Buzz was silent. I turned to face him. His eyes were glassy and shot through with red. "This is off the record and unofficial," Buzz said in hushed tones. "You tried to drag me into the shit the last time, and you saw how that turned out for you. I don't want my name on this, but I'll tell you, it wasn't a gun. No knife, either."

He smiled, but not from any joke.

"Those trigger-happy fucks shot him over a tape recorder," he said. "Yeah, he had one of those mini tape recorders in his pocket. He was pullin' it out of his jacket pocket when the cops broke in. Probably was recording his conversation with the governor. Cops said it looked metal, like a gun barrel. Personally, I just think they like to shoot first and make sure later. They're keepin' a lid on it for now until they can look into this a little more and come up with a better motive. You know how it is. Throw some dirt on the corpse, make him look mean and menacing, so the public don't question the shooting. Even though the guy was armed with a tape recorder. Don't worry, they'll do a good job draggin' your boy through the mud."

"A tape recorder?" I said.

"Don't you reporters use them all the time?"

"I never do. Pen and paper for me. But Braxton, he used them. Sometimes, I'd hear him at his desk. He'd rewind the tape, and it would make those squeaky sounds. But I never heard the actual recordings. He used an earphone, just stuck it in his ear and typed away."

"Sounds like a good system," Buzz said. "He gets his quotes and if anyone ever hollers that they were misquoted, he has them on tape." Buzz considered this for a moment. "I don't know, though. Accurate quotes are one thing, but they're not worth dyin' for. Sure enough, it was that damn tape recorder got him killed."

"I guess it did," I agreed, knowing Buzz liked his irony. But I didn't have time for the tragic poetry of the situation. I was thinking about something else Buzz said about the quotes. If there was ever a problem, Braxton would have the people on tape.

I returned to the newspaper and was surprised to find that the staff still hadn't learned of Abe Braxton's fate. Then, I realized that it made sense. Police were trying to keep the identity secret until they could track down Braxton's well-traveled parents. The fact that the Braxtons were rich and had ready access to top-flight Boston attorneys probably added to the precautions. The cops didn't want the family to hear about Braxton's death on CNN.

The lack of new information didn't stop our local TV anchors from droning on about what they dubbed "an extraordinary chain of events in the midstate." They recapped the late-night shooting at the governor's mansion, then worked their way backward, hitting the highlights of the crisis at Three Mile Island, the unsolved Christy Denza murder, and even managed to touch on the Herb Bucher embezzlement case, which seemed like ancient history now. Most of the newsroom staff remained huddled around the TV.

This distraction gave me the perfect opportunity to do what I promised myself would be the last of my own reporting on these sordid stories. I walked through the newsroom without anyone noticing, not even Jacquelyn Towers, who was as rapt as anyone by the TV news.

I ventured to Braxton's cubicle and sat down behind his immaculate desk. Not a scrap of paper was out of place. He favored political mementos, and his collection of buttons, bumper stickers, and other such memorabilia from presidential campaigns dating back to Ike was in prominent display around his desk and on his cubicle walls.

I reached for a desk drawer and pulled. Locked. Where would he keep the key?

Most reporters didn't bother to lock their desks, and those who did it out of habit usually left the keys in the locks or close at hand on their desks. I didn't see Braxton's key anywhere.

Son of a bitch probably kept it with him, I thought.

I lifted up some notebooks and moved around a few books. Then, I spotted one of those cheap rubber change purses, the kind shaped like an oval that kindergarten kids use for their milk money. It looked completely out of place there on the back corner of Braxton's desk.

I reached for it. It was blue with white letters so faded from use that I could barely read them. Upon closer inspection, I made out the words: "Winters 2000." It was a trinket from Winters's last governor's race. I shook it. There was something inside. I pressed the ends, and the slit in the center opened. I saw the keys, just two, joined by a wire ring. I shook them out of the kiddie purse and slid one into the desk lock. It fit nicely. I waited a beat, made a wish, and turned.

It worked.

I slid open the drawer and saw the boxes—boxes and boxes of little tapes, the kind that fit into micro-cassette recorders. Each of the little tapes was marked with a date. I saw a tape for the day after Herb Bucher died. There was one for the following Monday, when I went to Sharps with my story of Bucher's embezzlement and Braxton went ballistic. There was one for the day Christy Denza died. There were tapes for the days leading up to the press conference, as well as for days surrounding the main event: Danny Denza's unannounced visit to Three Mile Island. But there was no tape for last night, when I confronted Braxton with the information from my "source," and he decided to make a nighttime call on Governor Winters.

Might I hope that Braxton kept tapes of everything? Of all his conversations? That he didn't erase them?

Of course he wouldn't erase them. He had a bad little habit of keeping a voice-activated mini recorder in his pocket. No wonder he was so paranoid about tape recorders last night when he wanted to talk about my secret source. He'd been recording everybody. Not only recording, but cataloguing the stuff, and keeping it all under lock and key at the newspaper. Braxton wisely kept his tapes away from his apartment, where Winters might be able to get at them, like I was sure he could have gotten to Christy Denza's things. At the paper, guards were on duty around the clock, and no one entered without a security badge.

Of course he kept them. These tapes were his misguided insurance policy in the political games he was playing.

I grabbed the whole box, locked the drawer, and returned the key to the plastic change purse. I still needed one of those mini recorders, but I didn't want anyone to ask questions.

I glanced across the newsroom. Jack Towers was still among the group of staffers surrounding the television. I headed for her vacant cubicle. Her desk was a clutter of paper, notebooks, and empty water bottles. I gently lifted things until I saw the carrying strap of her tape recorder peeking out like a mouse's tail from under a bloated copy of the county budget. I grabbed the device, pressed a button to make sure the batteries had juice, and then slipped it into my pocket.

I walked unnoticed out of the newsroom.

39

I headed for the privacy of my Ford Fiesta and the refuge of the flask of whiskey that I hoped I'd kept filled in the glove box. I settled into the seat, placed the box of tapes on the passenger side, and reached hopefully for the glove box. The silver flask shone back at me like a treasure. I grabbed it, and it felt at least half full. When I couldn't make it all the way to a bar, it was reassuring to know a little refreshment was as close as my old shit car in the parking lot.

I twisted open the cap and took a soft slug. The whiskey was warm from being in my car, which had been baking in the spring sun. The warmth made the taste even better, more comforting somehow. It warmed me all the way down, returning something that had been absent inside me. I set the open flask between my legs and fiddled with the small tape recorder. I pressed a button and heard Jacquelyn Towers's sweet voice.

"When did you start your collection?" she asked, actually managing to sound interested.

A housewife with a rough smoker's voice launched in to a long explanation of her life's work collecting refrigerator magnets. I clicked another button, and the irritating voice was silenced. I pulled out Jack's tape and ran my fingers over Braxton's recordings. I settled on the day of Herb Bucher's funeral, the day I sprang my story on Braxton and Sharps, and later had my first conversation with Governor Winters. I didn't bother to rewind. I just pressed the larger of the buttons and the voices started.

It was Governor Winters, but he sounded different. Not commanding and confident, like at his press conferences, but small, weak, and whiney.

"This just fucks up everything, doesn't it? The fat bastard's gonna ruin me, take me down with him. It's all fucked now, all our plans." The governor sounded near tears.

"Easy, Lowell. This doesn't affect any of our plans." It was Braxton. His voice was steady and calm, comforting even. "It just causes us to accelerate some things and hold off on others. The key here is not the scandal, but how you deal with it. It's like a rain cloud, either the cloud blows over or you stay and get soaked. You control both of those things. To help things blow over, you go with full disclosure. Put all the records out there, let them see what the fat fuck was stealing. Who cares? But you've got to answer me one thing, and you've got to be straight. This is when it counts, Lowell."

"What?"

"Did you have anything to do with it, Lowell?" Braxton asked. "Is any of this going to lead to you? Is there any proof that you knew?"

"No," Winters shot back, indignant. "Hell, no. I didn't know what that fucker was up to. He just brought in the money. He was a cash cow, and I didn't question it. Everyone liked him well enough. I just tried to stay out of the way of his mouth when he was eating."

"Excellent. That's all I needed to know," Braxton said, sounding pleased. "We release everything, and you're as shocked as anyone by the allegations. You promise a full, open, and independent investigation. Then, you move on. You get out from under the cloud."

"Yeah, okay," Winters said. "Anything else?"

"There's going to be a press conference," Braxton continued. "You're going to have to play governor, and you're going to have to do it well. All the buzz will focus on what the scandal may do your presidential hopes—"

"No shit," Winters added impatiently.

"So," Braxton interjected, his voice not masking annoyance at the interruption. "We start a little buzz of our own. We start the press sniffing around on a new story—one we create. We put out word that the administration is going in a different direction. It wants a fresh start, and it's bringing on a new communications director. We set the stage for Christy's departure and my eventual arrival."

"Christy?" Winters sounded pathetic, like a junkie losing his crack dealer.

"Lowell, we knew it would come to this sooner or later," Braxton said, being strong for the both of them. "We both anticipated this change once things shifted into full campaign mode. Christy would be moved off stage, and I would be moved on."

"We never talked about firing her," Winters protested.

"Do you really think she'd take a demotion any better? You're fucking her and you don't even know her. Fact is, she'd probably take that worse. This she'll be able to understand. There's a scandal. The natives are restless, and sometimes you have to make a sacrifice. Well, she's the blond-haired, blue-eyed sacrifice."

"I can't do it," Winters said.

"I'll write the letter for you. It should be delivered after the press conference. I'll start the rumors today. She'll have a diminished role at the briefing. That'll really get the press talking. Then, you'll sack her after work with a very sympathetic dismissal letter. And you'll have taken a large step away from this unpleasantness."

"I'd better," Winters said.

"Don't worry, Lowell. Of course, we'll keep the second part of the restructuring—the part where I come aboard, save the day, and lead the campaign to the White House—secret for now. Timing is everything, and I can still be of some use at the paper. I want to keep a close eye on this Holcomb. I want to find his source. This is a washed-up obituary writer we're talking about. He's getting his information somewhere. We'd do well to find whoever is pissing in his ear."

"An obituary writer?" Winters sounded confused as I clicked him off.

I popped out the tape and rooted for another. I picked one for the day before Christy was found dead. It was the day my story on Herb Bucher broke, and Winters called his press conference, just like Braxton had wanted. And sure enough, the rumors were flying that the pretty blond press secretary would be out on her sweet ass. I wanted to hear what happened later, when they sacked her. Was there more? I was sure of it, yet I almost didn't want to know.

The machine screeched as it sped forward. I stopped it, pressed play and heard a familiar female voice.

"What the hell are you doing here?" It was Christy.

"Waiting for you," Abe Braxton answered. "Long day, wasn't it?"

"Too long to be out here talking to you." Keys jingled. They must have been outside her Second Street apartment. Braxton had waited for her there on the night she died. The night she was murdered.

"Wait, Christy, we have to talk. I'd like to explain some things. We want you to understand."

"What's to explain? I already got his fuck-off letter at work. Or should I say, your letter? He wants me out but isn't man enough to tell me himself," Christy shouted. "He gives me a letter? Says circumstances have changed, and all that bullshit? Don't worry, I already cleaned out my desk. Or should I say *your* desk. That's some candidate you'll be working for, such a great leader he can't even face me. He's man enough to fuck me, but that's only when he's takes his Viagra. 'The little blue fuck pill,' he calls it."

"Christy, please keep your voice down," Braxton said calmly. "You're not being very smart. We can't afford to have a problem here. That just can't happen. We're just asking you to sit on the bench for a while, take one for the team."

"Why don't you take one for the team—right up the ass," she snapped. "I won't be dismissed like this. I have options, too. The governor should realize that. Tell Lowell it's piss-poor strategy to make an enemy of his fuck buddy just when he's about to start a presidential campaign. The press just can't seem to get enough of those political sex scandals. I would have thought you'd have given him better advice, Abe."

"Christy," Braxton said in an even tone. I could see him smiling that sick smile of his. "We're not going to have a prob—"

The tape cut off and went to static. I pressed the forward button, but there was nothing. Braxton had erased it, but not all of it. Not the beginning.

• • •

I picked the tape for the very next day.

"I'm not even going to ask you about Christy," Winters said nervously. "Like we don't have enough problems, now we have a staffer floating in the river."

"Ex-staffer," Braxton corrected. "Remember, Lowell, you fired her last night. You have a copy of the termination letter on file. Might want to release it to the press. It's very well written, very sympathetic. The administration needed to move in a different direction. All the usual political euphemisms."

"Jesus Christ," Winters grunted. "That'll look great. I fire her, and she ends up dead."

"All indications are it's a suicide. The young woman, distraught over just having lost the job she loved, took a dive into the Susquehanna. It's all very unfortunate. So, you put on your best frown and make this sweet young girl sound like an office angel. Everybody loved her. It was just one of those difficult political decisions to let her go. Circumstances had changed, and she should have understood. You thought she understood. What a loss, you say. What a tragedy. Just do what you do best, Lowell. Go play governor, and let me worry about the details."

"Fuck you, Braxton," Winters said. But he didn't mean it. He knew Braxton was right. I could tell.

Next, my finger went to the tape for the day I called Winters about the picture of Christy and him in Mexico and then sprung the news about the semen that I'd found. I was getting good with the tape recorder. I fast-forwarded right to the good part:

"We've lost control of this situation," Winters said, panicked. "There's no getting out from the cloud, now. I have the administration where everyone dies. My press secretary jumps in the river. First, it's a suicide. Then, it's murder. Now, I was fucking her. People are never going to forgive me for this. Every time they look at me, all they'll see is that damn Polaroid they're going to plaster all over your fucking newspaper tomorrow morning. You think they had a field day with Condit? Wait until they get done with me. I thought you said you could control this fucker Holcomb? But he keeps fucking us in the ass."

"Holcomb is the least of our worries." Braxton was slow and steady, always so soothing with that deep voice of his. "In fact, Holcomb is the one thing we have going for us. I have to do some more checking, get all of the facts, but by Monday, this story will be about Holcomb and what a fuck-up *he* is. He's made a lot of mistakes. We can't afford to make any. I want statements from everybody involved in your alibi for that night. In fact, I want every one of them available for a press conference."

"A press conference?" Winters sounded bewildered.

"Yes, Lowell, a press conference. Monday," Braxton said, his voice pregnant with the thoughts flooding his mind. "But first, we get a meeting with the D.A. We lay out your story, show them there's no possible way you could have been involved in this crime. We make the whole allegation of an affair irrelevant. We get the D.A. to publicly exclude you as a suspect."

"He'll do that?" Winters sounded hopeful for the first time.

"After we give him your airtight alibi, he'll have to," Braxton said. "You'll even take a polygraph, but not one administered by your lawyers. One the police and the D.A. control. We keep your lawyers out of it. We don't fall into the Condit trap. We make ourselves available to the authorities. We go to them. Then, we go before the press, and we answer every single question."

"It won't make a difference." Winters sounded glum. "This is gonna be a feeding frenzy. They'll chew my ass. They won't care whether I'm a suspect or not. Condit was never a suspect, but that was always the last little line at the bottom of every story. It didn't mean a fucking thing."

"Condit didn't have someone vulnerable like Holcomb. We attack him," Braxton said. "No, better yet, we bait him into attacking you. He gets the first question at the press conference. We don't tip our hand. We let him think there's some blood in the water. We let him go at you, and then we come at him. We question where he got the picture."

"I don't know where he got it. He said it was a source."

"Probably the brother, but he's another story," Braxton went on. "This semen sample, that's the real stain—for *him,* not us. I checked with the coroner. There was no semen on the body. Something's not right. We need to get a state cop over there to talk to that coroner, and we need access to the full autopsy report. We might as well have the old bone collector at the press conference, as well. He could come in handy."

"So we do all this. We trash the reporter, and I get cleared," Winters said, still sounding depressed, ever the fatalist. "So what? The story's going to be on everyone's breakfast table tomorrow. They'll see the photo, and people will make up their own minds. They'll think I got off, that I pulled some strings. I'll be another O.J., for crissake. The people won't elect President O.J."

"You're right," Braxton considered, thinking, weighing. "We still have a symbolic problem, and they are the worst kind to have. People love symbols. Tomorrow, the symbol will be that picture. The problem is you've been defined by events, powerful events that have been out of our control. The only way to counter that is to have an event of our own, one that we control."

"The press conference?" Winters asked timidly.

"No, that's small-time. It'll be good theater when we cut Holcomb's balls off, but it's nothing. People won't remember. As soon as they see a politician on TV answering questions, they get bored and tune out. We need a spectacle, something so big it will crowd out everything else. We need to make you a hero, Lowell."

"How?"

"Don't worry about that," Braxton said. "You just get ready for that press conference. That's first. I'll prepare your grand spectacle and your new image. Remember, no scandal is too big, if you're a big thinker."

I grabbed the tape for the day of Winters's press conference, even though I knew what was coming. It was the day I played right into Braxton's plans. No, I wasn't interested in reliving my embarrassment. I wanted to hear the meeting that I was sure came later. The meeting between Braxton and Danny Denza.

The tape screeched under the strain of the fast-forward button until I found the brief snippet of conversation:

"What're you doin' here?" Danny Denza asked. "You keep callin', sayin' you're diggin' into things, but I never see you print nothin' in the paper. You say you can nail Winters for my sister, but you never print anything."

"We have a problem in that regard," Braxton said gravely. "May I come in?"

"I guess." There were footsteps as they walked into the kitchen. I heard Danny snatch what I was sure was an open beer bottle from the table.

"Want one?" Danny asked.

"No thanks. I guess you didn't catch the news today."

"Been busy. Buried my sister yesterday."

"Well, Danny, that reporter friend of yours—the one you went to with that picture of Christy and the governor—he just blew everything for us. I wish you would have come to me, instead."

"Whadda you mean?" Danny asked, annoyed. "And I told you before, I didn't give him that picture. I don't know where he got it."

"Well, your buddy went off half-cocked, shot off his mouth at a press conference today, and the governor squelched him." Braxton sounded disgusted with the outcome that he, himself, had carefully orchestrated. "How many times did I try to tell you that this story was delicate? That it was going to take a lot of work and careful planning to break? That you couldn't tip your hand too soon? I tried to tell you, but you put your faith in Holcomb. Well, he just got shot down, and he took our case with him."

"You're sayin' the governor's gonna get off? He's gonna get away with killin' my sister?"

"I don't see any way we can touch him now, Danny. Holcomb fucked up everything. He came at Winters too soon, without enough proof, and the governor was ready for him. Winters sandbagged him and snuffed the story. I don't see any way, not now."

"I can't let that happen," Danny said.

"I just don't see it," Braxton repeated. There was a long, pregnant pause. "Unless." Braxton announced his idea tentatively, almost dismissing it before he spoke. "Unless, you did something on your own. Unless you were willing to take up the cause and make the governor answer for your sister. You could make him answer."

"How? I should just call up the mansion? I don't think so."

"No, you use your talents," Braxton said. "You're a smart man. You know the power and knowledge that you possess could pose a threat—something that would give Winters no choice but to deal with you."

"I don't wanna hurt anyone."

"You wouldn't have to, Danny," Braxton assured. "Just the threat would be enough. I know the perfect place."

The tape cut off, and I reached for my flask. Empty. I must have drained it unknowingly as I listened to the tapes. I noticed then that I was sweating. My shirt was nearly soaked through, especially where my back pressed up against the vinyl car seat. I'd never bothered to roll down the car windows, and I'd been slowly roasting myself. My mouth was cotton. My tongue felt two sizes too large.

There was bound to be more—much more—on those tapes, but I had to get out of that car. I gathered up the tapes and grabbed the recorder, and I headed for the newsroom.

I had an announcement to make and a gift to give.

And of course, an obit to write.

40

I FELT PRETTY SICK WHEN I GOT BACK TO THE NEWSROOM. I was still hot as hell, and the booze was working me over pretty good. Of course, everything that I'd heard on those tapes was doing a number on both my head and my stomach. My brain felt too big for my skull, and my stomach was sloshing like a stormy sea. I knew it would be asking a lot for me to stand up and say my piece, but I was determined.

A large group of staffers still surrounded the newsroom television. Bill Sharps was there, of course, Jack Towers, too. Her beautiful and not-too-cynical eyes were a study of concentration as the TV flashed images from the governor's mansion.

The noon news lady was talking in breathless bursts, as if this was such a big story that she had to hold down her own excitement in order to get it all out:

"We still do not know the identity of the person who was shot and killed by a member of the governor's state police security detail. Authorities say that after gaining admittance to the mansion last night, the suspect argued with and threatened the governor . . ."

I'd heard enough as I walked up behind the group and prepared to deliver my own report.

"I have an announcement, everybody." I spoke to people's backs. They were reluctant to turn away from the TV.

"Hey, man, the news is on," someone said without turning around.

"You want news? I got news," I said, louder. People broke their stares and looked at me with pathetic expressions. I must have looked like shit—sweaty, sick, and half drunk. Jack Towers stood to get a better view.

"You all want to know who that was down at the governor's mansion?" I said. "You've been craning your necks all day watching the tube. I decided to do a little reporting. I paid a visit down at the morgue."

I had everyone's full attention now. Bill Sharps even turned down the volume on the breathless bimbo on TV.

"You've been drinking," a young reporter near me accused.

"Yes, I have. So what?"

"What is it?" Sharps said from his seat. The crowd between us parted, and I saw his eyes searching mine. "What is it that you know, Lenny?"

"This is gonna be my last scoop for a while, so you better listen up." There was no looking past me today. I demanded attention. "So, you all want to know who paid that late-night visit to the governor's mansion?" I said. "That's the big story today, huh? Yesterday, it was Three Mile Island. Last week it was Christy Denza. Before that, Herb Bucher. There's always something to keep us going, isn't there? We're junkies for it. We need the adrenaline rush. We say it's our jobs, but really, we need the fix."

People looked at me strangely, some clearly disgusted, others just impatient. But they kept right on looking, all of them.

"Well, today's big story is gonna hit a little closer to home," I went on. "Guess it's better hearin' it from me, one of your own, though most of you don't think of me that way."

Deep interest returned to the faces that watched me.

"What happened at the governor's mansion, the person who was shot? That was Abe Braxton. That's who it was."

A murmur swept the room. People looked at each other blankly. A woman, I think she worked in features, began sobbing.

"How do you know for sure?" someone demanded.

"Told you. I paid a visit to the morgue. Abe Braxton was laid out on the table, a hole in his chest no bigger than a dime. He's gone."

"The hell was he doin'? What were he and the governor arguing about?" someone asked, not really expecting an answer.

"There's gonna be a lot of talk about that," I said. "I have my own ideas, but it's not for me to say. Told you, I'm done with my scoops. That's for someone else to investigate. Let's just say Braxton had some deeper ties to the governor, and things went sour. I can tell you this, though, he didn't have a weapon. The metal object they keep talkin' about on TV? Abe's mini tape recorder, nothing more."

"Christ," Sharps said, his eyes showing pure bewilderment, utter disbelief. "The paper's going to take a beating on this. You can't have reporters running around threatening the governor and getting themselves shot." Sharps talked as if this unprecedented occurrence was listed in some manual of newspaper management.

"I better call the publisher," he continued, sounding like it was the last thing on earth he wanted to do. "We'll need to get our lawyers on this. It's gonna make us look like shit."

"Some of it probably will," I agreed. "But that's for another day. It'll all come out in time. For now, Braxton was one of us. I'll be the first to say I didn't like him, but he was a reporter for this newspaper. That means something. At least it does to me. We owe him a respectful obit. I owe him that."

The room fell silent. People were actually pondering my words. They were thinking about what I had to say, and they were remembering Braxton, the good and the bad. The silence went on for a good long time.

"If you'll excuse me," I said. "I have an obit to write."

I went to my desk, but noticed that many staffers remained, standing there like statues, faces blank. This was one story that didn't excite them. It didn't get them off. It didn't get them high, just left them hollow. I thought then that maybe Braxton had taught us all something—that it was good to actually *feel* a tragedy once in a while, instead of just thinking about the story. His death reminded us that, reporters or not, we were still human. I looked at the silent group of newspaper people once more, then turned to my computer. I was preparing to write Abe Braxton's obit when I felt a familiar presence. I glanced up to see Jack Towers leaning over my cubicle wall.

"Jesus, Lenny, I can't believe this. I mean I hated the bastard, but I feel sick about it."

"I know. We all do. The bad news is, we'll get over it. In the end, this is gonna be one hell of a story. You have no idea where this is gonna lead."

Jack's eyes widened. The excitement was still there, just under the surface.

"You gotta stay on the story," Jack insisted. "You have all the sources."

"Not me. I'm the obit writer, remember?"

"You don't have to be," she protested.

"I want to be." I smiled confidently at her. "This would be the perfect story for a young, ambitious reporter who sees herself at *The New York Times* one day. That's the kind of reporter who should be on this."

"I wish. They got me on features, remember?"

"Not anymore. Not after these." I handed her the box full of tiny tapes, along with her tape recorder, which I had borrowed without asking.

"What's this?"

"Your career," I said. "Just play it smarter than I did when you go at Winters. By the way, there's a vacancy covering the governor. It should be you up there bustin' his balls and keepin' him outta the White House."

"With these?" She nodded at the tapes.

"Damn right, with those. You've got enough there to roast his ass real good—and make quite a name for yourself in the process. Who knows, maybe the *Times* takes some notice. You can start the fire tomorrow. We give Braxton one clean day."

"But where do I say I got them, the tapes?" Jack Towers asked the question innocently, like a little girl.

"From a source," I said.

"A source?" She considered it. "A good source?"

"Sure. Why not?"

"No, not just good," she changed her mind. "The best."

41

I WATCHED JACK TOWERS CROSS THE NEWSROOM, AND I FELT clean. The scores had been settled. Christy and Danny Denza would get the truth they deserved. And Winters would soon get what he deserved—and it would not be the White House. Jack would get her career. And Abe Braxton would get a clean obit. As clean as I could write it under the mysterious circumstances of his late-night visit at the governor's mansion.

I spent most of the early afternoon working on the final story in this wretched chain of events. I made all the necessary calls, gathered the proper quotes, and relied on the latest police statements. Braxton's obituary would prove to be a good deal longer than the customary five column inches.

**HERALD REPORTER SHOT DEAD
IN ARGUMENT WITH GOVERNOR;
NO WEAPON FOUND ON BODY**

By Lenny Holcomb

Herald political reporter Arthur Abraham Braxton, who covered Gov. Lowell Winters's administra-

tion for the newspaper, was shot dead by police inside the governor's mansion during what authorities say was a threatening argument with Winters.

Braxton, age 29, was unarmed and never physically assaulted Winters or any of his staff during the incident.

It is still not known why the two were arguing in the governor's private study at around midnight last night. But earlier that evening, Braxton had placed several calls to the governor's private line, and Winters agreed to an impromptu meeting, authorizing Braxton's unscheduled admittance to the residence.

IT WASN'T GOING TO HAPPEN TO ME, NOT TO ME.

Officers with the governor's security detail entered the study after the argument broke out. They said an irate Braxton refused to leave and appeared to make a move toward the governor. Police say Braxton then reached for his coat pocket and retrieved a metal object, prompting one officer to fire. Braxton was shot once in the chest at close range.

It wasn't until after the fatal shooting that police determined that Braxton was unarmed. The object was a small, silver tape recorder, a device many reporters use to record interviews. Police continue to investigate the incident.

I HAD PLANS, BIG PLANS. LIFE IS JUST ONE LONG STORY, AND I WAS DETERMINED TO WRITE MY OWN TICKET.

"The governor was closer to Abe than any other reporter in the state," said a capitol newsroom source. "Whenever the governor had news, he'd go to Braxton first, because he trusted him to get it right. I just can't imagine what might have happened between the two of them."

Governor Winters released a prepared statement calling Braxton's death "unfortunate" and expressing his "deepest regrets" over the tragedy. However, the governor would not elaborate on what prompted the unusual late-night meeting or what sparked the shouting match between himself and the reporter. He said such matters are the "province of an ongoing police investigation."

Officials with the Herald also declined comment on the specifics of the incident, saying they'll await the investigation's conclusions.

Publisher Angus Merrin paid tribute to Braxton for his three years of covering the capitol for the newspaper. "Abe Braxton was a fine young reporter," he said. "He could have been a great one."

But Merrin took pains to point out that Braxton was not working on any assigned story when he requested the impromptu meeting at the governor's mansion. "I can't explain what may have led him to behave in the way that's been described by police," said the publisher. "I'll let the investigation answer those questions."

I WASN'T GOING TO LET THEM DO IT TO ME. THEY COULD NEVER BREAK ME. I'D NEVER LET THEM TURN ME INTO ONE.

When word finally broke that the dead suspect was Braxton, shock swept the Herald's newsroom.

"This really hits home," said a staff member. "I just can't believe it, no one can. Abe Braxton was a straight-laced professional. He always got the story, and he never even seemed to break a sweat doing it. I have no idea what could have set him off."

Braxton is survived by his parents, Lyle and Wanda. Mr. Braxton is a renowned heart surgeon, and Mrs. Braxton, a Harvard professor. They reside in a suburb of Boston, but were vacationing in the Fiji Islands when notified of their son's death.

I DID IT. I KEPT MY VOW. I NEVER WROTE A SINGLE OBITUARY.

JOURNALISM CAN KISS MY ASS!

42

Abe Braxton had done everything—all the lies, all the manipulation, all the violence—to avoid becoming a broken-down, ink-stained creature of journalism, like me. In some small way, he did it to avoid ever having to write a single obituary. This business—the endless cycle of news gathering—would never catch up with him now. It was as fitting an epitaph as any for our Abe Braxton.

He had other plans for himself. Indeed, he did.

First, he had the idea of covering Winters all the way to the White House. Then, that winter in Mexico, the plans changed. Why not use his prime position on the paper to help the governor in exchange for career rewards later? Why not use the paper before it used him?

Things just got out of hand. In the end, it was the governor—and Braxton's own ambitions—that used him. Used everyone.

It would come out, what Abe and the governor had done. Jack Towers had the tapes, and she had the talent to get the rest of the story. Winters would go down as a co-conspirator, and Braxton would come off as a lying, recklessly ambitious manipulator, not to mention a murderer. People would think he had done it all in exchange for the promise of some plum White House job with a big title, lots of exposure on programs like *Meet the Press,* and plenty of face time with Larry King.

But those things were merely the perks.

A part of him had just wanted a sure ticket out of this place, this business. A little protection from the beast in the basement, those hungry presses that demand feeding every night. He wanted—needed—to keep intact his no-obit streak.

For a long time, I wondered what Abe Braxton would think if he knew that it all would end with me writing his own obituary. He was so arrogant, so sure of himself, he probably never even conceived of such a thing. He never saw it coming.

Me? Perhaps, I served as a little added motivation to fuel Braxton's grand scheme. I represented the ghost of a future he feared most.

Hell, most of the time, even I lamented my own existence, loathed my lot in life. I never wanted to turn out like I had. But, I had my own ways of escaping. My mind would wander, as I've said. I had my booze. I had the satisfaction of being a reporter again, a real reporter. Occasionally, I'd have my stories. And, for those fleeting days, I had Jack Towers and my dreams of her.

But there was such a cost. And after all that had happened, I was still just Lenny Holcomb. Screwloose Lenny to certain staffers of this newspaper. The obit writer to everyone else.

Yes, I would go back to my old job at the *Herald,* but I would never again be the ghost of the newsroom. My instincts would see to that.

• • •

I decided to leave work early that day. I had it in my mind to go home and do some writing. Some real writing. I resolved to record these strange and tragic events, putting them down on paper. I'd tell everything, exactly as it happened. And I'd begin with how it all started, with the obits, of course.

I figured I could write my story at night and keep my mind sharp doing it. By day, I'd type the obits. And from time to time, when my instincts moved me, I'd have a story or two, as well. I promised myself that I'd continue my journalistic pursuits by looking into Glenda Jackson's unnecessarily painful death at Sunset Hospice. I hoped to get the truth for her, just like I'd gotten it for Christy.

But before I left the paper that afternoon, I read over Abe Braxton's obituary—his real obit—one last time. And I wept when I did. I wept for Christy Denza and her brother, Danny. And, yes, I wept for Braxton. Maybe him most of all.

I wept because he was a young reporter, and I am an old one. And because I know life writes us all one hell of a story.

It's worth reading to the end.

Being an obit writer will teach you that.

—30—

Acknowledgments

THE JOURNEY OF A FIRST NOVEL FROM MIND TO MANUSCRIPT, first draft to publication is a long and winding one. There are many people to thank for helping me along my journey.

First, to Amiran, for the love, support and patience on that long road. And most of all, for keeping my ego in check once we got to where we were going. Please put up with me through future books.

To my dad and brothers, Dave and Rick, and their families, who have kept the family tree firmly rooted in Johnstown, Pennsylvania, my hometown. You provide that solid anchor of a place called home.

To all the early readers of this story who were so generous with their time and so kind with their support and encouragement. Thanks to my love, Amiran; my best friend, Jack Sherzer; fiction-lover Jerry L. Gleason; blood-and-guts crime reporter Ted Decker; writer and copyeditor Bill Peschel; and friends Angela P. Swinson, Victoria Zellers, Anita Young, and others. You gave this upstart author the instant gratification of being read.

To accomplished newspaper editor Cate Barron, who not only was kind enough to read an early version of an earlier manuscript (not this one), but edit it, line by line. You showed me the right way to revise and instilled in me the strength and the ruthlessness to cut my own beloved words. Lesson learned. I think it shows in this book.

To my agent, the wise, wonderful Jane Jordan Browne, who passed away in February 2003. You saw something in an unsolicited manuscript, then guided and challenged me until we realized its full potential. It was a long two years of work, but you found my book a good home at a fine publisher. Thank you.

To my editor, Kevin Smith at Pocket Books, for taking a liking to old, cantankerous Lenny and giving me a shot at a mystery series. You've made this whole, complicated process of publishing seem easy.

And last but not least, to all my friends and colleagues at *The Patriot-News,* the Harrisburg newspaper where I work. I hope you all get a kick out of this book and read it in the same fun, entertaining spirit in which it was written. Just remember, it's fiction. I made it up. It goes without saying that the newspaper in this story bears little resemblance to the *Patriot*. Most days, it's a good place to work and not a bad place for a writer.

Thanks all around—JCL.

© Amiran White

JOHN LUCIEW has been a working journalist for more than fourteen years, writing at various newspapers in Pennsylvania. Born in Johnstown, Pennsylvania, he lives, writes, and practices journalism in Harrisburg. This is his first novel. He is at work on a second Lenny Holcomb mystery, forthcoming from Pocket Books.

9 781451 646825